GHOSTED

A GOTHIC REVERSE HAREM BULLY ROMANCE

STEFFANIE HOLMES

GHOSTED

From the author of *Shunned*, the Amazon top-20 bestselling bully romance readers are calling, "The greatest mindfk of 2019," comes this chilling new dark paranormal reverse harem romance.**

Ivan, Titus, Dorien.
These Bad Boys of Baroque may play like angels,
but they're determined to make my life hell.

When my mom got sick, my dreams of a career in music imploded. That is, until Madame Usher wafts into my life like a ghost from the past, offering me the chance to study at the exclusive Manderley Academy – a music school for the most gifted and wealthy.

It's an offer I can't refuse – free room and board at the gothic mansion where elite students immerse themselves in mastering their art. But there's a catch, and it's a big one.

I'm her slave.

I clean the rooms. I polish the piano keys. I serve her and the three pretentious a-hole guys who rule this school.

I must endure their bullying in silence. Even when they destroy my things, sabotage my performances, and try their best to drive me from Manderley.

Rich. Arrogant. Cruel.
They won't have the poor little charity case ruining their fun.
They've heard me play.
They know I'm a serious contender for the prestigious Manderley Prize.

These broken muses aren't used to losing, especially to the help.

But they're not the only ones haunting me.

Something twisted and evil shrouds Manderley Academy. Maybe my bullies are the least of my problems. Maybe Dorien, Ivan, and Titus aren't the ones behind the strange noises in the walls, the warnings scrawled on my mirror, and the gruesome murders on the school grounds.

Maybe...maybe Manderley's ghosts are real.

A dark mystery unfolds around musician Faye de Winter in book one of this gripping gothic college reverse harem bully romance by USA Today best-selling author Steffanie Holmes. Warning: This tale of three spoiled rich boys with unsettling secrets and the girl who refuses to put up with their shit contains dark themes, a creepy house, a smoldering second-chance romance, college angst, cruel bullies and swoon-worthy sex.

Grab a free copy *Cabinet of Curiosities* – a Steffanie Holmes compendium of short stories and bonus scenes – when you sign up for updates with the Steffanie Holmes newsletter.

*To Niccolò, Johann, Wolfgang, and Franz –
the original Bad Boys of Baroque.*

"One need not be a chamber to be haunted,
One need not be a house;
The brain has corridors surpassing
Material place.

– Emily Dickinson, *One need not be a chamber to be haunted*

FAYE

Beep beep. Beep beep.

The machine echoed in my ears like a drumbeat sounding my doom. The sound of everything I'd worked for scattered to ash.

The sound of my mother slipping away from me.

I leaned back in the hard plastic hospital chair, rubbing my burning eyes. I had no idea what day it was or how long I'd been sitting there. A cramp shot up my leg – a dull ache that had nothing on the searing pain in my heart. I stretched out my leg, gasping as the cramp arced down the muscle.

It's like they deliberately make hospital rooms as uncomfortable as possible. Because watching someone you love waste away doesn't suck enough.

My foot brushed the violin case on the floor. Before I knew it, I held my instrument in my hands. The chin rest perfectly fitting my body and the familiar weight of the neck against my fingers gave me comfort. It felt as natural as breathing to run the bow across the strings, to play the familiar trembling notes of Bloch's *Nigun.*

The Swiss composer wrote this piece in the memory of his

mother, and it's based on Jewish improvised chants. The idea is that by losing yourself in music, you become closer to God. Right now, I felt like strangling the big bastard in the sky for what he'd done to my mom, but I wasn't playing for him.

Nigun was one of my mother's favorite pieces – I learned it to play for her fortieth birthday. She'd hosted her party in her chic warehouse office in the East Village. All her investors and the executive team watched me in awe while she glowed with pride.

Beep beep. Beep beep.

Now, I played it beside her hospital bed, to an audience of one.

The doctors say she might be able to hear music inside her coma. This might be my only shot at speaking to her, at drawing her back.

Mournful notes rang out as my bow danced over the strings. The grey hospital room came to life in that moment, the sterile edges washed away under a wave of lament. I fancied I saw the shadows of others who had sat in this same chair to cry over their loved ones. I conjured their pain and made it my own.

Music *was* magic.

I needed a little magic right now.

As I played, a cloying scent reached my nostrils. Fake floral – like the bowls of potpourri my grandmother used to leave around her house. Old English roses and hyacinths drenched in sticky toffee and covered in mothballs. The scent tugged at a forgotten memory, a ghost of the past.

My pinkie finger slipped on the string, causing a dull note. I winced, forcing myself to ignore the smell, and kept playing. It happened sometimes when I was lost in the music – the melody conjured images, smells, or feelings from deep in my subconscious. They felt real until I set down the bow, and then I'd realize how stupid that was. *Obviously,* I didn't conjure scented memories with music.

It's just the smell of the hospital disinfectant or something. Don't get distract—

No, it's not. Deja vu tugged at me, bringing with it an ugly foreboding. *I've smelled that* exact *scent before.*

I reached the end of the piece and lowered the bow. A familiar ache settled along my arm – pain was another thing I never felt until after I stopped playing. I once smashed my foot while climbing on stage. I played Beethoven's entire *Violin Sonata No. 9* standing on a broken toe, and I didn't even notice.

Someone clapped.

What the fuck?

I jumped out of my skin.

My eyes flew to my mother, but she lay in the bed, immobile. The machine beep-beeped behind her. I whirled around.

"Brava." A woman stood in the corner of the room. I hadn't noticed her come in. Her Eastern European accent seemed so out-of-place in this ordinary hospital in the shittiest part of NYC. That wasn't the only thing about her that was odd – an old-fashioned floor-length gown in black lace and linen clung to her ample figure, and she clutched a large carpet bag with gold clasps. The fake floral smell rolled off her in waves. "You are still talented."

I set down the violin, angry she'd intruded. "This is a private room." The one indulgence I'd made in this entire shitshow, so I could grieve and hope and rage in private. And soon even that would be gone unless I came up with more cash.

"I am aware. I wish to speak to you, Faye de Winter."

How does this strange woman know my name? Her presence tugged at me, the deja vu growing stronger. That smell and her voice were so familiar. Even that black dress sparked some hint of memory, but I couldn't think where I'd have occasion to speak with such a woman. She looked like she'd got lost on the way to a Twilight fan convention.

Beep beep. Beep beep.

Tension sang in the air between us. I didn't want her here, infecting my mom's space with her scent. But I had to know why she knew my name and why'd she'd sought me out. I sighed. "Yeah?"

"Perhaps you do not recognize me. I am Madame Usher."

That name pierced my heart like an arrow.

Of course. The perfume. How could I forget the way it made me choke during music classes, or how it clung to my father when he came home from his private lessons?

I hadn't seen Madame Usher of Manderley Academy since my mother pulled me from her classes when I was nine years old. Alongside her husband on piano, she had been an accomplished violinist in her day but now ran an elite conservatory in the mountains offering expert tutelage for only the most exceptional musicians. She used to come to the city to teach a handful of super-rich students – children and adults, including me and my dad. But ever since Dad's disappearance, her name had been poison in our house, never uttered.

"I see that you remember now. It has been, what, nine years?"

"Ten." I would turn twenty this year.

"You were just a tiny wisp of a thing back then, but you mastered your Bach. The only person I heard play the Chaconne from *Partita No. 2* better was Donovan."

"Don't talk to me about him," I hissed.

"I see you've inherited your mother's bitterness."

"Get the fuck out." I jabbed my finger at the door.

"Excuse me?"

"You don't come into *my* mother's hospital room and accuse her of being bitter. I'd be upset too if I found out the husband who I supported through an expensive music education was fucking his teacher."

"Such foul language." Instead of retreating, Madame Usher stepped into the room and closed the door behind her. "You should know that I loved him with a passion I only ever reserved for music. My husband was a convenience – for the sake of our international career, it made sense to marry Victor. But when

Donovan and I played, it was as though we made love through our instruments."

I balled my hands into fists, resisting the childish urge to jam my hands over my ears. "Read my lips – I. Don't. Want. To. Hear. This."

The smile on Madame Usher's lips boiled my blood. "He planned to leave your mother, and I to leave Victor. We were to run away together. But then he disappeared, and I have never known such pain before or since."

"Get out," I growled, stepping toward the call button. "Or I'll have you removed by security."

Bitch.

Madame Usher continued as though I'd never spoken. "After your mother removed you from my classes, I kept my eye on you, Faye. You might think of me as a guardian angel, hovering in the background, waiting for Donovan's talent to blossom within you. Your father always believed you would one day surpass him, but I admit, I had my doubts. I do not accept just anyone into my tutelage, and you were never serious about your studies, always running about with Dorien."

Dorien Valencourt. I closed my eyes, remembering the little boy who'd been my only friend growing up. Dorien took piano lessons from Victor Usher, but we always paired up for ensembles and recitals. Dorien was rich in a way my family could never hope to be – we practically lived in poverty to fund Dad's career and my tuition – but I was too young to understand the gulf between us or why the other rich kids shunned me so openly. I just knew Dorien's slate-grey eyes gleamed with joy whenever I showed up in class. We'd been the twin terrors of Madame Usher's junior city school. The day Dorien placed his pet iguana in the baby grand and it jumped out just as Victor Usher sat down—

No. I couldn't think about Dorien now, not on top of everything else. That pain still cut too deep.

"Dorien was never serious either, and he's done well for himself," I shot back.

"Ah. So you have followed his career?"

Even if I'd never wanted to hear his name again (which I definitely didn't), I couldn't help but see Dorien everywhere. Every week there was a new article gushing over Broken Muse, the ensemble Dorien formed with two of his friends. The music press delighted in following the trio –who they'd dubbed the Bad Boys of Baroque – as they tore up the European scene with their antics. They were my age, but their flamboyant playing style, modernized Baroque costumes and strings of exotic lovers were giving the stuffy Classical world a playboy makeover. Early last year they stopped touring and dropped off the face of the earth – no one knew where they were, which only added to their mystique. But I wasn't going to give Madame Usher the satisfaction of revealing I knew any of that. So I ignored her question. "Tell me what you want, and leave."

"I've come into the city to speak with music teachers and private schools. For months I've despaired at finding a student to fill our last open place. Your school's music teacher put your name forward, and although I initially dismissed it because of the usual dross she tries to send me, the memory of your father's talent encouraged me to seek you out. I've had a devil of a time tracking you down, but eventually, the trail led me here. I'm delighted it did. There is no need for you to audition – I've heard enough to offer you a place at Manderley if you want it."

If I wanted it? The fuck was she kidding? It didn't matter that I hated her guts. Of course I wanted it. Saliva pooled on my tongue, as if the very thought of stepping inside that hallowed mansion made me hungry.

Beep beep.

The machines pulled me back to reality. Mom's mysterious sickness. The mountains of medical bills. The two jobs I'd been working in an attempt to pay them off. I shook my head. "I can't."

"Faye, an offer like this is not extended lightly, and it will not be offered again."

Don't use my first name. We're not, nor will we ever be, close. I gestured to the prone figure on the bed. "She needs me."

"You do not understand." Madame Usher moved to the end of the bed, standing over my mother and looking down at her with pursed lips. "I am not merely offering you a place at Manderley, but a chance at a future. I expect every musician who graduates to go on to a stunning international career. You cannot do that tethered to a hospital bed. We have the means to help you."

"Help me how?"

"Your tuition will be paid by my late husband's endowment fund. I shall provide your room and board, and an allowance for clothing and necessities. Most importantly, I will pay your mother's medical debts and move her to a more advanced facility closer to the school, so you can visit her on weekends. In exchange, you will extend your services to the school."

"My… services?"

"You will cook meals, keep the house and rooms clean, make sure the instruments are stored correctly, that sort of thing."

"What did your last maid die of?" I muttered.

Madame Usher's mouth tugged at the corner. "A broken neck."

I sucked in a breath. *Is she serious?*

Madame Usher nodded to my phone on the nightstand. "I will not dredge up that unfortunate incident by speaking of it aloud. Look it up if you still have your penchant for morbidity."

She referred to the fact I'd been a strange kid. I was obsessed with horror books and ghost stories. Still was. My favorite thing to do on a Friday night was curling up in bed with Mom and a stack of junk food to watch a spooky film. I knew all the tropes by heart, but I never got tired of hiding under the covers from ghosts and monsters.

I picked up the phone and tapped a line into the search bar. A few moments later, the headline popped up: "MAID DEAD AT ELITE MUSIC ACADEMY." The maid had been found crumpled at the bottom of the stairs – a nasty fall. A terrible accident. The journalist took a kind of morbid delight in describing the trauma to her skull, suggesting the angle of her body meant that she'd been pushed. Police investigated, but they eventually ruled her death an accident, although the journalist enjoyed speculating otherwise.

Knowing Madame Usher, she probably folded the towels wrong.

Madame Usher frowned at my phone. "As you may be able to guess, it becomes difficult to find new help when the press has made every attempt to suggest your maid died of foul play. Hence, I was inspired to seek you out. We can help each other."

A charity case.

I sank into the chair. The plastic creaked as it sagged under my weight. I was never supposed to be a charity case. After Dad disappeared, taking all our hopes of living off his music career with him, Mom swore that we de Winter women would make our own way in the world. She was sick of working sixty-hour shifts as a taxi driver to support a man's dream. She went back to school for business, and built a successful PR firm from the ground-up. After years living on the skin of our asses, we had money. We moved into a gorgeous East Village townhouse. Mom paid for the best violin tutor money could buy who wasn't Madame Usher. I went to a fancy prep school where I was ignored because I wasn't 'old money,' but the students were all little shits, so I didn't give a fuck. We took vacations in exotic places like Vietnam and Istanbul. We weren't mega-rich, but we were comfortable. We didn't need anyone or anything but ourselves.

Except, as it turned out, we also needed health insurance.

Mom's illness crept up on us without warning. One moment she was taking her team on a spa vacation in Hawaii to celebrate her best year ever, complaining the resort food gave her stomach cramps, the next she was lying unresponsive in the back of an ambulance. I called our insurance company to pay the bills and discovered Mom had forgotten to pay her premium, so they had canceled our coverage.

What started as bouts of nausea and cramping turned into a host of strange gastrointestinal problems, and then her kidneys started failing. She'd been deteriorating over the last two years, in and out of the hospital, while they did tests and tried medications and dialysis, but nothing worked. Every new treatment, every flight to a different state to try some new diagnostic machine, stretched our dwindling savings. I sold the townhouse. I graduated high school (barely), moved her to this cheap-ass chop-shop hospital, and took two jobs to try and keep up. Then, a week ago, she slipped into a coma, and the doctors still had no idea what was wrong with her.

What medical dramas on TV don't tell you is how fucking expensive it is to keep someone on life-support. If I didn't come up with some way to pay the bills soon, I'd have no choice but to shut her off.

My mom was my whole life. I wasn't saying goodbye. Not yet.

I'll do whatever it takes to keep her alive.

If that means bowing and scrubbing for this witch, just call me Cinder-fucking-rella.

I leaned over the bed, pressing my lips to Mom's forehead. How odd it was to see her this still. Mom was always bouncing off the walls, a ball of boundless energy. "I won't slow down – you slow down, you die," she admonished me once after she'd nearly walked out of the house with her underwear on her head because she was so excited about a client's TV appearance. "The only time I'll lie still is if you put me in a coma." Fate is a fucking cruel mistress.

Beep beep, the machines admonished me for my betrayal.

I straightened up and picked up my violin case, hugging it to my chest. All through Mom's illness, even as I sold off our possessions, she forbade me to sell my violin. She had it custom-made by an artisan luthier as my thirteenth birthday present, and it was the most precious thing I owned.

So I'd kept it, even though I'd all but given up hope of a career in music. The money Mom set aside for college had been eaten by her medical bills in the first three months. This was a second chance for both of us – for her and for me.

My father walked out and left us with *nothing*. If I took Madame Usher's deal, then at least something good came of his *trahison des clercs*.

The smile that crossed Madame Usher's face was chillier than the winter I'd just survived in my shitty, non-heated apartment. "Your father would be so proud. Faye de Winter, welcome to Manderley Academy."

2

FAYE

*W*ell, fuck.

A week passed since I accepted Madame Usher's offer. During that time I walked out of my hotel receptionist's job and worked my last shift at the dive bar. I packed Mom's things and filled in the paperwork to have her transferred to a first-class suite at a private hospital an hour's drive from Manderley.

I balanced my laptop on my knees as I leaned against the bare wall of my apartment – refreshing the school's website a million times, poring over the images of the opulent Victorian bedrooms, grand rehearsal spaces, and sprawling gardens.

But *nothing* prepared me for seeing Manderley Academy up close for the first time.

I shouldn't start there. I should start with the limo.

The motherfucking *limo* they sent to pick me up.

Madame Usher told me to wait on the curb with my bags at 7AM sharp. She had no idea women my age shouldn't chill out alone on street corners in my neighborhood. Or maybe she did. I wouldn't put anything past that witch.

I fingered the knife in my pocket as I peered both ways down the street. *Please, get here soon.*

A gang of guys with huge shoulders and mean expressions loitered on the corner opposite, eyeing up the white girl with the violin case and all her possessions in a duffel bag nervously jumping from foot to foot. The skin on my neck started to prickle. I stared the guys down with my best 'don't fuck with me' glare – a look I'd perfected long before our move to Bushwick. That look was all that stood between me and certain destruction at my old prep school.

One of the guys jumped off the curb and made his way toward me, his swagger all business, his smirk unmistakable. *Fucktrumpets. This is just what I need.*

My mind whipped through my options and was just choosing an optimum escape route when a black limo tore around the corner. The guy leaped back as the tires bumped over the curb. The side mirror scraped along the side of a parked car, and the insane vehicle jerked to a stop in front of my building.

"What the fuck?" the guy across the street cried out as he fell on his ass in the ditch. His friends guffawed, all four of them staring at the tinted windows like they were sure some famous rapper was about to emerge.

I agreed with the guy's sentiment. *Who the fuck drives a limo into Bushwick? This dick is blocking the street, so the car Madame Usher sent won't be able to park—*

The driver's door swung open. A stout old man with white hair and a neatly-pressed waistcoat hopped out and slid open the passenger door. "Can I take your bags, ma'am?" he asked me.

I hugged my violin case to my chest and shook my head before I realized he was here for *me.*

"Um… yeah. Sure." I handed him my bag, and he whisked it away. I settled into a plush leather seat, rested my violin case against my legs, and surveyed the minibar. Tiny bottles of hooch crowded the shelves beneath the touchscreen. There were even snacks. My stomach rumbled with desperation – feeding myself hadn't been a priority lately. While most kids my age were dealing with the Freshman Fifteen, I'd lost at least sixteen pounds since Mom got sick – not that it had made much dent in my ample *derriere*. I usually ate a plate of fries or nachos at the bar, but that would be my only meal for the day. I grabbed a candy bar and bit into it, letting the gooey caramel pool on my tongue.

I could get used to this.

"Did you want to say goodbye to your friends?" the driver asked as he slid into his seat, indicating the guys on the corner.

I wound down the window and flashed the one who'd approached me my middle finger. "They know I'll miss them."

Not.

The driver stomped on the gas. We flew off. *Goodbye, Bushwick.* I didn't even look back. I was happy to forget this part of my life.

The driver pressed a button on the dash, and his friendly voice boomed over the intercom. "My name is Harrison. Madame wanted to be here herself, but she has a lot to do now that classes are in session, so I have the honor of escorting you to Manderley. I'm the driver, groundskeeper and general dogsbody for the estate."

I finished my candy bar and picked up a bag of potato chips. Leaning over, I rapped on the glass divider. "Roll this down."

"I'm not supposed to—"

"It's a long drive, and I'm not having a conversation through the intercom like I'm the Duchess of York. We're the hired help, Harrison – we gotta stick together."

Harrison flashed me a toothy grin as he pressed another button and the glass rolled down.

"That's better. So, Harrison..." I leaned over through the window and offered him a potato chip. He looked like he was going to say no, but then his eyes twinkled and he reached into the bag. "How long have you worked at Manderley?"

"Forty-three years I've worked for the Usher family." Harrison puffed out his chest with pride. "Just like my Pappy before me. I grew up at the house, running around in the forest with Victor Usher. We were boyhood friends before he became master of the house, but he was always good to me. He said I'd have a job with the family for as long as I wanted it."

I couldn't imagine living and working at the same house, year in and year out, for your entire life. I was like my mother, whose Mexican blood bubbled to life when she traveled. Music was supposed to be my ticket to seeing the world. Now, it would be the noose around my neck. And Madame Usher was my executioner. "What about Madame Usher?"

"I still remember when he first brought her to the house," Harrison tapped the wheel as he sped through a set of lights, completely oblivious to the drivers honking on either side of us. "Back then, Manderley was just the family home, although it was always filled with music. Victor Senior was quite the fiddler, and Mary taught her son the piano. Victor met Gizella while touring Europe – she was first violin for the Hungarian National Philharmonic when he premiered his *Nocturne*, and it was love at first sight. They eloped to Spain, and he brought her home – his new bride, but she was anything but blushing. She walked through the door like she owned the place, and before long she ruled the house with an iron fist. They'd been married less than a year when she convinced Victor to shuffle his parents off to a retirement home and open the music school."

"She sounds like your favorite person."

"Pardon me, Miss. I shouldn't speak ill of the Madame. She allowed me to stay on after Victor died last year. These old houses aren't much common anymore – I'd be hard-pressed to find a new groundskeeper's job. I'd probably end up raking grass at the big golf course." The horrified look on Harrison's face told me exactly what he thought of such a career change.

"Did you know the maid who was killed?"

"I did, I did. Clare… such a sweet girl." Harrison's fingers tightened on the wheel. "I was the one who… on the staircase… I was mending a broken pane in the library when I heard the scream. I've never seen anything so horrible in all my years. Her neck all twisted, her eyes wide, and her mouth was open like she was still screaming."

"I read in the paper the police decided it was an accident."

"Accident my foot." Harrison's jaw clenched. He looked like he wanted to say more. "She was pushed."

He sounded so certain that a cold chill ran down my spine. *Blast the fucktrumpets – what have I walked into?* "Tell me what happened."

"Clare was carrying on with one of the male students – a real charmer, using his wealth and good looks to take advantage of her sweet nature. She told me with stars in her eyes that he planned to take her to Europe on his next tour, and ask her to marry him under the Eiffel Tower, all sorts of girlish fancies – but he never intended any of it. He had women on speed dial all across the world, but Clare couldn't see it. It boiled my blood, it did – in my day we learned how to treat a lady right."

"I can tell you're a gentleman of the highest order." I smiled, and Harrison beamed and puffed out his chest. I noticed a wedding ring on his finger, dirt smeared between the delicate filigree. The smile fell from his face as he continued his story.

"One night, I found Clare in the pantry, sobbing. She wouldn't tell me what was wrong, only that she'd had a fight with her fella. Two days later, she was dead. And *he* was there, fawning over her body, crying that she'd fallen."

"You think he pushed her?"

Harrison nodded. "I *know* he pushed her. That bastard's still there, swanning about like he's God's gift to music. Mark my words, Miss Faye, you watch yourself around those students, especially the young men. They've all got sticks shoved so far up their asses you could wave 'em about like lollipops."

I laughed at the image, but Harrison's words unnerved me. If he was right, and a murderer was still at the school...

Don't be ridiculous. This is real life, not a horror film. The police would have questioned this guy. If they let him go, there must be a good reason.

We drove out of the city and into the mountains. Tall trees loomed over the road, and I made Harrison open the sunroof so I could stick my head out and bask in the fresh air. My hair whipped around my face, and for a moment I forgot that I was penniless and alone. For a moment, I was free.

Then the weight of my mother's illness and my agreement with Madame Usher slammed down on my shoulders. I slid back into the limo and yanked the sunroof shut.

We passed through a few small towns and a larger city, where Harrison pointed out the gleaming hospital building on the hill. "Your mother's already settled in her new room. She has a lovely view over the river. I've seen to all the details."

On the other side of the city, we turned into a winding wooded road that curled up the mountains, zigzagging through dense forest and over bubbling streams. I was just thinking about rolling back the sunroof again when the road ended at a set of wrought-iron gates nearly entirely obscured with vines. Beyond them, a small brick gatehouse peeked from between the trees.

Harrison rolled down the window and the crisp mountain air rushed in, washing over me – a primal exhalation that reminded me of being on stage with the audience's collective breath releasing as the music pulled them under.

"Welcome to Manderley." Harrison pushed a button on the dashboard, and the gates swung open. A narrow driveway snaked through the woods. Branches scraped the side of the limo as we inched our way forward, and it was impossible to see anything through the thick trees and towering cones of vicious-looking thistles. Here and there I saw the edges of stone walls – these gardens had once been well-kept, but now the mountains had crept down upon them unawares – nature reclaiming what was hers.

I remembered all the famous musicians, composers, and conductors listed in the brochure who supposedly visit Manderley every year. I couldn't match up the glittering black-tie galas in the pictures with this overgrown, neglected driveway.

Just when I thought the road couldn't get any narrower, it widened out into a circular drive, surrounding a dried-up fountain – Cupid peered out at me from behind his lyre atop a weed-choked plinth. Beyond it, I got my first glimpse of Manderley Academy.

The place is insane.

If you were looking to cast a creepy house for a gothic horror film, you'd come to Manderley. The gabled roof chewed at the bitter sky with serrated teeth. Twin turrets jutted from the corners, and walls of grey stone stood like the battlements of a castle, immovable against the progress of time. A wide porch wrapped around the front – a later addition, by the looks of it – held up by elaborately-carved wooden poles and wreathed with delicate iron railings. Dormer windows along the roof loomed over me, catching the sun on the glass – gleaming eyes watching. Judging.

The driveway fanned out in both directions, leading off to stone and wooden outbuildings scattered deeper in the trees. I recognized what might've once been a stable. At any moment I expected to see a horse and cart roll by or to hear someone yelling to bring out the plague victims.

The only nod to modernity was the row of cars parked in a small clearing under the trees. A Porsche, a Jaguar F-type, a little pink Corvette, some kind of enormous blinged-out pickup truck

... all of them freshly buffed and polished, despite the danger of tree sap looming directly above them.

"Thanks," I said to Harrison as he pulled my duffel from the trunk and handed it to me.

"A pleasure, Miss de Winter. If you'll forgive me, normally I'd come inside with you, but I need to collect the wood before those clouds roll in. I believe I'll be seeing you later when you begin your work." Harrison doffed his hat at me and set off toward the outbuildings, whistling a merry tune.

He seems nice enough. A little odd, but you'd have to be to live in the middle of nowhere waiting on rich, snooty musicians who park their fancy sports cars under trees. I bet they weren't the ones cleaning them.

I shifted my violin case to my other hand so I could grip the iron balustrade as I ascended the steps. Up close I could see that the house was as shabby as the grounds. Shingles were missing from the roof, and weeds choked the drain pipes and snaked up the crumbling stone walls. It was weird how Manderley was so prestigious, only accepting a handful of students every year, and yet the place had been allowed to deteriorate into such a state. It was a far cry from the polish of the brochure. I inspected the rotting wood of the steps as I climbed. *These don't look structurally sound—*

FUCK.

The plank cracked under my boot. My violin case went flying as I dropped straight through the porch. I pitched forward, throwing out my hand to catch myself before I face-planted into the door.

How I managed to look graceful on stage when I was such a klutz in real life was one of life's great mysteries, like the fact there existed people who enjoyed black jelly beans.

I winced as I looked down at my leg buried in the porch nearly up to my upper thigh. My foot dangled free in the darkness below, and for a brief moment I imagined all the rats and critters that might be down there, and a shudder ran through me. A stinging bite along my calf told me I'd scraped off a ton of skin on the jagged edges of the rotting wood.

Dickweasels. So much for a great first impression.

I struggled to free my leg, but I didn't quite have the upper body strength to push myself up. I glanced behind me, hoping Harrison was still around, but he'd driven the limo off somewhere. I threw my head back, ready to yell for help.

A long velvet rope dangled down the side of the door, extending up into the heavens. I wriggled and bopped and scraped and eventually managed to wrap my fingers around the knot on the end. I gave it a sharp tug, half expecting it to bring the roof caving in on top of me. Instead, a deep gong sounded from within the house.

The door flung open. On the threshold stood the most beautiful girl I'd ever seen.

Honey-blonde hair cascaded over her shoulders in tight, silken ringlets. It must take her hours every morning to get her hair to behave like that, framing her Californian good looks – tanned skin, eyes like the Pacific Ocean, a nose that was just made for looking down on the plebs. Soft, bow-shaped lips curled back into a smile that was anything but friendly.

"Hi." I waved sheepishly from my hole. "My name is Faye de Winter. I'm a new student here, and I seem to be having a disagreement with the porch. Could you give me a hand or get Harrison or something—"

"You can't come in here."

Her voice dripped like honey off a spoon, sweet and summery. She sounded like she was singing as she spoke. But beneath all that saccharine sweetness was a stinger that would cause serious damage if I crossed her. Apparently, just my existence was enough to bring out this girl's claws.

I shrugged, as if it were no big deal, as if I got stuck in porches every day. "I told you, I'm a student here, so—"

"See this?" She stepped backwards, gesturing to the grand stone arch, polished wood paneling and antique sideboard in the hall behind her. "All *this* is for the students who can actually *afford* tuition. You may be sitting in on our classes, but you're not one of us. You're a *servant*. Use the servant's entrance."

"But—"

She slammed the door in my face.

3

FAYE

*B*itch.

Twatface.

Cockpoodle.

I glared at the door, screaming my most imaginative insults inside my head.

Guess I'm on my own. Fine. Whatever. I'd been on my own for a long time. De Winter women looked after ourselves. I worked two jobs, graduated high school with a 3.8 GPA *and* aced my Sibelius piece for violin exams, all while managing my mother's money and dealing with her useless board of directors and being by her bedside every chance I got. I'd done all that, so I could pull myself out of this fucking porch.

I grabbed the velvet rope again. The dong sounded inside the house, but I figured no one was coming. I leaned back against the rope, sitting as much as I could on the porch and bracing my other leg against the door as I hauled myself up.

Doooooooong.

The gong continued to ring as hand-over-hand I hauled myself out. Sweat dripped down my face. Finally, my leg flew free, and I bounced onto the porch in one piece.

Mostly in one piece. A jagged cut opened down the side of my jeans, enough so I could see the long scrape and dribble of blood. I rubbed off the dirt and spiderwebs as much as I could, but there was nothing I could do about my ruined outfit until I got inside.

Guess I'd better find the servant's entrance.

I picked up my violin case and hobbled around the side of the house, my leg stinging. The blood boiled beneath my skin. That blonde girl didn't even give me a second to explain myself. She could see I needed help, and she'd slammed the door in my face. Now I had to go inside and serve her food and clean up after her.

I guess I have to get used to being talked to like that.

As I hobbled and fumed, I passed under a window partially obscured by creeping ivy. The pane was open a crack. I stopped in my tracks, arrested by the music flowing from inside.

The lightest flutter on the keys made the piece sound effortless, but I recognized it immediately as Liszt, *La Campanella*. Liszt is one of the hardest composers to play since the rotten bastard loved to create knotty compositions that seemed to defy the laws of physics. If you made even a couple of mistakes, the whole thing sounded like complete shit, so it was gutsy to add a piece like that to your repertoire.

This musician wasn't just playing Liszt, they created *magic* with Liszt. The skips and runs carried with them a wild passion that evoked the master's unconventional style, but with a playfulness that was completely unique.

I couldn't help myself. I set down my violin and stepped onto the raised garden bed, craning my neck to peer through the window. The music drew me up short, grabbing my heart in my chest. I needed to see who could play like that.

I squinted into the darkened room, my breath catching in my throat as I struggled to make out the shapes of furniture and people. A girl sat at the piano, her delicate features bent toward the keys, her eyes heavy-lidded as she *felt* her way through the piece. A waterfall of white-blonde hair – perfectly straight and shimmering like threads of silver – cascaded down her back. In the shadows, I could just make out the folded legs of the tutor, sitting in rapt contemplation.

The pianist was a tiny wisp of a thing, everything about her light and effortless, her eyes closed, her features serene. How did a girl like *that* channel the kind of raw emotion that made tears prick at the corners of my eyes—

"Ms. de Winter," a sharp voice broke my reverie. "What do you think you're doing?"

4

FAYE

I jumped at the voice, slamming my head into the stone lintel. Red welts danced in front of my eyes.

At least I'm not thinking about the pain in my leg anymore.

Rubbing my head, I turned to face Madame Usher. She stood on the path in another of her sweeping lace gowns – this one black and purple – her hands on her hips and an expression of utter disgust on her painted face.

Great. Because this day couldn't get any worse.

"Skulking around the grounds and peering in windows like a cat burglar," she tsked. "This is not the conduct of a Manderley student. Under my tutelage, you represent not just me but all the graduates of our fine school. I will not tolerate this kind of anti-social behavior. Do you understand?"

"I was trying to find the entrance, and I—"

"A simple, 'Yes, Madame Usher' will suffice." She hit me with that smile again, the one that promised pain if I didn't obey.

I bit back a hundred wicked retorts. "Yes, Madame Usher."

The words tasted like sandpaper. I hated having to bow and scrape for this woman – the bitch who'd seduced Dad with all her promises, leaving Mom broken and me without a father.

"Good. Follow me."

I jumped down from the garden wall, sending a jab of pain through my skull. I must've hit the lintel harder than I thought. As I bent to pick up my violin case, Madame Usher's mouth pinched like she was sucking a lemon.

"We enforce a strict dress code. I realize you've been living 'in the hood', but your hobo-chic style will not be tolerated here."

What's she talking about— Oh, right. I glanced down at my torn and filthy jeans, which now boasted a few dead leaves and dewy patches from the overgrown garden. "I fell through a rotting board on the porch. I was hoping to change before I saw you—"

"When I want you to talk, Ms. de Winter, I will make a request."

Okay, fine. It's going to be like that.

Her demeanor made no sense to me. In the hospital, she claimed to still love my father. She was impressed by my playing. She even used the word 'delighted.' But now she seemed almost annoyed that I was here.

For a slight woman, Madame Usher walked fast, with purpose. I had to jog to keep up, which only made my leg and head hurt more. She led me along a wide path and through a small iron gate into a kitchen garden overgrown with weeds. A narrow wooden door broke the monotony of the brick wall. Madame removed a set of keys on a metal loop and selected one, turning the ancient lock until it clicked.

How was she planning to let me in if the door was locked?

The door opened onto a short hallway, cloaked in shadows. A single fluorescent bulb swung from the ceiling, barely penetrating the corners.

She showed me into the first room – a narrow pantry stacked with supplies. A whiteboard on the wall detailed shopping lists and menus in delicate, looped handwriting. The floor had this gritty feeling, like someone had upset a salt shaker but never bothered to clean it up.

The cupboard opposite held cleaning supplies. Another led to a laundry with an ancient washing machine and drying racks suspended from the ceiling. I half expected there to be a hand-cranked wringer and a stone for grinding flour.

The final door led into a low-ceilinged kitchen. One entire wall was taken up with an old-fashioned wooden stove with cast-iron pots and pans suspended from a rig that wouldn't look out of place in a sex dungeon. Dark mahogany cupboards lined both sides, with wooden tops scuffed and marked with age. A narrow window above the sink looked out across the back garden and outbuildings, over a bubbling stream and down the mountain valley beyond.

This place is unreal. I've stepped back in time.

"Harrison will cut the firewood. The woods around the house are part of our estate, and we also manage the forest on this side of the mountains – thinning the trees is an important part of management, but that's Harrison's concern. It's up to you to monitor the household wood supply and let him know when you're running low. The oven is wood burning, and there are three fireplaces on this floor, plus one in every bedroom. During winter you'll need to light the fires in the morning and bring up the wood to the bedrooms. I provide a weekly budget for food and cleaning supplies. All of this is detailed here." She opened a drawer and showed me a leather-bound ledger, the corners stained with flour-dusted fingertips.

In the center of the room, a farmhouse table with bench seats groaned under the weight of at least ten boxes. Flies buzzed lazily around the pile, and I noticed some weird red stains on the corner of the cardboard leaking onto the table.

"This is the last grocery order. It's a few weeks old now. We've been ordering catering from the village since Clare..." Madame Usher left the sentence hanging. "It is not sufficient. You'll need to clean this up and make a new order for what we're missing. The details are in the ledger."

I stared at the pile, appalled. "You just left all this food here to rot?"

She sniffed. "I've been a little preoccupied with preparations for the school year – and the police snooping around the house, asking unsavory questions about Clare's accident. The other students don't even know how to boil an egg. They have more lofty concerns. Here are your keys."

An loop of keys sat on the kitchen table, identical to the ones Madame Usher held. I picked them up, surprised by the weight of them. Lots of locked rooms in this house. Lots of secrets.

Dread settled in my stomach as Madame Usher led me out of the kitchen and down a narrow hallway to emerge from a small door under a grand staircase. *The* staircase where Clare had fallen to her death.

I stood in the entrance hall I'd seen earlier. Thick velvet drapes hung from the front windows, allowing only a sliver of dull light through the gaps. Patterns leaped at me from the floral carpet and the gilded moldings to the painted decorations on the heavy wooden furniture and the faded Victorian wallpaper. From this angle, I got a good look at the portraits crowding the walls. Previous teachers, students, and patrons of the school, judging by the number of fancy wigs and instruments.

Faint snatches of music echoed through the lofty room, snatching at the lifeless details of the house, threatening to bring the patterns to life.

I noticed an empty square on the wall at the foot of the staircase. The wallpaper stood out in vibrant colors – women clothed in sheer shifts surrounding a basket floating in blue-tinged water – showed that a painting had been recently removed.

"What happened here?" I pointed to the empty square. "Did someone take up a career in the evil jazz and have to be excommunicated?"

"That portrait has been sent for repairs." Madame Usher

started across the entrance hall, her skirts sweeping behind her. "Do not trouble yourself with it. Follow me."

She led me down a wide hallway lined with even more antiques and gilded portraits. My feet sank into a heavy rug. Here, the Liszt grew louder, the sound muddied by another voice – a haunting violin melody from behind a different closed door that rose and fell through the piano, playing a completely different song. The two compositions meshed together into something dissonant and vaguely threatening.

"We have three practice rooms on the ground floor. These must be shared between all students." Madame flung open a wide door to reveal an azure-blue parlor. Velvet chairs lined the walls, facing inwards to scattered music stands and a second grand piano – a Bösendorfer, by the look of it. *Wow, they only make like, a few hundred of those a year. Madame Usher must be hella loaded.* "This is the Blue Room. The others – the Yellow and the Red Rooms in the turret – are currently occupied. You may book slots on the sign-in sheets located on the noticeboard in the hall."

"Wow." I'd seen the pictures in the brochure, but being here in person, surrounded by all the heavy furniture and gilded finery… all I could think of was how long it was going to take to dust.

"We have lessons and guest lectures in the morning, from 8 until 11 in the Red Room or the Ballroom. At 11AM we break for lunch. In the afternoon, you will have your private lessons with Master Radcliffe. When you are not in lessons, you will be practicing in groups or alone, completing your assignments, or attending to your household duties. We offer regular opportunities for students to perform in the community and abroad, and we also give several recitals, galas, and showcases throughout the year. Many of the top conductors, patrons, and industry professionals will be in attendance, so it is important you participate and that you continue to meet our high standards. At the end of the year, Master Radcliffe and I will choose one student to accept the Manderley Prize. That student will be awarded $200,000 and is practically guaranteed an international career. It is unlikely you will be in the running for this, given your sub-standard education after you left my tutelage. But nevertheless, I believe in equal opportunities, and I'd love nothing more than to award this to Donovan's child."

"Gee, thanks." *Because the only thing worthwhile about me is the fact I'm his daughter.*

She continued without acknowledging my reaction. "These rooms must be kept immaculate. If the housework is not kept up to our standards, you will not be allowed to continue here as a student. I will show you the bedrooms."

I nodded, the ball of dread inside me spinning faster. The study program she just described would be intense on its own, and I'd have to keep this huge house with all these antiques clean and cook on top of it? It sounded impossible.

Obviously it's impossible. She's made it that way on purpose.

As soon as the thought occurred to me, I knew it was true. I had no idea why, but Madame Usher *wanted* me to fail. But then why was I here? She didn't have to invite me to her rich school or pay for Mom's care. She could have just ignored my teacher's recommendation, pretended she never knew I was still playing the violin. So what was her deal?

I didn't understand, but I was determined to find out.

I expected us to return to the entrance hall to ascend to the second story. Instead, Madame Usher led me down a narrow corridor, past two wide mahogany doors opening into a grand ballroom with yet *another* grand piano, to a narrow flight of plain wooden steps.

The servants' stairs.

We ascended to emerge at the end of another long, wide hall. On each door was a gilded plate displaying each student's name and instrument.

TITUS THIBODEAUX, CELLO, I read as we walked past. Thibodeaux? I wondered if Titus was any relation to Amos and

Delphine Thibodeaux, the famous New Orleans Classical duet who injected their jazz heritage into their performances.

AROHA RAWHIRI, PIANO... Someone inside practiced a dissonant Russian piece. HEATHER DANVERS, VIOLIN... IVAN AND ELENA NICOLESCU, VIOLIN AND PIANO... I wondered why they shared a room. Were they married? Interesting – students usually entered a conservatory like Manderley straight out of high school, or even before they were eighteen. How could they get married so young?

"...expect these ensuites to be tidied and the sheets changed every week. Other than that, the students are responsible for their own rooms. There are guest suites on this floor for parents or visiting musicians, and you'll need to dust—"

Madame Usher's voice receded into the background. The door on the far end of the hall hung open. I stepped in front of it, and curiosity drew my gaze inside.

Sprawled across an enormous canopy bed hung with blue curtains was the most beautiful guy I'd ever seen. He was my age, but the look in his slate-grey eyes was older and dripping with sin, like he'd seen some shit and was responsible for most of it. Soft lips set into a cruel slash as haunted eyes flickered over my body.

Familiar haunted eyes.

Eyes I'd recognize anywhere.

It can't be.

I willed myself to turn away, but my gaze drew down his naked chest, across the ink that curved around his pecs, down impossibly sculpted arms to his hands, where treble clef tattoos danced across long fingers.

It was none other than Dorien fucking Valencourt.

My childhood friend, the boy who'd torn my heart out and stomped it so hard that I'd never open it for anyone else, shot me a wily smile as his fingers stroked the most enormous cock I'd ever seen.

5

———

FAYE

*D*orien Valencourt.

This is impossible. Of all the gin joints in all the world, how can he be here? There's no way.

Sound the fucktrumpets, I'm doomed.

My throat dried. I tried to tear my eyes away, but they'd fixed on that cock like I was radar and it was a German U-boat – a rigid vessel plundering the oceans...

Ahem.

Dorien slid his perfect body off the bed. He didn't bother to throw a towel over himself or pull on a shirt or anything, because the universe was not that fucking kind to me. As he strode toward the door, my mind flicked between past and present.

Dorien's shit-eating grin as he smeared peanut butter into another student's clarinet. Dorien embracing me with joy when we found out we would be in the same advanced class. Dorien's cold eyes stripping my soul bare as he told me we weren't friends anymore—

Me with my eyes ringed in red, sitting in that uncomfortable plastic chair in Mom's hospital room, staring in rapt attention at my computer screen as it played a montage of Dorien's concert footage from his last tour with Broken Muse. My body responding with fire and flame as those same inked fingers danced over the keys.

The other two musicians playing with Dorien were hot as sin, too, but that just made things worse. An African American cellist shredded his bow across the strings, his beaded cornrows swinging around his head as he contorted the music to his will. He turned his head toward the camera, and the instant my eyes met his midnight orbs I felt a sizzle run down my spine – a magnet pulling me into the screen, into a twisted world where a guy like that would notice a girl like me. Then the camera flicked to the violinist – a white-haired beauty with eyes of pure ice, whose long fingers curled around the strings with such exquisite grace an unshed tear squeezed from my eye. And I thought I'd already cried all the tears I had in me...

As the memories flooded me, recognition flashed in Dorien's eyes. His stride faltered for just a moment, but he regained himself, wiping over his expression with a hardness that sent a shiver down my spine.

"Stay out of my private room, trash." Dorien's voice was like music on my body, strumming me in all the right places even as he insulted me.

The door slammed in my face, the sound ricocheting through the house like a gunshot. From Aroha's room, I heard a bow screech across the strings and someone curse.

Dorien, what's happened to you?

The old Dorien, my childhood best friend, was a total ham. He was always playing practical jokes and trying to make me laugh when I got too serious. He loved to make people laugh, to make them adore him.

I saw nothing of that bright, fun little dude in those stony eyes. All the fun had been sucked out of Dorien's soul. Sure, he was fucking gorgeous beyond belief, but what good were brooding good looks and playboy ways if you were shriveled up inside?

His soul may be shriveled, but his dick—

I had to bite my lip to stop myself salivating. What was wrong with me? Get a grip, *Faye*. *You're here so your mother can get the best medical care, and that's it. You're definitely 100% not here to chase after a guy who already rejected you once.*

If Madame Usher noticed Dorien's nakedness, she seemed unperturbed. She continued my tour past a row of guest suites, bathrooms, another tiny practice room, a small gallery/storage room filled with instruments donated to the school, and a library in a double-height room filled with dusty old books and scores no one had ever read. I nodded and listened with half an ear, my mind occupied with Dorien.

What changed him?

Why is he here?

Dorien didn't need Manderley. He already had an international career. Having the prestigious program on his resume might look good, but so would touring internationally as a soloist or with the other two Broken Muse hotties, and he couldn't do both at once. That dead, haunted look in his eyes – he didn't want to be here. So why was he?

I bet it's his parents. Even when Dorien was being a complete shit, he loved the music, and he wanted so badly to do well. His parents pushed him hard – his mother always sat in the back of the class, her eyes burning holes in his back as she memorized his every movement to criticize later. They were both super odd – I went to their house once for Dorien's birthday, and his father made us play in this room that had no furniture and only a box of wooden blocks – but Mom said that was just how old money people were. They seemed to like me, though, although it was primarily my father's fame that interested them. I always wondered if they were the reason Dorien broke up our friendship, but I didn't want to make excuses for his dickweasel behavior—

With a start, I realized Madame Usher had stopped in her tracks. I skidded on the heavy carpet in an attempt to halt my momentum before I slammed into her. I succeeded, but it threw me off-balance. My flailing hand caught a vase, toppling it off the edge of its stand. I lunched and caught it before it smashed on the floor.

"Watch yourself." Madame Usher gestured to a heavy wooden door at the end of the hall with a NO STUDENTS sign engraved on it. "I live in the east wing of the house. No student is to enter my private rooms unless invited. Disobeying this rule will result in an *immediate* expulsion. Do not take this lightly, as I have dismissed students before."

I nodded.

"Master Radcliffe lives in the stable house toward the rear of the grounds. He joins us for meals unless he is traveling. You've met Harrison already – he lives in the gatehouse you saw when you came in. If you need to know where to find anything, he's the best person to ask. I'll be too busy with the school to be concerned with small details. This is the first year I'll be running our program without Victor, and it must run flawlessly. Any questions?"

A million, but none I wanted to ask her. "Where's my room?"

"You will be on the third floor. Follow me."

Up another flight of stairs, so steep and narrow I had to hug my violin case to my chest in order to fit. We emerged on a small landing, the walls of clapboard sloping inward at such a steep angle I had to stoop as I climbed up. Madame Usher pulled a string and a single, bare bulb lit the space.

We were obviously in the attic of the house. Facing me were three doors. I assumed that when the building was used as a stately home, servants lived in these rooms. It seemed fitting then that I'd be given one. Madame Usher found another key on her ring and shoved it into the lock of the middle door.

"We had these rooms remodeled three years ago when we employed Clare. The room on your left is your bathroom – this outside door is blocked off, so the only access is through your room. The other door must remain locked at all times," she said. "We use it for storage, and it contains many old tools and other odds and ends. It becomes a health and safety issue if students are wandering inside, so I've not given you a key for it."

She swung open the middle door to reveal a surprisingly large space. The walls sloped toward the center of the room, and a dormer window cast cool light across the grey shag rug and comfortable – if worn – furniture. A white brass bed made with cream sheets faced the window. A stack of blankets rested on a carved wooden chest. The stone chimney rose through one corner of the room, so at least I would stay warm when the downstairs fire was lit.

Sticking me in the attic was obviously another part of Madame's plot to humiliate me, but she'd have to do better. The room was actually pretty cool – it had more personality than the ritzy suites downstairs. I set my violin case beside the chair at the window. "Thank you."

I hovered there, waiting for her to leave. When she didn't, I upturned my duffel bag on the bed and picked through the clothes I'd hastily shoved inside, pulling out my two concert dresses to hang on the rack beside the window, and a spare set of jeans to change into.

"What are you doing?" she demanded.

"Unpacking."

"No time for that." She glanced at her watch. "It is past ten. We dine promptly at eleven. You need to get back to the kitchen."

6

FAYE

*A*n hour of frantic chopping and sautéing later, I had prepared a passable lunch with what I found still usable in the fridge and pantry – herb-encrusted lamb medallions, a warm chorizo and sweet potato salad, and some stale bread that I'd sliced into croutons and grilled with a little garlic and served with a caramelized onion preserve I'd found on the shelves. Mom may not have been a virtuoso dickhead like my father, but I learned a lot from her – namely, how to rock the fuck out of a bare kitchen.

Bringing the heavy plates of food into the dining room was another matter entirely. It was another chance for my natural coordination to shine. As I rounded the corner of the staircase, one of the croutons slid off the plate and landed preserve-side down on the hallway rug.

Great. That's going to leave a stain. Remember to pick it up later.

Talking and laughing echoed off the high ceilings as I entered the room and got a first look at my fellow students.

Dorien Valencourt sat at the right-hand side of Madame Usher, where he held court over the table. He must've just said something hilarious, because the honey-haired girl who left me stuck in the porch tossed her hair over her shoulder and laughed. Her laugh sounded like water trickling down a waterfall.

The white-haired waif I'd seen at the piano sat beside a boy who… wait a second.

It was the violinist from Dorien's videos, I was *sure* of it. He and the girl looked practically identical – the same perfectly-straight silver hair, arresting eyes and sharp cheekbones. While she had the appearance of a pixie, he was a dark elf, the kind that lured you off the path into a magic circle where he'd make wild love to you and then cut your head off and suck out the blood. He placed his hand over his sister's, his icy gaze sweeping me with that a menace that made it clear he was as dangerous as he was beautiful.

Twins. That explained their identical last name, but not why they shared a room. Wouldn't they want their own space?

Across the table from the twins was a girl with curves like mine (maybe we could be friends…) – her skin a deep, rich brown, and her eyes sparkling with mischief. She wasn't African American, but I couldn't place her features. She wore a tight leather skirt and a black tank top that showed off swirling black tattoos across her shoulders and only barely covered her tits, as well as an attitude that told the world to fuck right off. She bent her head to speak with a guy I immediately recognized as the third Muse from Dorien's video. He could only be Titus Thibodeaux. In the dim candlelight, he *was* the spitting image of his father Amos, except that Titus' smoky eyes – the edges tinged with midnight – shared none of the maestro's warmth. He looked like he'd spent the day at back-to-back funerals with a quick stop in between for a root canal.

Madame Usher sat at the head of the table, and a white-haired man with soft grey eyes and a slightly-hooked nose faced her on the other end. Master Radcliffe, I guessed. A rare musician who had mastered three instruments, the brochures made a big deal about his presence on Manderley's staff. He was the only person who smiled at me as I approached the table.

Dorien Valencourt stood as I slunk forward, my knee stinging from where the porch bit me. He wore clothes this time, thank fuck, although his skintight black jeans and fitted red shirt with Baroque embroidery on the collar and cuffs did nothing to disguise that hot-as-sin body beneath. A hand reached out to me, those treble clef tattoos dancing over his fingers, and I imagined what it would feel like to have those hands dance across my naked skin—

I stiffened, my hands trembling. *Is he coming to speak to me? Is he going to lead me to my seat like a gentleman and—*

Dorien's eyes trailed across my body, searching my rumpled t-shirt and torn jeans for something he didn't find. He turned away with a snort of disgust and grabbed a decanter of red wine from the sideboard, pouring the dark liquid into crystal glasses.

Madame Usher nodded to me. I set the platters in the middle of the table, then stepped back awkwardly, not sure what to do. Did I sit at the table, or did she have a closet somewhere where Harrison and I shared a bowl of gruel?

"Join your fellow musicians," Madame Usher commanded me.

No closet for me. Counting that as a victory, I pulled out the only empty chair – next to the one Dorien had vacated. Six heads whipped around. Six pairs of eyes stared me down.

"Students, this is Faye de Winter. She will be joining us for the master class on violin, as well as taking over duties from dear departed Clare."

"There's only supposed to be six students," Titus broke in, his deep voice rumbling over my bones. Cornrows tumbled over his shoulders as he grabbed for the meat, narrowly missing dragging his hair in the food. "Master Radcliffe never takes more than six students, and Victor isn't here any longer to teach piano, so—"

"The Master has accepted Faye as a favor to me, as we're in need of domestic help. Her father is *the* Donovan de Winter, my greatest love." Madame's eyes glazed over, and for a moment she was lost in some memory of my father. Funny, so was I, although I doubt we saw the memories in the same way.

"He *was* my father," I corrected her. "Now he's taking a dirt nap."

Across the table, the brown-skinned girl snorted. Madame Usher gave no indication she heard me. "If Faye has even an ounce of his talent, then she will be a serious contender for the Manderley Prize."

This was the opposite of what she told me, but it was obvious from the six hostile glares around the table that Madame wanted me to be hated.

Dorien handed out glasses to everyone except the male twin – he of the sapphire eyes. It was weird to be drinking alcohol at lunchtime, on what was technically a school day, when I bet most of us were still under twenty-one, but I'd been at prep school long enough to know there were different rules for the rich and snooty. When Dorien came to my glass, he'd finished the decanter, so he had to open another bottle. He fiddled with some aerator device on the lid, then filled my glass to the rim – double the amount of alcohol than he'd given the others.

"Why didn't you save yourself the effort and hand me the bottle?" My voice dripped with sarcasm as I tried not to spill on the pristine white tablecloth.

"I bet that's how they drink wine in the *Bronx*." Dorien let the word drip from his tongue, the plosive slapping me across the face. Interesting. How did he know where I'd been living? When I knew him, we lived in the East Village.

If Dorien knows about Mom's illness and our fall from grace... could the floor just swallow me now?

My fingers curled into fists. I could flatten Dorien's perfect nose. It would even things out between us if he had a ruined face to match my ruined life, but that was probably exactly what Madame Usher wanted – the perfect excuse to get rid of me.

Not to mention the fact that messing up a face that perfect was a cardinal sin.

Remember, you're not here for yourself.

It took a buttload of self-control to uncurl my fist and hold my glass like I was grateful for it. As long as I toed the line, Mom got the best medical care money could buy. Maybe these fancy new specialists could figure out what the cut-rate chop-shop Dr. Frankensteins at the last hospital could not, and bring her back to me.

Now that I knew Madame Usher set me up to fail, I was more determined to stay, to win, and to find out exactly what her story was. Why was she so determined to have me here if she also wanted me to fail? Why offer to help my mom when she tried to steal her husband? And why *now?*

My scraped leg stung, and I knew I'd trailed cobwebs across the rug. Under their scrutiny, I felt myself coming apart. They all wore designer clothes and smiles of cut glass. Ivan ran his hands through a feathered haircut that probably cost more than a month's rent at our Bronx apartment. The brown-skinned girl, who I guessed was Aroha (was that Hawaiian? I didn't think I could ask) wore several large rings on her fingers, the diamonds twinkling beneath the flickering candles.

Dorien's eyes flicked over me, stripping away my clothing with his mind, the way his music laid my soul bare. I shuffled in my seat beside him, completely naked. He smirked – a mean expression. He didn't like what he saw.

An awkward silence settled over the table as everyone sipped their wine and stared at the food as if it might sprout tentacles and devour them all. Madame Usher frowned at my wine glass until I took the hint and sipped. It tasted foul, like rotten apples soaked in feet. I hoped she didn't expect me to drink the whole thing.

Finally, Master Radcliffe leaned forward and picked up the platter of lamb. "This looks delicious." His voice had a melodious tenor to it, as though he was still within a song. He scraped three medallions onto his plate, along with a generous helping of salad. That seemed to be an unspoken cue for everyone else to dive in. I waited until all the students had food on their plates before leaning in to serve myself. They hadn't left me any lamb (greedy bastards) so I loaded up with salad and bread. I'd need it to soak up the wine, which was already making me feel ill and, judging by Madame Usher's furious glances, I was expected to finish.

"So, Faye, please tell us about yourself," said the Master in his pleasant tone. "Who have you been studying under?"

I was about to say, "Ms. Finch for History and Mr. Sacks for Mathematics," when I clicked that he was referring to my music teachers.

Eyes bored into me. "Emma Garrison," I muttered into my plate. My tongue stuck to the roof of my mouth, and there was this strange harshness in the back of my throat.

Across the table, snickers were muffled with napkins.

"Emma Garrison? I can't say I've heard of her. Is she with the Berlin school?"

I shook my head. *Is he deliberately baiting me, or does he not know?* "She's… independent."

"What Faye means is that she's been under the tutelage of *amateurs*," Madame Usher offered up. "This Ms. Garrison is her high school music teacher – and their music program is far from distinguished. Such a waste of rare and exquisite talent. You'll have your work cut out for you, Maestro."

Across the table, Aroha choked back a snort. She tried to cover up the sound by crunching on some bread, but my skin bristled.

What did I expect? These rich assholes had been studying under accomplished masters since they were still in diapers, while I had to give up my expensive lessons *twice* so we could survive. The gaps in my knowledge put me behind them before we'd even began.

"I remember your father well," Master Radcliffe continued. "We met on several occasions at symphony events in the city. I saw him perform Sibelius with the London Philharmonic, and it was one of the most sublime performances I've ever encountered. The world was not ready to lose him."

I nodded. What else was there to say? I hadn't been ready to lose him, either. Too bad I had no say in the matter. One minute, Dad was yelling at Mom that she didn't appreciate his need for artistic space after she'd worked twenty-two hours straight to cover his flights to Venice and couldn't understand why he'd been home all day and hadn't cooked dinner. The next, he'd disappeared without a trace.

A memory surfaced that I hadn't thought of in a long time, that I'd shoved into that little black box in my head of things too painful to think about. A much younger, much skinnier Madame Usher standing in our doorway, her lips wet with crimson lipstick and her faux floral scent bowling through our house like Hurricane Bitchface. My mother facing her with a rigid back and hardened eyes. The pair of them sitting opposite each other at the kitchen table, untouched cups of coffee and an unopened white envelope between them. Nine-year-old me sitting on the stairs and straining to listen, but they spoke so low and in such harsh voices... when Madame Usher left, she carried the envelope and wore a satisfied smirk that didn't reach her eyes, and Mom stopped crying. She didn't shed a single tear for Dad after that.

I did the crying for us both, and a fat lot of good my overactive tear ducts did, sobbing over a man who I now knew was nothing but a rotten cheater.

I still didn't know what they'd said that day, or what was in that envelope.

"—Victor's most accomplished pupil," Madame Usher was still gushing about my father. "Donovan was to be the shining star of Manderley Academy, but the fates had other ideas."

I wished the Master would change the subject before me and my steak knife took a trip to stabby town. Instead, he reached for a second helping of salad. "You aspire to a career in music?"

"I don't know." That was the honest answer.

"If you don't know, then why are you here?" Madame Usher snapped.

More giggles from across the table. Only the waifish girl – Elena – looked uncomfortable.

"I'm here because you were in desperate need of my culinary skills." I popped a piece of chorizo in my mouth. As if she didn't know – I couldn't go off on a world tour while my mother still lay in a hospital bed.

The conversation moved on to discussing an upcoming recital the students were giving at a museum in New York City. An animated debate broke out over which showpieces they should perform. I longed to join in, but I'd never heard them play, and I got the vibe my opinion wasn't welcome.

Beside me, Dorien dominated the conversation. As he teased Ivan about his fingering technique, I caught a hint of the mischievous boy I'd grown up with. Being this close to all three Muses made my body light up and my stomach twist in ways I didn't understand. I averted my gaze across the table, but Titus's dark eyes bore into mine with unsettling intensity, as if he saw nothing wrong with cutting me open to study my entrails. I decided staring at my food was the best option. Between glances up from my salad, I noticed the honey-blonde (Heather?) hanging on Dorien's every word, nodding in agreement to whatever he said.

Yes, Dorien. Of course, Dorien. Polish your cock for you, Dorien—

"Oops." Dorien knocked my fork off the edge of the table. "Let me get that for you."

It's fine, I wanted to say, not wanting him any closer. But my mouth didn't work. Too much hot in this room.

As Dorien bent over to reach under the table, his head drew

close to my thigh. His breath tickled the bare skin behind my knee, where my jeans had torn. I sucked in a breath. Fire shot through my limbs.

Dorien hesitated, his body stiffening. A lock of dark hair fell forward, brushing my thigh. He whipped his head around to glare up at me, his lips dangerously close to… to… places a guy that hot had never been close to before. My body reacted instantly, all the fire inside me converging between my legs. I clamped my thighs together, but it was too late. A faint gasp escaped my lips… a gasp Dorien Valencourt heard.

Dorien's lips curled back into a smirk. He knew exactly what he was doing, hovering over me like that. What a Dickweasel.

"You like this?" He arched a perfect eyebrow. My tank top had ridden up, and his lips blew hot air against my already-burning skin. I could almost imagine him as the Dorien I used to know. *Almost.* If not for that coldness in his eyes.

"I'd like my fork back," I managed to choke out.

Dorien sat up, leaving me flushed. He dropped the fork onto my plate and leaned toward me. Carpet fluff rolled off into my food, but I didn't care. I hated the sizzle that swept through my veins as his breath tickled my ear.

"You don't belong here, Sprite," he whispered. "And we're going to make sure you know it."

7

DORIEN

uck.

Faye de Winter.

Double fuck.

My mind spun, and I struggled to push out any coherent thought other than the mountain of trouble I'd brought down on my own head. When Madame Usher informed me the Master wished to offer a place to Faye de Winter, I told myself it didn't matter. I stopped caring about Faye a long time ago. I'd be able to do what I had to do to keep my place at Manderley.

I lied to Madame.

I lied to myself.

Next to me, Faye hunched over her plate, her skin deliciously close. She stared at her salad like it held the mysteries of the universe. The wine stained her lips with a hint of red, like the blush of an intense kiss.

My skin crawled with her scent. Lavender and orange blossom – a distinctive perfume. The scent of my childhood. Of another time, when I'd been happy, free, not trapped in a night-mare of my own making.

I'd steeled myself for seeing Faye again, but the minute she appeared in my doorway it all went to shit. I pulled that stunt in the bedroom to throw her off, to show her right from our first meeting that she was *nothing* to me, but that was a lie, too. I'd known it as soon as I slammed the door and my dick sprang to life in my hands.

Then she waltzed into the dining room with that defiance blazing in her eyes, her clothes all torn and filthy and exuding 'don't fuck with me' from every pore. She wore her half-Mexican heritage with pride – that tumble of black curls down her back and that slightly broad nose turned up, like *she* was too good for *us*, instead of the other way around.

My Faye. My Sprite.

The sooner she was gone from Manderley, the better.

Heather let her gaze fall to Faye's glass, then turned to glare at me, the question obvious on her face. I kicked her foot under the table. Heather could fuck right off if she expected me to explain myself to her. My little fork stunt wasn't part of the plan, but it worked. Too well. I gritted my teeth as I remembered Faye's tiny gasp, a chink in that armor she wore, a hint that the fire scalding my skin was also burning her up inside.

I intended to disarm Faye, to wipe that defiance off her face, but her scent… it sent my head spinning, in a good way what was so fucking bad. My dick was hard again.

For a moment, I fancied I saw a pale face in the corner of the room, hiding in the folds of the curtain. But I blinked, and realised it was just the light falling in a certain way.

Get control, Dorien. Don't let her disarm you. This isn't about you.

I tried to focus on the discussion, anything to take my mind off Faye. I noticed Titus had that sparkle he got in his eyes when someone new walked into his life. He always wanted everyone in the room to love him, and they usually did. I hope his desire to be needed wouldn't fuck up our plan.

Master Radcliffe had turned his attention to Elena and the piece for the upcoming recital. While Elena discussed the merits of the different song choices in her breathless voice, I caught her brother's gaze. Ivan sat ramrod straight, and the venom in his eyes could have poisoned us all.

Of all of us, Ivan had the most to lose to Faye, and that was saying something. I'd seen that look in his eyes before. Once on our last tour, we'd been delayed at the airport in France for sixteen hours, and the airline could only get us to Canada in time for our show if Elena took a later flight. Ivan let *certain facts be known* with his typical Romanian sledgehammer personality, and ten minutes later all four of us had seats in first class.

I cut in with my opinion, trying to insert myself between Elena and Radcliffe, to lead the conversation somewhere that made Ivan less stabby. I kicked Heather again, and she finally took the hint and stopped glaring at Faye long enough to contribute.

I jabbed the lamb on my plate, chewing hard. It looked amazing, but all I could taste was cardboard. Cardboard flavored with lavender and orange-blossom. Unable to help myself, I reached across the table for the pepper and snuck a look at Faye. She sipped her wine again, her hair curtaining her face – a wall of protection against the world, against me.

I hated myself for what I was about to do, but I hated *her* more.

Ten years ago, I told Faye de Winter I never wanted to see her again. Now, she tore through my life like a fucking hurricane. If I didn't strike first, she'd destroy everything. That scent already dragged me under. Those fire-rimmed eyes would burn down everything I'd worked for. She'd ruin me.

I had to ruin her first.

8

FAYE

You don't belong here, Faye. And we're going to make sure you know it.

Dorien's chilling words haunted me all afternoon as my nausea grew worse, mingling with Harrison's warnings and visions of the last maid sprawled at the bottom of the stairs. My stomach churned as I stacked the dishwasher, and I kept looking over my shoulder, expecting to see Dorien or one of the other students sneaking up behind me, brandishing a knife.

By the time I finished in the kitchen, the house sang with faint, stolen notes of perfection as the students practiced. I hiked back to my room to change into a pair of black dress pants and grab my violin. During the day, the attic had heated to an unbearable temperature – a combo of pre-Victorian construction and heat rising through the house. I cracked the window and went to the bathroom to splash cold water on my face, but it did nothing to stop my churning stomach or the flush of sickly heat pooling in my cheeks – heat that had nothing to do with the warm attic and everything to do with those three unnervingly beautiful guys who already seemed to hate me for no reason.

I was heading back downstairs to find a spare practice space when Master Radcliffe stepped out of the music library.

"Faye, I wondered if you might accompany me to the ballroom," he said. "I'd like to hear you play, so we can get a sense of where you are. It's not often I teach students with your... unorthodox training."

He meant my *lack* of training, but he was polite enough not to say it. So far, the Master was the only person in this freak show haunted house who treated me like a human being. But I still found him intimidating – he'd been a superstar a decade ago, but he'd given it all up abruptly to teach at Manderley. There were rumors of a mental breakdown because of the pressure of his career, and of a scandal hushed up, but his warm brown eyes peering at me from behind bifocal glasses betrayed only kindness, and I needed some of that right now.

"Sure. I'd love to play for you."

Master Radcliffe held out his arm and I looped my hand in his, indulging in the old-fashioned and chivalrous way he accompanied me down the main staircase. Already, Manderley seemed like a house stuck in time.

He shoved open the doors of the ballroom. I stepped inside, my stomach lurching as my gaze drew up to the crystal chandeliers dangling from the impossibly high ceiling.

"This room is nearly double-height." Master Radcliffe drew back the velvet curtains, casting a square of grey light across the piano. Outside the towering windows, the forest encroached, trees reaching sinewy fingers toward the windows. "I often imagine the bright parties and balls held in this room, the ladies in their muslin dresses dancing, the dynasties forged and the scandals whispered between gossips. This is my favorite room in the house. As you will soon discover, the acoustics are superb."

He sat down at the piano bench, crossing his legs and folding his hands on his lap. "Please, indulge me with some of your favorites from your repertoire. It will allow me to see your strengths and weaknesses. If you wish me to accompany you, you have only to ask." He tapped out the first bar of Bach's *St Matthew Passion*. "I still have a little fire in my fingers yet."

I rested my violin against my chin and started to tune. Nerves tingled along my spine, and my stomach lurched. For perhaps the first time, I crashed headlong into what it meant to be in a school like this. I knew I would be behind the other students, but I was so focused on Madame Usher's money funding Mom's care that I hadn't considered how it would feel to play for a *maestro*, to see disappointment etched onto his features.

While I tuned, Master Radcliffe kept up a running commentary about my father. "…most exquisite fingering I'd ever seen. He'd have gone on to be one of the greatest virtuosos of our time, if only he'd—oh dear." He winced as I made a bum note. "Do you need more time, perhaps?"

I need you to stop comparing me to that bastard. But instead, I smiled. "It's fine. It's nice to hear from someone who knew my father."

Nice like a hole in the head.

"He came to my summer school in its inaugural year," Master Radcliffe said. "He would have won a full-ride scholarship had he not been so distracted by… social pursuits. He allowed other students to pull ahead of him. I hope you will not make the same mistake."

"I don't intend to." To shut him up, I launched into Brahms' *Violin Sonata No. 3*.

I loved this melancholy piece and usually played it well, but the weight of my father's legacy dragged my arm. I knew as soon as I hit the first arpeggio that I was sluggish. My fingers stiffened on the strings. I closed my eyes so I couldn't see Master Radcliffe's mouth turn down with disappointment.

Halfway through my fumbling attempt at Vivaldi's *Winter*, the door creaked open. All six students slipped in to stand along the wall. Titus was a towering mountain in the corner of the room, his dark energy sucking the last dregs of life from my performance and pummeling them against his bulk. The twins' expressions were featureless, two porcelain dolls sitting on a shelf, silently judging me. Dorien's eyes bore into mine, his smile wide and dark and triumphant.

It was a smile that said, *I'm going to eat you for breakfast.*

My stomach twisted as humiliation burned on my cheeks. *They can't be here. They can't see me play like this.* I'd seen Dorien's dick in all its glory, yet *I* was the one stripped naked.

As I turned my back to the students, my stomach gurgled in protest. Hot bile rose in my throat. I swallowed, but the sensation only grew stronger.

Maybe it wasn't nerves twisting my stomach. Maybe I was going to throw up.

My fingers wobbled on the strings as I shuddered against the rising bile. A wave of nausea crashed into me, turning me about until I lost what little focus I had left. I fumbled my way through the final movement, not daring to take my bow lest I puke all over Master Radcliffe's shoes.

When I lowered my arms, my hands trembled. I knew I'd played badly. If I wanted to prove to Dorien and his posse that I deserved my place here, I'd fucked that right up.

"You have promise, but your technique lacks precision." Master Radcliffe stood up. He took my hand, turning my fingers over and curling them around in an awkward position. I leaned on him more than I should have as another wave of nausea hit me. "That is what comes from having a second-rate education. It may be too late to repair the damage. We will have to work very closely together to transform your technique."

Behind me, Titus snorted. Master Radcliffe looked over his shoulder, for the first time noticing our audience. "Shouldn't you be rehearsing your Elgar, Titus?" he remarked.

With a flash of his obsidian eyes, the midnight edges disappearing in the shadows of the ballroom, Titus stood. "Sorry, Master. We were curious about the new girl."

Dorien stood too. "We won't disturb you any longer."

Interesting. Dorien may strut about like he owned this place, but he respected Master Radcliffe enough to listen to him. I stored that information for later. Any potential advantage I had over Dorien Valencourt was going to prove useful.

Not as useful as a bathroom. I grabbed my protesting stomach as the bile reached the back of my throat.

"May I be excused?" I managed to choke out. Master Radcliffe nodded. I tossed my violin on the settee and sprinted shakily from the room.

"She hasn't even bothered to pack away her instrument," I heard Heather whisper as I jerked open the door. "Trailer trash like her have no respect for their art."

Luckily, the ground-floor bathroom was right across the hall. I slammed the door behind me and hurled into an old-fashioned toilet.

As I wiped my eyes and spat repeatedly into the sink, my thoughts spun faster than my stomach. *Why do I feel so sick?* I'd been fine on the drive, and I'd never had any kind of stage-fright. Nerves, yes, but nothing that would make me physically sick. I'd only started feeling strange after lunch, and it couldn't have been anything I ate because I cooked it all—

The wine.

I thought it tasted gross, but chalked it up to knowing nothing about expensive wine. I remembered something else – Dorien's eyes gleaming as he opened a new bottle. Just for me.

He put something in the wine.

Fucking dickweasel.

And I'd drained the whole glass like a fool, thinking they were testing me. I leaned my cheek against the cool mirror, not caring that I left a smudge I'd have to clean up later.

When I emerged from the bathroom, Heather and Titus waited in the hall. Heather smirked as I walked past. "I'd be sick too if I played that badly. Such a waste of a place at the academy. The garbage disposal plays better than you, that's why we call you trash."

I stalked past her without responding. Titus' immovable bulk towered over me as I headed straight to the noticeboard to see if any of the practice rooms were free. None were. In fact, the rooms had been booked for the rest of the week. Hastily, I scribbled my name in the two remaining gaps in next week's list. I knew I needed all the practice I could get.

I collected my violin from the ballroom and clambered back to the attic. By clambered, I mean I crawled on my hands and knees while doubled over in agony. My phone was still sitting on the bed amongst my strewn belongings. There was a text from the hospital saying Mom had arrived safely. I was too wired to finish unpacking. I dragged a chair under the window, turning it so I could face outside at the sloping, overgrown back garden and stream surrounded by wilderness, the tops of the mountains hidden in the mist.

I placed the violin against my chin and drew the bow across the strings, wishing I could use it to saw off Dorien's stupid gorgeous neck.

I pushed through the pain in my stomach as I launched into a fast piece, building a tremolo with my wrist on the upper part of the bow, then moving to the middle until the bow began to bounce. The harder I pressed, the more the bow bounced, and the faster I could play. My head bobbed as I kept time, the screaming notes echoing the pain gasping at my belly.

This is how I should have played for Master Radcliffe. If Dorien Valencourt hadn't sabotaged me.

As I played, my eyes flicked to the window. The woods, branches reaching toward the house like outstretched hands, waited to grab me and welcome me. It was the kind of woods that appeared in a children's picture book – like the illustrations in an old copy of *Grimm's Fairy Tales* my father gave me – filled with scary monsters and yellow eyes that watched you.

I shook off the melancholy thoughts. *I think the scary monsters are inside the house—*

Wait, who's that?

A figure stalked across the lawn, heading for the trees. A lighter flickered, and a curl of smoke circled a head of straight black hair. I recognized stylized tattoos on her bare shoulders. *Aroha.*

I wonder where she's going?

I itched to go after her, if for no other reason than to bum a cigarette. Behind me, my alarm buzzed.

Fuck. *Have two hours gone by already?* I grabbed my things and headed down to the kitchen. No time for cigarettes when you had rich cockpoodles to serve.

9

IVAN

"What do you think of the new girl?" I slouched into Dorien's room and tapped the door shut with my foot. Titus was already there, kicking off the wall so he could spin the desk chair around in fast circles. *He's far too large a person to be so energetic all the time.*

Dorien looked up from where he was draped across his bed, his eyes flashing.

"You're late."

"Elena's lesson ran over." Dorien didn't ask why I was sitting in on my sister's private class, or why I couldn't leave her there alone. He didn't have to, and I appreciated that. Dorien may be a *mägar*, but he kept my secrets like they were his own. I threw myself on the end of the bed, picking at a loose thread on the embroidered border. "What's the verdict on Miss de Winter?"

"Terrible violinist, but eminently fuckable." Titus scooted the chair over to the window and lifted the sash as high as it could go. He leaned outside and lit up a joint. Smoke curled around his lips as he held it out to me.

I shook my head. I needed that weed to get Faye de Winter out of my head. My body crawled with the awful sensation of being watched by invisible eyes, and I longed for something to take the edge off. But Elena hated drugs and she'd smell it on me. "I agree."

"I wouldn't put my dick in that. You don't know where it's been." Dorien scooted to the corner of the bed and leaned toward the window, grabbing the joint from Titus and taking a deep drag.

I didn't like the look in Dorien's eyes. He'd had the same look the night he handed me those plane tickets in Prague – the night he fucked our lives forever. It was the same murderous rage that burned bright as the police took him away for questioning after Clare's fall.

Watching Faye's face as she struggled through the Vivaldi should have brought me satisfaction. It was going to be too easy to break her, to go on with our lives. But all I felt was a dull ache in my gut. It was an ache borne of failure – in her eyes shone the defiance that coursed through my veins back in Prague, an echo of the man I might have been. Now I'd sold my soul to the devil to save my sister, and made both of us slaves. Not even the music was doing it for me these days. I made myself numb because numb was the only way to get through this, to reconcile the things I had to do.

Nothing made me feel anything except Elena's smile. I'd do anything to see that smile.

"You've met her before, right?" Titus took the joint from Dorien and curled his fat lips around it, swiping a cornrow out of his face. "You used to have lessons with her."

"Back when my parents were crass enough to let me hang around with plebs, yeah." Dorien leaned back on the bed and folded his arms behind his head. "She was mediocre then, too."

The way he said it, we all knew the truth. Faye de Winter was anything but mediocre. That was why she had to go.

"We're going to have to perform with her in ensembles." Titus was talking himself into action. He needed to believe the lie –

and he'd tell himself these fairy tales until they became facts in his mind. "She's going to drag down the reputation of the entire school, if Madame Usher bringing her here hasn't achieved that already."

"It won't come to that." Dorien's eyes fixed on the ceiling. He made a good show of pretending he didn't care, but that haunted look in his eyes gave him away – it was the same look he got when he sat down at the piano, when the music took him over, and it was the reason women flocked to him more than us. Faye de Winter had got under Dorien's skin, and that in itself was interesting. "We need to get rid of her."

I shook his head. 'Why bother? She'll eliminate herself with her masterful grasp of Vivaldi."

Titus laughed. Dorien did not.

"It's her first day. It's probably nerves." Dorien waved a dusty glass bottle in front of my face. "And the syrup of ipecac I put in her wine."

"The what?"

"It's this stuff the Victorians used to use if someone was poisoned to induce vomiting. Clare found all these strange old bottles in the chest in her room. I kept this one – thought it might come in handy one day."

Titus clapped Dorien on the back as he passed the joint back to me. "You're such a shit. No wonder she ran away so fast."

"That's fucking hilarious." *Dorien is dangerous. Right now he's on your side, but never forget he could do that to Elena if you cross him.*

"It was Heather's idea, and we've got a ton more where that came from. We'll make sure Faye leaves Manderley by the end of the semester. Nothing will come back to us." Dorien sat up again, grabbing the joint from Titus and hanging it from his lips. "This is our territory. We're invincible."

Invincible. I used to believe that. The three of us playing sold-out shows in London, Vienna, Berlin, the press dubbing us The Bad Boys of Baroque and unwittingly showering us in a mountain of beautiful women, the promise of bigger and brighter things to come. I'd sure felt invincible then, but then Dorien and I fucked it all up, and now we were all prisoners.

"Here's what Heather and I decided. No one is to talk to her. Don't acknowledge her. Don't insult her. Just act like she isn't there."

"Wait, why is Heather in on this?" I glared at Dorien.

He looked away. "Drop it, Nicolescu. She's got a stake in this, too. She'll keep your precious hands clean for Elena. As far as you're concerned, Faye's ghosted. We'll take care of the rest."

Dorien's wrath was one thing. Dorien making plans with Heather and not sharing with us? A shiver ran down my spine.

Faye de Winter better watch out, Dorien had her in his sights – he planned to enjoy toying with her, and the Prince of Darkness liked to break his toys.

FAYE

After another excruciating meal with the students, during which they all acted like I didn't exist, I slumped back to my room. My stomach and throat still burned from whatever Dorien put in my wine, and I barely picked at my food. As soon as I could excuse myself, I loaded the dishwasher and escaped to my room.

The stuffy air in the attic clung to my clothes. I pushed open the window to let a fresh breeze circulate. Voices and laughter rushed up to greet me. I peered down to see the students gathered around a table at the edge of the garden. Heather looked up and saw me. Her nose turned up as though I gave off a bad smell. Sighing, I stepped away from the window, flung my clothes on a chair and collapsed on the bed in my panties, letting the breeze brush my clammy skin.

The stomach cramps had mostly subsided, replaced by a dull ache. Whatever Dorien had slipped me in the wine, it seemed like I'd be better in the morning. But if they were spiking my wine on the first day, what fresh horror would wait for me tomorrow?

I pulled my phone from my purse and I was halfway through a text to Mom when I remembered, she wouldn't answer because she was in a coma. My beautiful, vibrant mother who'd brought grown men to their knees in the boardroom and on the dance floor had been felled by some mysterious illness, and I had no one left to talk to. It didn't seem as though I was going to make any friends at this school.

Instead, I rang the hospital and checked in with the nurse on duty. She'd been settled in okay – Madame Usher had been as good as her word and moved Mom to their best room. There was no change to her condition.

I scrolled through my contacts list, looking for someone to call. I had a few friends I'd hung out with in high school, mostly fellow music students, but I'd ghosted them when Mom got sick. Amelia moved to Boston to study architecture, and John was backpacking across Europe. I'd seen their pictures on Facebook, but we didn't really talk anymore. I had my excuse, but I was still a shit friend. I hadn't been there for them at all since school finished, and I couldn't call them now when I needed them.

Fuck it. I tossed my phone on the bed in disgust. I was Marguerite de Winter's daughter. I could handle a few rich dick-weasels.

I rolled over and picked up the battered paperback I'd shoved in my bag for the drive. It was this reverse harem romance set in a creepy gothic school called Miskatonic Prep. The main character, Hazel, is bullied by three rich kings of the school, but she holds her own and there's something about her that's not 100% normal—

Creak.

I jerked my head up at the noise. "Hello?"

Creak, creak, creaaaaak.

That sounds like footsteps.

I flung a t-shirt over my bare breasts and went to the door. I opened it gingerly, expecting to see someone on the landing. The square of light from my open door illuminated the narrow space. No one was there.

I must've imagined it.

I pushed the door shut and went back to bed. As soon as I sank into the sheets, the creaking started again. I paused, listening. *It's just the house settling, nothing to worry about—*

Creak, creak, creeeeak.

Nope, that's footsteps.

Definitely footsteps.

On this *floor.*

I slid out of bed, silently this time, grabbing the lamp off the bedside table and yanking the cord from the wall. The creaking continued as I crossed the room and leaned against the door, raising the lamp above my head as my fingers closed around the handle.

Creak. Crea—

"Fuck off," I yelled as I flung open the door and leaped into the gloom.

The creaking stopped.

My breath froze.

The landing was completely empty.

I swung in a circle, then leaned out to check the staircase. No one there, either. My blood rushed in my ears as my fingers tightened around the lamp. "Dorien, if that's you, I'll be reporting this as harassment. I don't care how rich your daddy is."

Silence answered me. I stood until my sweaty fingers could no longer grip the lamp, trying to figure out what the fuck was going on.

Back in my room, I slammed the lamp down and poked my head out the window. Down below, the students gathered around a wrought-iron table, passing a bottle of something around. I recognized all of them – the twins, Heather, Aroha, Titus... and Dorien.

How had he got back outside so quickly?

As if sensing my silent accusation, Dorien looked up. When his eyes met mine, he flashed me a smile that was all teeth and menace. He raked a hand through his hair – the moonlight painted his dark locks with shades of russet and crimson. A rush of heat coursed through my body, and I hated myself for it.

I couldn't be attracted to Dorien Valencourt, or any of the Muses, especially when they turned their ire toward me.

With a roar of frustration, I slammed the window shut and yanked the curtain across. A wave of exhaustion washed over me. I'd only been at Manderley one day and already I wanted to leave. I slouched over to the bed and wriggled under the covers.

But even though my body ached with weariness, I couldn't sleep. My skin crawled with the sensation of being watched. I flicked the light on, scanning the empty room, then flicked it off. But the feeling didn't go away.

And then, just as my eyelids fluttered shut, I heard it again.

The creak of footsteps against the floorboards. Slower now, more deliberate and careful. Only this time, I could tell that they weren't coming from outside my door.

They echoed along the wall opposite my bed.

The footsteps were coming from the locked storage room.

FAYE

Briiing.

I rubbed my eyes, trying to drag my brain from a disturbing dream. *What time is it? Am I late for my shift?*

As my eyes adjusted to the gloom, I stared at my sparse surroundings with confusion. *Did our apartment get robbed? Crap, is Mom okay? Is she...*

Then I remembered. Mom was in her new hospital, getting the best care money could buy. And I was in the attic room at Manderley Academy, about to start my morning duties like a maid of yore. It wasn't even light outside, and I had to be downstairs to make breakfast and clean the rooms before the day's lessons began.

I hadn't heard Dorien or whoever he sent to hide in the storage room again, probably because I buried my face in the pillow and refused to acknowledge their childish stunt. But I'd lain awake for hours, my senses on alert for the next evil trick. The old house creaked and groaned around me – each stirring a fresh wave of nerves, and every gust of wind rattled a windowpane with ill portent.

Now, in the warm light of the morning, I wasn't afraid. I was *pissed as hell.*

I pulled on the plain black dress Madame Usher had given me as a maid's uniform. The wool scratched my skin. *She's laying on this servitude thing a bit thick.* The dress was just another of her subtle digs at my status, marking me out as different from the other students, who all wore designer clothing and owned those expensive cars parked outside.

The zipper stuck. I grabbed it and jumped up and down, tugging until it pulled free. The dress was a little tight across my tits, but otherwise, it wasn't a bad fit. It was pretty unflattering – making me look broad and boxy instead of accentuating the hourglass shape of my hips – but I wasn't at Manderley to be admired. I was here to play music and get my mom the care she needed.

Speaking of which… I picked up my phone for the hundredth time and checked to see that I hadn't missed a message from the hospital saying she'd woken up. Nope, the universe wasn't that kind to me.

Dress on, all I needed was some foundation and a swipe of mascara and I was ready to face the Muses. I shoved open the door to the bathroom.

And screamed.

Scrawled across my mirror in blood-red were the words, LEAVE MANDERLEY.

TITUS

Faye's scream echoed through the mansion. I stared up at the canopy of my bed, red fabric covered in gold stars, and imagined I had the superpower of seeing through solid objects. I peeled away the fabric and ceiling and floorboards in my mind and pictured those feisty eyes wide with terror, her wild hair streaming down her back as she slammed the bathroom door.

My cock stirred, and I wrapped my fingers around it. I closed my eyes. I imagined she was screaming my name.

Faye de Winter.

Everything about her intrigued me. And I haven't been intrigued in a long time. Manderley bored me to death – the crusty old furniture, the dull compositions, the endless hours of practicing the same pieces over and over again. I longed to be back on the road – a new city every night, a new girl in my bed, the applause of the audience washing over me, drowning my veins in pulsing, exhilarating *life*.

Instead, I was trapped here, miles from anything interesting. The only thing to entertain me was Dorien's vendetta against the new girl. When Faye walked into the dining room carrying those trays, I saw something in her eyes I recognized – a wild animal trapped behind bars. She was so much more than her bedraggled clothes and mediocre performance let on. She was more than the ghost from Dorien's past, and if he took his head out of his ass for a second, he'd be able to see it, too.

Not that I wanted him to see it. I wanted Faye for myself.

My hand moved faster, and my cock jerked. Upstairs, someone stomped across the attic floorboards. I pictured Faye as I'd seen her last night while I hovered in her doorway, the key tucked in my hand, waiting for Heather to finish in her bathroom. Moonlight streaked across the bed from the open window, making a pale face appear on her clothes rack. I started, then realised it was just an optical illusion, the same way the moonlight danced shadows across Faye's serene features. Raven hair fanned out across her pillow, falling like ripples of a silken river over the duvet. Looking down at her stirred something inside me – a mixture of fascination, desire, and repulsion at myself. My parents always warned me Dorien was a bad influence, and now here I was, sneaking into a girl's room and watching her sleep like a stalker creep.

I thought about shaking the ankle that peeked out from beneath the sheets. I wanted Faye to wake up, to see us in her room, to scream and rage and wake up the whole house. At least it would shake the cobwebs out of this place.

I wanted her to throw herself at me, to feel her warm skin against mine as her fists pummeled me or her lips devoured me. Either option worked for me, although my cock much preferred the latter.

Instead, I had turned and followed Heather outside. We locked Faye's door behind us and returned to our rooms.

And now I was wanking while Faye freaked out over the message we left in her locked room.

I'm a fucking horrible person.

My breath came out in quick gasps as I pumped harder. *Fuck,*

fuck, fuck. This is sick. It's disgusting. But it's as close as I'll ever get to Faye de Winter.

I was forbidden to speak to her. Dorien's orders. That dude had been there for me more times than I could count. I didn't like to play by the rules, but this was one that I had to obey.

My body dropped back to reality. My cock softened in my hand as the vision of Faye faded from my mind, replaced by something equally beguiling but even more dangerous.

The secret hidden under my bed. The reason I couldn't get close to Faye de Winter. The shame that would eat me alive even as my soul petrified in this house.

The addiction I couldn't shake.

13

FAYE

What the fuck?

I swiped my finger through the wet letters and brought it to my nose. My stomach churned afresh. My mind flicked to Harrison's drawn face as he told me the last maid at Manderley had been murdered.

I scrunched up my face. *I don't want to do this.*

I sniffed.

Odd.

I'd seen enough horror films to expect the metallic tang of blood but instead, I smelled lipstick. In fact… I opened my eyes and rubbed the red between my fingers. Yep, that was definitely lipstick. The color looked suspiciously similar to the one Heather wore yesterday.

A juvenile prank. Just Dorien's style.

Dickweasels.

What concerned me most wasn't the stupid message, but the fact that one of the students snuck into my room *while I was asleep*. They couldn't have climbed in the window, which only left the door.

The door I'd most definitely locked.

I crossed the room in three strides and checked – still locked. I yanked the door open and inspected the mechanism. Nothing broken.

Which means... they have a key.

That probably meant they also have a key to the storage room next door. That would explain the creaking sounds last night. One of them must've hidden in there and waited until I went to sleep, then snuck in to write the message.

Dorien.

But no – I realized with a start that Dorien couldn't have done it if he was hiding in the storage room. I saw him with the other students hanging out around that table, and there was no way he could have made it from there up the stairs to the storage room without me hearing him – the stairs creaked more than an Edgar Allan Poe poem.

My heart leaped in my chest as I crossed to the window and drew back the curtain. Sure enough, there was the table, with an ashtray and an empty bottle of Scotch. They might've snuck up while I was asleep to do the mirror, but that didn't explain the footsteps. I couldn't see how anyone around that table could have been making the footsteps in the storage room.

Unless...

It must've been Aroha. She hadn't been with the group at the table, I remembered.

Great. So they were all in on it with the Muses. Dorien's hatred of me was personal, and I didn't understand it. He was the one who broke *my* heart. But whatever. We at least had a history. The others... they didn't even know me. Aroha didn't look like rich-bitch Heather. Something about her clothes and the tattoos and the way she carried herself told me she didn't give a fuck what anyone thought of her or Dorien's petty problem with me. So why was she sneaking around in the storage closet and writing messages on my mirror?

I turned from the window, squaring my shoulders.

I grabbed my violin case and thundered downstairs, not caring that I sounded like a herd of elephants charging through the silent house. I stood in front of the door to Madame Usher's private chambers.

They have a key to my room. I don't feel safe. Even as the resident charity case, that's unacceptable.

"Madame Usher?" I knocked. "I need to report something. Some of the students broke into my room last night and wrote things on my walls."

Scuffling sounded inside the room. I pressed my ear to the wood as a faint voice hissed something. There were a couple of dull thuds, then footsteps padded toward me.

The door flung open. Madame Usher blocked the door, her eyes blazing. "What did I tell you?"

"Yes, but—"

"I don't care if the house is burning down around us or a flying saucer lands on the roof, you *do not* disturb me. This would be grounds for expulsion, but on account of our arrangement, I will give you a second chance." She glared at me. "Don't do it again."

"Wait. I—"

The door slammed in my face.

"Morning, trash. Sleep well?"

I whirled around. Dorien leaned against his doorframe, wearing only a pair of boxers and a smirk that would raise the Titanic from the bottom of the ocean. The saliva dried on my tongue as I glimpsed the tattoos dancing across his naked skin. *Don't give him the satisfaction of looking. That's exactly what he wants—*

Yeah, turns out I have no self-control. My eyes swept over the hard lines of his torso. Dorien was sin itself – his unearthly angelic beauty hid the bitter pride and desolate state of his soul. I paused at the Gothic lettering spelling out a Latin phrase across his chest. *In Cauda Venenum.*

So different from the boy I'd known, and yet exactly how I'd pictured him. Dorien was always destined to be a rebel. Being the Bad Boy of Baroque was written in his future from the very first time he put red paint on Madame Usher's chair.

Why do the bad boys have to grow up so damn fine?

"No ghosts visit you in the night?" Dorien lifted one perfect eyebrow.

"Fuck you." I stormed past him. His scent hit me – the dark heart of cinnamon and frankincense, dappled with sweet violets. Pure lust shot with innocence. I longed to drown in that scent, to allow it to pull me under even as it warned me that I could lose myself in its depths. "And stay out of my room."

Dorien's cruel laughter followed me down the stairs.

~

Over a breakfast of granola, Greek yogurt, and frozen berries (if the students thought they were getting bacon from me every morning, they had another thing coming) Madame Usher informed us that Dimitri Solokov – the producer of the Moscow Philharmonic Orchestra – would dine at Manderley on Friday.

"Following your private lessons, gather in the ballroom this afternoon. You will each perform your best concerto for Master Radcliffe, who will choose one student to perform for Master Solokov."

My heart pounded. I'd only been at Manderley one night, and already Madame Usher dangled an incredible opportunity in front of me. To have Dimitri Solokov rapt by a solo performance… that was a fucking big deal. Even when Mom was rich enough to send me to the prep-school and my private lessons, I could never even hope for that kind of connection.

The other students continued shoveling food into their

mouths as if Solokov's presence was no big deal, as if bombshells like this dropped every week. Maybe they did.

I've walked into a whole other world.

Madame Usher rose, indicating breakfast was over. I rose, too, circling the table to collect the plates. As the students filed out of the dining room on the way to composition class, Titus drew up beside me, his broad shoulders blocking the door so I had to slow my step to avoid crashing into him. Damn, that boy was *fine* – that buzzed haircut with the cornrows down the middle, tied away from his face so they flowed down his back, the body of a freight train if locomotives modeled Calvin Klein, and those eyes of fire and brimstone. If Dorien was the Lord of Hell, then Titus was Demon-at-Arms. Too bad he'd already decided which side he fell on. He leaned in close to whisper in my ear, "Don't even bother showing up today. Fingering like yours is only good for strangling cats."

I didn't dignify Titus with an answer, but I shot him a look that I hope articulated how little I cared what he thought. His words only made me more determined to succeed.

His lips curled back into a smile. It wasn't warm exactly – the same fire in his eyes flickered across his face. "You drool in your sleep. It's adorable."

The words slammed into me. I stopped in my tracks, my body rigid. Behind me, Heather swore as she crashed into me. She shoved me aside without a word and stomped away. My head spun.

Titus was in my room. He watched me while I was asleep. Now he's smiling at me like that's not creepy at all.

He could have done *anything*. Fear rippled through me – a fear born of uncertainty, of knowing I was at the bottom of the food chain and these guys could do anything they liked to me without consequences. Clearly, they planned to do just that.

An image flashed in my mind – a maid in the same scratchy wool dress I now wore, crumpled at the bottom of the stairs, her neck bent at an impossible angle. Titus opened his mouth to say something else, but I shoved my way past him and fled toward the kitchen.

As I rounded the corner, my chest heaving, I glanced back over my shoulder and noticed Dorien glaring at Titus, who shrugged and pushed past his friend on his way to the practice rooms. *Weird. What's that about?*

In the kitchen, I dumped the crockery into the dishwasher without rinsing it. I had no time to collect myself, to reel from what I'd just learned. I splashed cold water on my face and rushed to the Red Room in the turret for composition. Master Radcliffe had already started the class. No one acknowledged me as I took my seat at the end of a semi-circle surrounding the piano.

For the next three hours, I forgot all about the shitty students and the note on my mirror and the scratchy dress and even Mom's illness. Music could do that to me – it was my escape from reality. Composition wasn't my strongest area, but the way Master Radcliffe explained and demonstrated the concepts held me rapt. When he played through a short piece he'd composed in the moment, tears sprung in my eyes. If I could be even *half* as good as him, I'd be a world-renowned *Maestra*.

I had to leave the class early to prepare lunch. It sucked dragging my ass from the chair and leaving the others to soak up the final minutes of Master Radcliffe's wisdom.

Yesterday, I'd hurriedly scheduled a food delivery. When I entered the kitchen, the table groaned under the weight of the bags. Harrison moved through the space, making the low kitchen seem smaller somehow as he shifted the meat and frozen vegetables into the chest freezer in the pantry.

"Thank you for helping." He'd just saved me a ton of time, and I know he was busy repairing the hole I made in the porch.

"'Tis my pleasure." Harrison dusted off his hands on his filthy overalls. "It's nice to have a break from the weeding. How are you finding the school?"

"It's… different." I flopped a salmon fillet onto the chopping block, wishing I was slapping the wet fish across Dorien's smug mouth or Ivan's icicle stare or Titus' glorious cheekbones.

"Those students are giving you trouble." It wasn't a question.

I nodded. "It's nothing I can't handle. They've got a key to my room. Do you have a spare lock to replace it?"

Harrison's face clouded over. "You need to tell Madame Usher."

"I did. She didn't want to hear it, so I guess I'm on my own."

"I'm making a trip into town tomorrow." Harrison dropped a stack of salmon fillets into the freezer. "I'll bring you back a new lock. Victor never tolerated their bad behavior, but the Madame lets them get away with…"

Murder, he was about to say. And a thought niggled at me – that the students weren't the only ones who wanted me gone from Manderley. If Madame Usher wanted me to leave without getting her hands dirty…

I thought of Titus standing over me in the darkness while I slept, and those footsteps pacing back and forth across the room. A horrible thought hit me – he admitted to being in my room, but Titus couldn't have possibly made those footsteps. *He'd been outside with the others. I saw him…*

The thought left an unsettled feeling in my gut. "Harrison, tell me straight – am I in danger here?"

"You be careful, especially of that Dorien Valencourt. He's her pet." Harrison looked like he wanted to say more. Instead, he slammed the lid of the freezer down and scurried away, like he couldn't bear to be in the big house a moment longer than necessary.

I dressed a shoulder of pork, covered it in foil, and whacked it in the oven to slow cook for dinner while I tossed vegetables in truffle oil and grilled the salmon steaks. When I carried lunch into the dining room, Dorien was on his feet again, pouring the wine. He started with the Master and worked his way around the table. I needed to cross his path to set down the platters.

"Excuse me," I mumbled under my breath. I balanced four plates in my hands. They were much heavier than his wine bottle.

Dorien pretended he didn't hear me, shifting his body so I ended up doing an awkward dance to get around him. As I stepped toward the master, Dorien stuck out his foot. I tripped, splattering juicy steaks and salad across the pristine tablecloth.

"Ew." Heather leaped back, clawing at her head. "She got tomato in my hair."

"Ms. de Winter," Madame Usher boomed. "Clean this up at once."

"But—"

"Not another word." Madame Usher stood up and held out her plate. "Salvage what you can. We will take our lunch in the drawing-room while you deal with the mess you made."

Fuming in silence, I scooped meat and salad back onto the platters, handing one to her and the other to Elena. I tried to meet the Romanian girl's eyes, but she kept her chin held high. She might not actively participate in whatever the Muses had planned for me, but she certainly went along with it.

By the time I'd scrubbed at the tomato stains on the rug and put the tablecloth on to soak, they'd polished off the food. They hadn't left a single piece for me. I grabbed an apple from the kitchen. While the others spread out across the practice spaces, I got a mop and bucket out of the storage cupboard and cleaned the bathrooms on both floors, then moved on to scrubbing the marble tiles of the Red Room until they shone. I dusted down all the antiques so the place would be perfect for Andrei Solokov's visit.

My chores done, I returned to my room and practiced for two hours. I chose Bartok's *Violin Concerto No.2* for my audition piece – I'd been wrapping my head around the fiery, conflicted music for the last year. When Bartok composed the concerto in the lead-up to the First World War, he was being attacked in his native Hungary for his anti-Fascist views, and the concerto reflects his frenzied state of mind. It perfectly matched my mood after learning about Titus' invasion of my privacy, and the fact that his confession didn't explain all the noises I heard. By the end of my practice, the notes hummed in my veins. I knew I played the piece with heart, with fire, and I'd give all three Muses a run for their money.

Back down in the kitchen, I roasted some vegetables and made *rotkohl* – red cabbage, cloves, bacon, and apples. A recipe handed down from my German grandmother on my father's side. We never saw her after my dad disappeared – I didn't know if it was too painful for Mom or if she suspected Grandma knew something she hadn't revealed. It was no big loss – the best thing about Grandma had been her cabbage. The bitter woman died a few years ago. We didn't go to the funeral.

Tension crackled in the air as I served dinner, with less joking between the students than normal. *Of course, tonight they weren't friends, but rivals.* No one spoke to me, but Ivan kept sneaking glances at me between bites – those intense icicle eyes sweeping over my face. His expression never changed – I had no idea what he was thinking, and it both terrified and angered me. The skin on my neck prickled with nerves, and I kept looking over my shoulder, certain there was some horror about to be visited upon me from behind.

Dinner finished in record time. I hurried to stack the dishwasher while the others went upstairs to change clothes and tune their instruments. By the time I arrived in the Blue Room – the largest of the practice spaces – sweaty and still wearing my wool dress, six perfectly groomed students lounged on all the available chairs, carefully avoiding acknowledging me.

I stood awkwardly beside the sideboard, trying to avoid looking anywhere near the guys. Madame Usher poked her head in. "The Master and I won't be a moment. Faye, pour us all a glass of port. It calms the nerves."

I went to the liquor cabinet and found the port decanter and eight glasses. I splashed a generous slug of the dark liquid into each glass and arranged them on a silver tray. The door opened, and Master Radcliffe walked in. As I held the tray out to him, Dorien slid his foot across the rug and kicked my ankle. I went down hard, the tray flying from my hands and splattering sticky port all over Master Radcliffe.

14

FAYE

The Master frowned at the red stain dripping down the front of his silk shirt. "I must change clothes."

He flounced from the room, leaving me alone with my six enemies. Heather no longer bothered to hide her laughter behind her hand. Aroha let out a booming roar that got Titus going, and soon Dorien was chortling, too. Elena and Ivan stared at the floor, apparently unmoved by it all.

Dorien pointed to the port stain on the floor. "Clean that up," he commanded.

I made the only possible response to such a request. I flipped him off.

"You're the servant. Do your duty. If that's not gone by the time Madame Usher returns, you'll pay."

"*You* clean it up," I shot back. "You're the one who tripped me. Do you think it's fun to pick on people, Dorien? You're like a spoiled only child throwing his toys out of the sandbox because he doesn't want to share."

Dorien's eyes flashed at me. "You don't know what you're talking about."

I snorted. "I know exactly what I'm talking about. Are you so afraid that I'll beat you? Why are you even *here*, anyway? International career not going so well?"

Something inside Dorien snapped. I knew I'd got to him; I just didn't know how or why. I clenched my hands into fists, ready to drive the knife deeper, desperate to hurt Dorien the way his insults hurt me, when Madame Usher entered the room. Her eyes immediately fell on the stain on the floor. "Miss de Winter, can you not perform one task without spillage?"

"Dorien tripped me deliberately—"

"You are accusing Dorien Valencourt to cover up your incompetence." Madame Usher flashed me with her cold smile. "Dorien has thousands of adoring fans waiting for him on the other side of Manderley's walls. He has no need to resort to petty pranks. You will clean that immediately. And then you will go to your room and think about whether you really want to be here."

"But the audition—"

"You will not be auditioning."

Her words hit me like a punch in the gut. It was one thing to be ordered around like a servant. I could handle that if it meant Mom was safe. But to be deprived of this opportunity because of Dorien's assholery? I gulped back the venom that danced on my tongue.

Madame Usher took a seat on the velvet chaise under the window, spreading her skirts around her. "Hop to it, girl. There's carpet cleaner under the dresser. You better not be here when Master Radcliffe returns."

"Yes, Madame."

I loathe you. I hate you.

Mocking eyes burned into me as I knelt down and located the spray. On my hands and knees, I scrubbed at the stain. Above my head, Dorien and Heather held court, clinking their glasses together as they gloated over my humiliation.

"Too bad you can't whip insolent slaves anymore," Dorien mused, and there was a wicked edge to his voice that made something warm and wanton slither down my spine and pool between my legs. I hated him so much in that moment, but not as much as I hated myself for wanting him.

"Trash like her is probably gagging for it," Heather giggled. My ears rang with rage. "What a waste of perfectly decent port."

"It's not a waste. There's a fine view from over here," Titus' murmur reached my ears.

His friends laughed. My cheeks burned with humiliation. I stood, smoothing the front of my dress, now creased and covered with fluff from the rug, and tucked the cloth into my pocket just as Master Radcliffe entered again, his shirt swapped out for a new one. He sat behind the piano and indicated for Dorien to begin. I hovered by the door, my violin clasped at my chest, hoping Madame had changed her mind and—

"Get out," she rasped. "For your insolence, you will be confined to the school grounds this weekend. Allowing the use of Harrison for driving is a privilege, not a right."

"But I have to visit my mother—"

"You should have thought of that before you made a mess of my home. Don't make me regret bringing you here, Miss de Winter."

The door slammed shut behind me, echoing down the hall.

I slumped against the door, my body vibrating as the first fluttering notes of Dorien's concerto reverberated through the door. Even when I was part of the most elite music academy in the country, I was still shut out.

I can't see my mother, and it's all his *fault.*

It would be bearable if Dorien was a shit musician, but when his fingers touched the keys he created magic. He didn't just play Beethoven, he made love to Beethoven. He fucked Beethoven slow and steady from behind. Dorien made Elena's performance from the other day seem like a novice.

I tore myself from the door, determined not to give him the satisfaction of listening any longer. Brilliant musician or not,

Dorien was intent on seeing me fail, and he'd convinced all the other students to help him. Something Madame Usher said nagged at me. *He has no need for petty pranks.*

She was right – Dorien had already made a name for himself in the Classical world. He had fame and fortune and groupies galore. He didn't need Manderley or the prize. And yet, he was going to great lengths to drive me away.

Dorien Valencourt saw me as a threat.

That knowledge bolstered me. I curled my fingers into fists. Dorien may have meant something to me once, but now he was just another hurdle in my way. I'd survived my mother's mysterious disease – dealing with the Bad Boys of Baroque was nothing compared to that. Not only would I keep my place at the Academy and ensure Mom had the best medical care, but I would finish the year with the Manderley Prize, and I'd rub it in their self-righteous, chiseled, gorgeous faces.

15

FAYE

It turns out, Dorien's efforts to sabotage me were in vain. Master Radcliffe chose Elena to play for the visiting conductor, with Ivan accompanying her on the violin. They practiced all day in the Red Room while I worked on my composition in the smaller Yellow Room. Listening to the twins through the walls was like a lesson in concert performance. Elena had that kind of rare talent that would leave audiences broken and haunted, glued to their seats after the house lights came up, unsure if they'd yet returned to the real world.

And Ivan… he was a masterful violinist, but it was clear to me that he hung back, allowing his sister to shine. Odd, because I'd seen him play with Dorien and Titus in the videos – he was as fast and furious as either of them. Ivan could hold his own and command a stage. Yet, when he played with Elena, he became background noise.

After a while, I set down my violin and picked up my duster to clean the bookshelf beside the window, watching grey clouds move across the mountains and the trees bend in the approaching gale while I listened through the wall. I couldn't imagine Ivan being anyone's background noise – not with those intense blue eyes and those cheekbones that could cut glass. And yet… he seemed happy to let his sister take the limelight. Another mystery of Manderley, one I was unlikely to solve while everyone ignored me.

The storm grew more intense. Rain rolled down off the mountains and pooled in low spots on the lawn, creating muddy puddles that reflected dark clouds the exact color of Dorien's eyes. Harrison had to cancel his trip into town – he couldn't drive on those roads – which meant I wouldn't get my new lock until next week.

Dimitri Solokov arrived during the peak of the storm – rain sleeting sideways into the windows, thumping a steady rhythm that kept me company while I worked.

The gong echoed through the house, signaling someone had arrived. When I emerged from the practice room, Madame Usher was greeting the producer in the hall, draping his sodden coat over the antique stand. She snapped her fingers at me and pointed to the Blue Room. I knew what she wanted – drinks must be poured.

"Faye is a charity case," she explained to Master Solokov as I held out the tray of drinks. "Out of the goodness of my heart, I've accepted her into Manderley's program in exchange for her service. I shan't think I'll do it again. Her father was Donovan de Winter—"

Solokov's face lit up at the mention of my father's name.

"—alas, she does not share his talent. On a good day, she can strangle Vivaldi out of her violin, but I wouldn't expect more than that from her."

I bit back a retort. *It doesn't matter how she treats me and what she says about me. I'm still here in her school, learning from Master Radcliffe. She's still paying for medical care for a woman whose husband she tried to steal. I still have as much of a chance as anyone else of winning the Manderley Prize.*

I left them to talk as I returned to the kitchen, where I'd laid out an assortment of hors d'oeuvres for Solokov's visit. Tonight, I'd gone all out into my mother's Mexican heritage, serving up esquites, crispy deep-fried chimichangas with salsa roja, and cinnamon churros with a dark chocolate dipping sauce. Hearty, warming food for staving off the cold. I reached down to grab the trays and noticed something.

Someone had taken three of the chimichangas from the tray.

I smirked. If someone thought stealing a few nibbles would scare me away, they had another thing coming. I rearranged the food so the gaps weren't noticeable and took the trays out to the Blue Room, arranging them on a table in the corner.

I half expected Madame Usher to ban me from the room, but she seemed to have forgotten about me as soon as Master Solokov arrived. Harrison had lit the fire, and it blazed with welcoming heat. I settled myself on the chesterfield by the fire, letting the warmth soak into my limbs.

The others filed in as they finished their practice and groomed themselves. Heather's curls caught the light, bouncing beneath the chandelier. Elena looked like an elf with her silver waterfall of hair streaming down her back. Aroha wore a floor-length dress printed with bold swirling designs that matched her tattoos. The three Muses filed in last, and I stifled a gasp.

They wore the black ruffled shirts and tight pants from their European tour. On anyone else, those outfits would be ridiculous costumes, but the three of them were unholy gods. Dorien's dark hair flopped over his eyes and curled around his collar, every inch the dark prince. Titus had to duck under the lower arms of the chandelier to avoid hitting his head. As he did, the cornrows trailing down his back fanned out, and the beads at the ends clicked together. That guy was just so big, it was hard to picture him playing a beautiful instrument with precision, and yet he could shred that cello like no one else. Ivan stood in contrast to them both, with his silver hair matching the threads of glittering embroidery on his cuffs and collar, and his Eastern European features hard and focused.

Dorien and Ivan took up places across the room, near Madame Usher, but Titus slumped down beside me on the low couch. His leg brushed mine, and sparks shot up my leg. My mind might've been disgusted at the idea of him sneaking into my room and watching me sleep, but my body had no such qualms.

When we were all gathered, Elena and Ivan took their places and performed their piece. As the music flowed through me, the warmth of Titus' leg penetrated my skin until I could feel it in my bones, and his scent danced across my nostrils – red musk and myrrh, cut with fragrant roses – its intensity conjured by the music and by the electric attraction I felt to him.

Something is seriously wrong with me. I've spent far too many hours cooped up in Mom's hospital room with only elderly doctors for company. A week at Manderley with the Bad Boys of Baroque and I've turned into a mess of hormones.

I tried to focus on Elena's fingers and Ivan's solemn notes, but Titus' presence loomed large beside me. Every breath he took and every subtle movement of his body translated through that square of skin where we touched until I was a mess of want and frustration.

I refused to look at him, instead focusing on the grim features of our Russian visitor. Solokov's expression gave nothing away, but when Elena lifted her hands from the piano he rushed at her, collecting her fingers in his, and kissed the knuckles of her hand.

"You will go far. You should already be in Europe, not wasting away in this stuffy school."

In her seat, Madame Usher bristled and looked to Ivan as if to demand his support. Ivan slunk back into the shadows by the door. It was Master Radcliffe who came forward to stand beside Elena. He threw his arm around her shoulders.

"Elena is my star pupil," he said, and there was a hint of challenge in his voice. "Like a delicate flower, she must be allowed to bloom at the right time. Too early and she will wilt, her beauty fading."

Madame Usher rose from her seat, and everyone started talking at once, surrounding Solokov and offering him drinks, food, a place to sit. Titus turned his body to me. He didn't say anything, but there was a confidence in his broad shoulders that told me I didn't want to be near him. I shot up and darted around the group to the door. To where Ivan lurked like a vampire in the night.

I leaned my back against the wall beside him, my fingers brushing the paper, feeling a crack where the wall met the wainscoting. A faint draft tickled my fingers. "Your sister is so talented."

Ivan glanced up at me. This close, his eyes became shards of sapphire – facets of twinkling beauty catching the light. So clear they drew me in until I lost myself in their depths, toppling into a lake of frozen emotion.

He turned away, his lip jutting out – a deliberate and conscious movement to avoid answering me. Ivan fixed his gaze on his sister in the center of the room, surrounded by the adoration of teachers and students, while he stood here, forgotten. Across the room, Dorien swept his head up and caught Ivan's gaze, and an unspoken conversation flickered between them.

I slipped out of the room. I knew I wasn't wanted. Madame Usher wouldn't let me speak with Solokov, and the others were intent on ignoring me, so what was the point? I clicked the door shut behind me—

Down the hall, a door slammed. The sharp *BANG* of wood cracking against the frame echoed through the walls, trembling the vases on their plinths.

I whirled around, my heart leaping into my chest. "Who's there? Harrison?"

No one answered.

I stalked down the hall, glancing into the rooms on either side of me, searching the shadows for an answer. The door to the Yellow Room was shut – the only one in the hall, and I knew I left it open earlier – the heavy wood held back by a brass stopper.

It's okay. It was just a gust of wind blowing the door shut. Someone must have opened a window. Which was ridiculous, because of the raging storm outside, but the Yellow Room was at the back of the house, where the eaves hung lower, and it could get quite stuffy.

My fingers closed around the handle. My breath came out in short gasps. *It's nothing. It's just this creepy old house capturing your imagination.* But I couldn't stop the niggling, tight sensation in my chest, the scratching on the back of my neck that signaled someone watching me.

Willing my heart to return to normal, I pushed the door open and stepped inside. The windows were all closed, and there was no breeze in the room. *Of course, the storm could have rattled the frame so much the window slid down.* I gulped back the lump in my throat as I crossed the room. The skin along my arms prickled, overwhelming me with a sense that I wasn't alone in the room. I scanned all around, but I couldn't see anyone, and there was nowhere for someone to hide unless they crawled into the piano.

My fingers shook as I drew back the curtains. All the windows were tightly latched. Not a breeze or draft touched my bare arms.

So how had the door slammed shut? *Everyone's inside the Blue Room.* It couldn't have been any of them.

Except for Harrison… I cupped my hands against the glass, but I could barely even see the gatehouse lights through the downpour. I picked up the house phone from its cradle beside the window seat, my hand trembling, and dialed his extension.

"Gidday," Harrison's gruff voice answered.

The words rushed out. "Hi, Harrison, it's me. You weren't just down at the house, were you? Specifically, in the Yellow Room?"

"Not me. I didn't want to be a bother while Madame entertained her guest, so I knocked off early." I could hear a TV blaring in the background. "Why do you ask?"

"The door slammed, but there's no one here, and no windows open. And—" I paused. I couldn't explain the weird feeling in my gut without sounding insane.

"Always strange noises in that house." A crunching sound as Harrison opened a packet of something. "Knocking in the walls. Footsteps where there should be no footsteps. Cold spots. Clare complained about food missing from the kitchen."

I remembered the three missing chimichangas, and a fresh wave of unease rocked through my body. "You might've mentioned this before."

Harrison munched on his dinner for a moment. "But it can all be explained, can't it? Rats stealin' the food, drafts between the walls, old houses creaking and settling, rotten rich kids pulling pranks."

"Yeah. You're right. Thanks, Harrison." I hung up the phone and turned back to the door.

I wanted so badly to believe he was right – there was a logical explanation for what happened. Of course, if this was a horror movie, Harrison would be the killer for sure – the harmless old groundskeeper with a sordid past and thirst for blood.

But I knew Harrison couldn't have been here. He picked up the phone in the gatehouse only a couple of minutes after the door slammed. Even a fit person couldn't have made it back down the driveway in time, and not in this storm. Besides, the windows were all latched from the inside. There was no way out of the room unless someone crawled up the chimney like Santa Claus.

My eye caught the bookshelf beside the window.

I froze.

I *knew* when I dusted that shelf earlier today it had been

perfectly in order. Now, several books had been pulled out and scattered across the floor.

I gathered up the books and shoved them back onto the shelf. A sliver of ice crawled up my spine as my fingers curled around a battered leather volume.

Grimm's Fairy Tales.

Odd, it looked *exactly* like a book I had when I was a child. My father got it for me as a gift when he returned from a tour of Germany. He used to read a chapter to me every night before I went to sleep. When he was on tour, he'd call me as often as he could from the other side of the world, and we'd read the stories together over the phone. He did the best voices – I broke into giggles at his rumbling monsters and cackling witches. When he disappeared, I threw the book into the trash.

Lightning cracked outside the window, and the raw energy of the storm sizzled in my veins as I held that book in my hands, memories I didn't want to recall flooding my mind.

I flipped open the cover.

My heart flew to my throat.

The book clattered from my hands, the frontispiece falling open on the floor.

There, written in looping script across the corner of the page, was the message:

MY DARLING FAYE,
MAY ALL YOUR DREAMS COME TRUE
LOVE DAD

DORIEN

After Elena's performance, Madame Usher dismissed us so she and Radcliffe could talk shop with Solokov. In the hall, Heather threw her arm in mine. "You should have been the one playing for him," she said. "You know you're the most talented pianist here – especially when I accompany you. Madame only chose Elena because she's exactly *his* type."

"Mmmm." My gaze fell to the stairs, where Ivan and Elena walked hand in hand, their heads bowed in hushed conversation. Heather had so many reasons to be jealous of Elena – who was a hundred times the musician Heather could ever hope to be – but Radcliffe's attention was not one of them. Ivan's hand on Elena's shoulder trembled with rage as he led her to their room, the door slamming behind her. I thought about following Ivan, trying to calm the rage that had already threatened to unleash itself tonight, but I was in no state to be a good friend. Besides, he had Elena, and that was all that mattered. For now.

Faye slipped out after the performance. Madame flashed me a satisfied smile that felt like something slimy crawling up my spine, and I knew that old witch had something planned, something she hadn't told me. I didn't like not knowing shit, especially when Madame Usher was involved.

But I couldn't just warn Faye, not without risking everything. I couldn't speak to her, and she despised me, which was exactly what Madame Usher wanted. I needed to *think*. I needed to know why he hadn't fucking messaged me in two weeks. I needed the silence to stop so I could figure out my next move on this fucked-up chessboard with enemies on all sides—

"Dorien," Heather's shrill voice pierced my thoughts. "You're not listening to me."

"Not one bit," I growled.

She leaned against me, rubbing her cheek against my shoulder and staring up at me with heavy-lidded eyes. I'd seen the look on hundreds of girls – in the front row of concert halls in Milan, in the lineups of Amsterdam whorehouses, in Clare's deep brown irises. "Come up to my room, and I'll find ways of taking your mind off Elena. I stole a bottle of port from Madame's stash. We could drink it together and—"

"No." I kicked open the door to the kitchen, and rushed through to the back door and out into the night.

Rain droplets splattered my face and clothes, but I didn't give a fuck. I needed air. Inside the house, I felt like I was choking on the lies and the shit and Faye's goddamn intoxicating scent.

I walked to the back of the garden, following the overgrown path toward the gazebo. The storm had eased off, though a bitter wind still tore at my exposed flesh and the rain splashed into puddles between the gnarled tree roots. My fingers fumbled in my pocket. I tugged out my phone and tapped the screen, cupping my hand against it to protect it from the rain. No messages.

Don't panic. He said he'd text when he could. Just because you haven't heard from him doesn't mean he's in trouble.

I scrolled back to his last text, my eyes flicking over the words even though I knew them by heart.

Father Aaron took my shoes today.

Six words. Six measly fucking words. I scuffed the ground, my sock squelching where the water had soaked through. The wind whipped my hair across my face, flogging the strands against my skin – a self-flagellation that didn't feel nearly perverse enough. Even though it was still technically summer, the mountains could be unforgiving.

Over the roar of the rain, I caught the wafting notes of a violin. I glanced back at the house, but no one should be playing now. We had a strict curfew – no music after 10PM. It was almost midnight, and Solokov would be sleeping over in one of the guest rooms. No one would dare risk Madame's wrath.

Someone clearly didn't give a fuck about Madame's rules, and I had a feeling I knew exactly who that would be.

I followed the mournful notes down the path to the gazebo. I didn't recognize the melody, but I didn't have to for it to fill my chest and wrap around my heart. The melody had an ethereal quality to it, as though the music came from another place entirely – every note an invitation to fall through a hole and end up in some strange and forgotten fae realm.

A shadowed figure stood under the ruined structure, and I knew even before they came into focus who it would be. No other musician could make me step outside myself the way she could.

Faye turned in a slow circle, her eyes closed as she drew the bow over the strings. I'd heard flashes of the piece she played through the walls when she practiced, but here with the rawness of nature raging around her, she wove magic into the very air. Her fingers flew with ease over the arpeggios, and her bow made light work of the spiccato. The music lifted through the storm, bringing hope and light and beauty to this place of darkness. Her damp hair clung to the curve of her back, and I almost expected wings to sprout from between her shoulders or a sprite to peek out from behind her ear.

I drew forward, mesmerized, not noticing where I stood until my foot caught on a loose stone, kicking it into the side of the gazebo.

Faye's eyes flew open. The bow squeaked on the strings. The music stopped, and the spell that drew me to her broke. She glared at me and jabbed her bow toward the house.

"Go away."

"It's a free garden." I stepped closer. The moonlight played off her raven hair. She must have come outside when it was still raining heavily, because she had mud splattered up her legs and her dress was soaked through, the fabric clinging to her skin, revealing every curve of that fucking gorgeous body.

"You talking to me now?"

I let a slow smirk play across my lips. Even with that defiant flame in her eyes, she still couldn't resist rising to my challenge. "You're playing out in the rain when there's a perfectly good bed inside. Consider me intrigued."

"I don't have to explain myself to you, Dorien." Faye shook her head, and a sadness flickered in her eyes that reminded me so much of his desperation that I had to look away to catch my breath. When I turned back to her, that sadness had disappeared. "Why are you doing this? We haven't seen each other for ten years. I stayed away from you, just like you wanted. It's not my fault we ended up at the same school. So why are you so determined to make me leave? You of all people should know I don't fucking bend to anyone's will."

I never wanted you to stay away.

The thought tasted bitter. Or maybe that was just the decade of resentment that bubbled inside me. Because Faye was lying – she didn't bend to anyone's will, except mine. I told her to leave me, and she left me. And I hated her for it, but not as much as I hated myself.

That decision was supposed to hurt for only a moment. I was supposed to lock up my heart so I could forget Faye, so I would never again feel the sting as her heart broke in front of me, as tears drowned out the fire in her eyes. I told myself it had worked for ten years, as I wandered the earth a ghost of a person, an empty box without a key. But now the decision that cost me my only true friend threatened to destroy someone else I loved, and Faye had stormed back into my life and blown the box to smithereens.

Fourteen days and no text. He has to know I'd be going fucking crazy.

I closed the space between us in three strides. Faye yelped in surprise as my fingers circled her wrist, pulling her close so our bodies pressed together, chest to chest. Her heart danced a wild rhythm through the thin fabric of her sodden dress, matching the violence of my own. Red lips parted, and the urge... the urge overwhelmed me... to slip my tongue between them, to tease out the sorcery inside, to drink and drink of her until I burst with her magic.

But those six words ran around and around in my head, blurring together until they lost all meaning. Until I knew only one thing – that I had someone else to protect, someone who needed me more than I'd convinced myself I needed Faye.

Hurting her should come naturally to you. After all, you did it once before.

"Little hint." My fingers tightened around Faye's arm. She whimpered, but it wasn't a sound of fear. I strained through my desire, searching for a threat. "If you want to survive the next year, you should walk out the gates now and never come back. If you stay, I'll destroy you. That is my solemn promise."

My body buzzed with the urge to flip Faye over, to lift up that sexy skirt of hers, bend her over the railing, and enter her. How many times over the years had I wondered how she'd feel, the girl I let go – how hot and slick and inviting, how she'd push back against my cock and throw back her head and howl at the moon like the wild woman she was. I growled, low in my throat, and the sound was meant to scare her, but it sent a tremble of desire through her body that echoed in my own. Could she feel my cock hard against her thigh?

Fuck. Fuck. I'm in deep shit.

"Why are you trying to frighten me?" Faye whispered, glaring back at me with defiance, with triumph, as a prickle of unease jolted across my shoulders. The air around us shifted, disturbed by some foriegn presence. I wanted to look behind me, but I didn't dare break our gaze. "I'll never be afraid of you. I've seen real horrors, Dorien. I've lived through pain you could only imagine, and trying to keep me from my mother is not going to break me. To me, you're nothing but a scared little boy."

"You think you know me?" I growled. "You think you have a monopoly on pain? You're about to find out just how little you know. That boy you remember died a long time ago, and the man he grew into is callous and dangerous. I'll stop at nothing to get what I want, and what I want is for you to *leave*."

Faye smirked. "Funny. I could have sworn you were after something else when you grabbed me."

I threw her arm from me, sending her reeling across the gazebo. She yelped in surprise, but I couldn't hear it. I had to shut myself off to everything she was, everything she could be. I struggled to control my breathing as I rasped my parting words. "This is your last warning. Poor little Sprite. You're trapped in the spider's web, and you don't even know it. Leave Manderley forever, or you'll be the next ghost to haunt these walls."

17

FAYE

Still shaking from my encounter with Dorien on top of missing my visit with Mom and finding my father's book, I slammed the attic door and flopped down on the bed, kicking off my shoes. Going outside was a mistake, that was obvious. I'd spent a good hour being pummeled by the rain as I stomped around in the garden bed under the window, looking for signs someone had been there. But the only footprints were my own.

I should have gone to bed then, but as I tiptoed through the hall in my damp clothes with the fairy tale book under my arm, I could still hear the others in the Blue Room – Elena's tinkling laugh and Titus' booming voice regaling the group with stories from the last Broken Muse tour. I hadn't thought. I didn't even pause to change my clothes. I dumped the book beside my bed, grabbed my violin, and rushed out into the biting wind.

I just needed to *play*. Somewhere away from *them*. Maybe the wind would carry the notes to my mother. As soon as I struck the bow to the strings, I felt better. I closed my eyes and transported myself far from Manderley, to a different time and place, when Mom and I were happy and the future looked bright.

Dorien just *had* to find me and ruin it.

I shook myself, like a dog drying himself after rolling in a puddle, and threw myself down on my bed. I wished I could shake off the trembling in my fingers that had nothing to do with the cold. Heat pooled in my chest and other places I didn't want to think about.

When Dorien held me, his lips dangerously close, his stiff cock pressing against my thigh, how close had I come to leaning in to kiss him, to taste the cruel words flowing from his lips like honey?

"Cockpoodles," I muttered into my pillow. *This whole night is completely fucked up.*

I flipped myself over, turning on the lamp and pulling the book across the bed to rest on my knees. I pinched the familiar pages between my fingers, staring at those words scrawled across the frontispiece until they ceased to make sense. It *was* my father's book. *My book.* The grief from losing him came in waves of rage and despair, each powerful and uncontrollable. I'd tossed it away during one of the rages. So how had it ended up at Manderley?

And why did someone *want* me to find it?

18

FAYE

On Saturday a week after Solokov's visit, Madame Usher announced over lunch that he'd been so impressed he invited Elena to perform in Moscow over the winter break. I tried to smile, but it came out as a grimace. Across the table, I noticed Dorien's eyes were stormy even as he joined the applause.

Elena's pale skin glowed with joy, and the faintest smile tugged at the corner of her mouth. She turned to Master Radcliffe. "What about Ivan?"

"This will be a solo opportunity, Elena," Master Radcliffe replied in his friendly voice. "Don't be concerned. I'll accompany you to Moscow to ensure you're settled and see your early performances."

The smile slipped from her lips. Ivan reached across and squeezed her hand. Elena shook her head. "I can't go without Ivan. I *won't*."

Tension crackled across the table, although I couldn't understand why. My gaze fell on Ivan's face – his eyes shards of sharpened stone, ready to cut the Master down.

"You're going, and that's the final word on the matter."

Madame Usher glared at the twins. "You need to grow up some-time. *Both* of you."

Nothing more was said about Moscow, or anything else. Lunch finished in stony silence, Ivan piercing each person at the table with an icy glare. As I stacked the dishwasher and wrapped up the rest of the roast beef to make into sandwiches, Harrison walked into the kitchen carrying an armload of wood.

"I brought up fresh supplies. The forecast is for another storm to hit this week. Will we be visiting your mother this afternoon?"

"Hell yes." I slammed the fridge door and wiped my hands on my apron. "I can leave right now. I'll just need to run upstairs and grab my violin."

"Good. I'll meet you around the front in the limo. If you see Dorien, tell him I'm waiting."

"Dorien's going to be with us?"

Harrison's face darkened. "I don't like it, either, but his family lives near the hospital and it makes sense for us all to drive together."

I sighed. Obviously, saving the environment and all that. "I know why I don't like him, but what's your beef?"

"He was the one dating Clare when she had her accident."

My hand flew to my mouth. *Dorien?* I knew what Harrison suspected, could hear the accusation dripping from his words. I'd seen the cruelty in Dorien's eyes directed at me, but I couldn't believe the Dorien I knew would kill a girl.

But did I know him still? Dorien had more secrets than a heart-shaped box. Plus, he had tormented me since the moment I arrived, and once upon a time he cared about me. If this Clare crossed him, what would he do to her?

I slunk out of the kitchen and headed for the stairs. As I ascended, my gaze fell to that empty square on the wall where the portrait used to be. It hadn't come back from the cleaners yet. I wondered why Madame Usher, usually such a stickler for everything in its proper place, hadn't gone postal with them yet about its late return. *Maybe she reserves all her ire for her staff.*

I reached the first story landing and turned toward Dorien's room. He was already leaning against his door wearing a black t-shirt that clung tight across his shoulders over black jeans and combat boots. A leather jacket slung over his shoulder crackled as he moved. Curls of dark hair flopped over his eyes as he frowned down at his phone, running his fingers over the edge of his stubbled jaw. So effortlessly sexy – too bad he was such a fucktrumpet.

When he heard me coming, Dorien shoved the phone in his pocket, as if he were hiding some kind of national secret.

"Harrison's just bringing the car around front, so meet him there." I jabbed a finger at the staircase.

Dorien didn't acknowledge me. Fuck, I hated this ghosting thing, especially after what happened in the gazebo. I spun on my heel and stalked up the narrow attic stairs to my room.

I grabbed my purse and violin case and took the stairs back down two at a time, too on edge to care if I slipped and broke my neck. I missed Mom so much. If she'd been awake and coherent, she'd have advice on how to handle Manderley and Broken Muse. I could just imagine her with a cappuccino in her hands, sloshing hot coffee everywhere as she gesticulated wildly, regaling me with a tale of how she won over some difficult executives with her wit and acumen.

When I slid into the limo, Dorien was already inside, staring at his phone screen with a foul expression. I sat near the front, beside the bar, and rapped on the glass. Just because Dorien wouldn't talk to me the whole trip didn't mean that I had to endure his silence.

"Hey Harrison, you ever use the sound system on this thing?"

Harrison flicked on the radio knob, and a loud burst of static blasted through the speakers. "No reception until we get closer to town."

"No problem." I pushed the button on my phone to sync the Bluetooth, then hit my finger on the perfect playlist – the upbeat pop songs Mom loved to play while she cooked or pottered around the house.

Lady Gaga's voice blasted out the stereo. I sat back and sang along at the top of my lungs. I kept one eye on Dorien, who didn't lift his eyes from his phone.

Ten minutes down the road and three pop songs later, a vein was throbbing in Dorien's head. I flipped through my music list, choosing song after song I knew would drive him crazy. I put on 'Achy Breaky Heart' and Harrison belted out the words, his voice a wonderful rumbling tenor.

I kept up a stream of 80s hits – my mom's favorite music – and was having so much fun I barely noticed the drive go by. Harrison turned down a narrow country road. A high stone fence ran alongside the ditch, barbed wire curling around the top. Dorien stared out the window, still as a statue. The mood in the car turned frosty, and not even Prince's greatest hits could thaw it out.

Harrison pulled up outside a high iron gate – the only break in the stone wall for miles. Through the narrow bars I could just make out a crumbling driveway curving off into the trees, and a giant pile of garbage stacked beside the gate. Signs along the wall read KEEP OUT and NO TRESPASSING. A gabled roof peeked through the tops of the trees, like some kind of medieval fortress. "What are we doing here?" I asked. *This is a weird place to be running errands.*

Dorien had already flung open the rear door and clambered out. "Thanks." He nodded to Harrison. "I'll see you back here at 4PM."

Harrison nodded, tearing away from the gate so fast the back wheels spun out. I pressed my face against the back window, watching the gates swing open to admit Dorien. His black-clad body faded into the distance as we sped away.

"What was that?" I slid back across the leather seat and grabbed a bottle of apple juice from the bar.

"That's the Valencourt estate." Harrison gripped the wheel so hard his knuckles turned white. "I don't like to stick around. It gives me the heebie-jeebies."

"An accurate description." I studied the high stone wall and barbed wire as we careened around the first corner. I visited Dorien's home in New York City that one time, and it had been the usual decadent mansion of the elite. I'd pictured their country estate as rolling lawns and stables, not... whatever this was. "It looks more like a prison."

"Mmmmm. Dorien's parents haven't been seen in public for ten years. There are all sorts of strange rumors about the place."

I waited for Harrison to elaborate, but he didn't. We drove into the city, and Harrison dropped me outside the hospital. It took me a bit to get my bearings and find the correct ward, but finally, I stood outside a room with a DE WINTER nameplate on the door.

"Hey, Mom. How're things?" I slid into the chair beside her bed. No hard plastic here. The room was a bit like a 4-star hotel room if you squinted hard and ignored the hospital bed and the beeping machinery keeping my mother alive. "I'm sorry I couldn't come last week. I missed you."

I touched her hand, steeling myself against the warmth in her fingers. I always expected her to feel cold, lifeless, because of the way she looked. But that warmth gave me hope, and that hope kept me glued to her, paying the mounting hospital costs week after week.

Seven weeks she'd been in a coma. Her prognosis was slim because her kidneys were failing, and they didn't even know what was wrong with her. But I couldn't bear the thought of my vibrant, boisterous, forgetful mother gone from the world. And so I hung on, long after I should, but I couldn't quench the flame of hope that burned inside me.

"Are you Mrs. Usher?"

I whirled around at the voice. A youngish doctor stood in the doorway, her mouth set in a line born of late nights and grim results. I burst out laughing.

"I haven't been cast out from a gothic horror story, so nope, not me."

"Sorry." She glanced at the tablet in her hand, a strand of lank strawberry-blonde hair falling out of her bun and dangling over her face. "I have an Usher on file as admitting her, along with a man named Harrison. No one else has visited her since she arrived. I'm Doctor Henrietta Nelson, and I'm assuming you're the daughter, Faye?"

"That's me."

"I was going to call Mrs. Usher at the end of my shift, but since you're here now, I can tell you. We've had some test results back that have shed light on what happened. It appears your mother was poisoned."

19

FAYE

"Poisoned?"

Dr. Nelson nodded. "At this time, we can't assume it was deliberate – that's for the police to decide."

"The police? Are you saying it's…" I couldn't force the word *murder* from my lips. That word didn't belong in any sentence associated with my mother.

"There are two ways poison can cause damage in the body. One is by taking a large dose all at once. The other is when a patient ingests a small amount of a poison over a long period – each individual dose isn't enough to do any harm, and in some cases isn't even detectable on tests, but over time it builds up in the body until one day…" she looked down at my mother with concern.

"You think that's what happened here?"

She nodded. "We call it chronic poisoning – it was a common way poisoners administered arsenic during the 19th century, but we don't see it often in a modern hospital as people will usually go to their doctor with symptoms before it reaches this stage. This isn't arsenic, though – it's not something we've ever seen before, which is why your mother's doctors couldn't help her before now. I'll know more once our lab identifies the poison, which they're working on now as their top priority. The most likely culprit is some kind of unregulated supplement or non-traditional medicine. Was your mother eating or drinking anything outside of her usual diet, something those around her weren't partaking of?"

I squeezed my eyes shut, trying to remember. "She used to have these special herbal teas. Her assistant would order them in bulk and make one for her each morning. Mom said they helped her memory and cognitive skills, but they tasted so bitter and gross I never wanted to drink them."

"Would you have access to any of these teas? If they're the source, it would help us identify the poison."

"I doubt it." The teas had probably been thrown out when the office was cleared out by the liquidators. "But I can check."

Poisoned.

Dr. Nelson must've seen the horror on my face, for she stepped into the room and placed her hand over mine. Her stoic features crumpled into something like a smile. "I know this is hard to hear, but it might be good news. If we can find the source of the poison, there may be a way to create an antidote. Some of your mother's internal systems have been damaged, but the coma has halted the breakdown of her organs. I don't want to get your hopes up until we know what we're dealing with, but there is still hope to cling to here – more hope than most."

I nodded. My fingers closed around my mother's, squeezing as hard as I dared. "Okay. Thank you."

"Don't thank me yet." She stepped back, rearranging her face back into her practical mask. "I'll do everything I can for her. But Faye, you need to speak with the police and find out anything you can about this tea. If that's the source of the poison, it needs to be pulled off the market immediately. We deal with a number of cases of health complications from people taking herbal reme-dies made with dangerous ingredients. Wellness is big business, but so many of those products are untested. If we could save other lives…"

My other hand curled into a fist. "Don't worry – I'm not letting them get away with this."

Dr. Nelson left, and I pulled out my violin. I usually played *Nigun* for my mother, but today, I was too on edge from the news to do that piece justice. Instead, I launched into Paganini's Caprice No. 5, filling the room with brashness and light and fury as my thoughts whirled around me.

Poisoned.

My head spun. It didn't make sense. It was something out of a bad murder mystery. Dr. Nelson seemed to believe it might be the fault of an unscrupulous herbal tea company, but there was another option. One I didn't like to consider, but had to.

Someone could have laced my mother's tea with poison. My first thought was her assistant, Natalie, who made the tea and who had long coveted a larger role in the company, but it could have been anyone with access to the storage room where the tea was kept.

But why would someone want to poison my mother?

~

The police came by later that day, and I gave them my statement and a list of names of people I remembered working at Mom's company, as well as a description of the tea and its packaging. They took another statement from Dr. Nelson, then left me alone to play for Mom again.

Next thing I knew, Harrison rang to say he was downstairs. I packed away my violin and kissed her warm cheek. In the hallway, Dr. Nelson strode past, clipboard in hand. "Thank you," I called out to her. "This is the first time in two years we've had anything like an answer."

"I'll call you if we learn anything else." She patted my shoulder. "You play beautifully, by the way. Next time you visit, do you think you'd be interested in playing for some of our other patients? There's not much to cheer them up around here – I think they'd love to hear beautiful music."

"I'd love to."

Outside, Harrison had parked in a pick-up zone right outside the doors. I slid into the backseat and gave a start as Dorien's features came into view, emerging from the darkest corner of the limo. Seeing that smirk twisting across his lips and knowing my mother lay upstairs with poison in her veins tore me up inside. I couldn't deal with any of his shit today.

"I finished with my chores early," Harrison explained. "I even picked up a new lock for your room, which I'll install as soon as we get back. I decided to swing out and pick Dorien up first, to give you a little more time with your mother."

I nodded, a lump forming in my throat. I wanted to thank Harrison, but if I opened my mouth, I'd burst into tears, and I refused to cry in front of Dorien.

"Would you like your music on again?" Harrison asked as we pulled out of the parking lot.

"No thanks." I sunk back into my seat, my mind still reeling from Dr. Nelson's news and the statement I'd just given to the police.

Across from me, Dorien's eyes flicked to mine, their deviant depths plunging into me, trying to draw out my secrets. "What's got your tongue?"

I ignored him.

Dorien leaned forward, clasping his hands together and resting his elbows on his open knees, giving me this tantalizing glimpse of his toned thighs, of the buttons on his crotch tugging at their seams. Those eyes swept over me, and for a moment I was back in the practice room at Madame Usher's New York City school, with Dorien grinning wickedly at me from behind the piano.

Back when things were simple.

I shook my head. He wasn't getting his hands on this secret. He already knew too much about me, had too tight a grip on my heart. But Dorien never took no for an answer. His eyes tugged at mine. In their fathomless depths stirred all sorts of depraved and deviant things, all the rumors and stories of his exploits, all the promise of what I might feel in his expert hands. I could forget myself in Dorien's eyes, and I had to be careful because right now that thought was way too tempting.

"You're upset." His words burned my skin like fire. It wasn't a question. "Is it your mom?"

"You don't care."

"Faye…" The way his mouth lifted up at the edges as he spoke my name, and how his eyes revealed the deviant thoughts he kept for his own amusement… *fuck*. I'd tell him all my darkest secrets if that look was really for me.

"I'll tell you about my mom if you tell me why your house is surrounded in barbed wire," I shot back.

Just like that, his eyes turned to stone. Dorien leaned back, folding his arms over his chest, walling himself up in a private prison. And although I was grateful for the space from him, part of me longed for him to break through what bound him and tell me what he was hiding, so that I could break too, and share the pain I carried by myself for so long.

But it was not to be. We drove the entire way back to Manderley in stony silence, regarding each other with wariness from opposite ends of the limo while Harrison's warning played over in my head.

Who are you, Dorien Valencourt? What do you have to hide?

20

FAYE

My days at Manderley faded into each other – one lonely hour after the next. The students continued to ignore me. At mealtimes they'd talk around me, filling the room with news of their upcoming recitals and visits with friends. Most nights one of them would shuffle around in the storage room to keep me awake. I bet they took turns – they always emerged for breakfast so well rested, whereas I looked like a crack panda 24/7.

That didn't bother me so much. At least, I told myself it didn't bother me.

My new humiliation was ensemble work, where everyone had to go off in groups to work on concertos. The twins were inseparable, and Ivan's sapphire shards made it clear he'd stab me if I got close to his sister. Aroha and Titus had a definite flirtatious thing going – a jealous seethe ached in my belly at the idea of being stuck in that sandwich – and Heather seemed permanently attached to Dorien's hip. I left the room whenever they played together. I told myself it was because it was such a shame to see Dorien's talent dragged down by Heather, the succubus who sucked the life out of every piece of music she played. But really it was the jealousy again.

Which was fucking ridiculous, because it wasn't like any of the Muses wanted to pluck my strings. But it was more that I wanted them to see me as an equal, as someone worthy to share their spotlight. It was like being picked last for teams in gym class, only a hundred times worse because unlike gym, I was actually *fucking good*.

At the violin, maybe not the sex. I'd only done *that* once before. Not that I wanted to get vertical with any of the guys. I had no desire to have Ivan's cold eyes locked on mine, or feel Titus' enormous hands on the small of my back, or feel Dorien's cock…

Nope. *Not at all.*

It was a moot point since none of them would talk to me. The only people who so much as uttered a word in my direction were Master Radcliffe, during our lessons, and Madame Usher, to snap at me for some perceived infraction.

Still, I had the music. I filled my head with Master Radcliffe's knowledge. The hours I got to spend alone with my violin lifted my spirit. But what surprised me was how much I'd started to enjoy composition. For the last two years I'd done nothing but work dead-end jobs, try to get my schoolwork done, and sleep in that cursed plastic chair while Mom underwent tests. Being able to learn something for the sheer pleasure of it lit a flame inside me I thought had been extinguished forever.

One evening after returning from another visit to my mother (no change, no results from the lab yet), I was in the kitchen, planning menus for the following week and chopping and roasting a bunch of vegetables I could use over the next few days. I figured out that if I took each Monday as a prep-night, I'd be able to get most of the food cooked, giving me more time during the week to practice.

While I stood at the stove, caramelizing onions, I noticed a figure dart from the porch toward the trees. *Aroha*. Without thinking, I switched off the stove, flung my hoodie over my shoulders, and headed after her.

I cut through the walled garden and emerged on the overgrown path leading down through the trees. Moonlight glinted off Aroha's leather jacket as she picked her way around the ruined gazebo and continued deeper into the forest. I followed, wondering if I was making a huge mistake. *This is how girls in horror films get stabbed or exsanguinated or eaten alive...*

The path emerged into a small clearing. It might once have been beautiful – a ring of trees surrounding a domed glasshouse. But neglect had wreathed the structure in weeds, had broken several glass panes, and had given the plants inside a life of their own. They overgrew their pots with such vivacity they tangled together into an impenetrable mess that spilled out through every available crack and cranny, trailing vines and delicate floral tendrils across the forest floor. Aroha sat on an upturned terracotta pot, wreathed in the shade of some strange plant with weird, elongated leaves. A cigarette dangled from her lips.

"Piss off, trash," she muttered when she saw me, but the words had no venom.

I shifted my weight from foot to foot. Aroha had spoken to me, of her own accord. Sure, it might have been to insult me, but it showed one thing – Aroha didn't conform to the rules Dorien had put in place. Foolish hope surged in my chest, the kind of hope borne of loneliness and desperation.

I lifted an eyebrow. "Can I bum a smoke?"

Aroha shrugged. I took that as an invitation. I grabbed another pot and upturned it, plonking down on the damp surface beside her. I picked up the cigarette box gingerly, expecting her to snatch it from my hands. She stared at the box as if she was debating it, then shrugged again. I tipped a cigarette from the packet and brought it to my lips. I didn't really smoke – I tried it a few times at my shitty school in an attempt to fit in. It turns out smoking doesn't make dorky music geeks cool unless you looked like Dorien Valencourt. Who would have guessed? Sometimes I shared one with the other staff after a late shift at the bar – Creepy Cory couldn't be around cigarette smoke because of his asthma, so it gave me a break from his lewd comments about my body.

Silence stretched between us.

"You come out here a lot?" I asked.

"If you'd said you wanted to talk, I wouldn't have given you a ciggie," Aroha snapped without looking at me.

My turn to shrug. "Fine."

I took a long drag of the cigarette, letting the smoke fill my lungs. A calmness swept over my body. This almost felt normal.

"I come out here because sometimes I can't stand it in that house," Aroha said, tapping her diamond ring against the terracotta. "All that fancy furniture. All those dead eyes staring at you from the walls. It feels like a time capsule or a dead person's house after they've passed on. I like being out here where things are living, reclaiming the edges of the estate. It reminds me of home."

"Where's home?" I asked, daring to continue the conversation. Loneliness ached inside me. I didn't realize how much I'd missed just interacting with another person, just how much I longed for my mother's boisterous laugh. Aroha reminded me of her in some ways.

"New Zealand. My parents run a church. We used to live right on the edge of a mountain range called the Waitakeres. I spent my childhood climbing trees, shooting rabbits, catching eels in the creek. Then Dad decided to become a preacher and we moved to the city, and then they shipped me off here." She sounded bitter about it, but that might have been her reluctance to talk to me.

Ah, her accent made perfect sense now. "Do you miss New Zealand? It must've been interesting to grow up there."

She shrugged. "It's normal, I guess. There aren't exactly wild hobbits running around everywhere like most Americans assume. My family is Maori – the indigenous people of Aotearoa, New Zealand. We used to live on our marae – that's like a meeting house for our community. I was practically raised by my aunts and cousins. There was always music and laughter and games. My parents gave up a lot when they moved to the city, and the city didn't always accept them in return. It's the Pākehā world."

"Pākehā?"

"White people." She elbowed me in the arm. "They sent me to a Catholic boarding school, all prim and proper and white as fuck. There were no traditional instruments, so I learned violin instead."

"But you love the music." Aroha adored atonal pieces, which she played with a loose aggression.

"Of course. But more than that, I love being a brown girl in a fucking white musician's world." She grinned. "Just you wait, trash. As soon as I get out of here, I'm gonna use this upstanding Classical education to bring my musical heritage into the spotlight. I've got plans, so don't you fuck them up for me by letting on that I tolerate your presence."

"How would that mess up your plans?"

"We're not supposed to talk to you. Dorien's orders. Usually, I don't give a fuck what anyone says, and you seem harmless, but the Broken Muse boys seem particularly keen to get you out of here, and they're a direct line to Madame Usher. I need her to like me or I won't graduate." A darkness passed over Aroha's eyes, but it was gone in a moment.

I leaned forward, dangling my cigarette between my fingers, my heart thumping. She knew something. "You think if you don't do what Dorien asks, he'll influence Madame Usher?" *Would he really mess with someone's entire career like that?*

Aroha shrugged. "Have you met Dorien? Dude is hot as sin, but he's got crazy serial killer eyes."

"Were you here when Clare… fell down the stairs?" I remembered just in time that I shouldn't reveal Harrison's suspicions to anyone, least of all a fellow student.

"Yup." She shuddered at the memory. I reached behind me, curious about the strange plant poking out from a crack in the glass. "All of us were in the house except the twins, who were at a recital. Clare was a bit cray-cray, sooooo obsessed with Dorien, but he— don't touch that!"

Aroha slapped my hand. Hard. The sting arced across my palm. I rubbed at the spot. "What was that for?"

"That's monkshood. It's highly poisonous. If you get the sap on your skin, it's bad news."

"How do you know?"

Aroha gestured to the greenhouse. "Duh. This whole place is a poison garden."

"A… what?"

"It's a Victorian curiosity. Apparently, one of the Usher ancestors fancied himself a botanist. He collected all these different poison plants from all over the world and grew them inside the greenhouse. He did lots of experiments and made some important scientific discoveries. Madame Usher warned us all not to go inside – apparently, some of the plants are so toxic you only have to brush past them to fall over and die. Look."

She pointed to a rotting wood panel above the shuttered door. I peered at it, unsure of what she was referring to, when carved letters came into view. A phrase in Latin: *In cauda venenum.*

The same phrase tattooed across Dorien's chest.

My mouth dried. "Do you know what it means?"

She snorted. "Right. Like I have time to study Latin."

Fuck. *Fuck.*

My mind whirred with impossible thoughts. Like why Dorien would have the same tattoo as a poison garden, and how I happened to find that out right after I learned my mother was poisoned. A vision of a crumpled body at the bottom of the stairs flashed in my mind again.

No, it's impossible.

Aroha must've seen something in my face because her expression softened. "Look, Dorien's not *actually* a serial killer. He's just a cocky shit. A fucking gorgeous one, but a shit all the same."

I grinned. "The word is dickweasel."

Aroha tossed her head back and laughed. "You're all right, trash. Come bum a smoke from me any time."

"But you won't speak to me inside the house?"

"Hell no. I'm not incurring their wrath. It's not just Dorien you've gotta watch out for – Titus and Ivan are no angels. Little word of advice, trash. Everyone at Manderley is running from something. The Muses make it their business to discover what that something is, and then they'll use it to twist you to their will. Hold your secrets close. Don't let them into your head, or they'll tear your heart out while it's still beating. That's what they did to Clare." She stood up, grinding her cigarette butt into the dirt with the heel of her boot. "We should head back."

As we walked back along the path, my eyes scanned Manderley's facade. From this angle, the house appeared even larger and more foreboding – straight out of a Bram Stoker novel, especially given the number of sexy Romanians wandering its halls. I felt a tiny glimmer of peace when my eyes landed on the window of my room. It had been my little square of sanctuary since Harrison changed the lock. I'd left the light on because the bulb at the top of the steps blew. I could just make out the outline of the edge of my clothing rack and—

I gasped.

There in the window, staring down at us through the glass, was the outline of a face.

21

FAYE

"**S**hit." I surged forward, crashing into Aroha. She wobbled in her high boots, throwing her arm out against a tree trunk to stop herself from falling over.

"What the fuck, trash?"

"Do you see it?" I jabbed a finger at the attic window.

"See what?"

"That face in my bedroom. It was looking right at us—" The face had gone.

"I don't see anything— hey, where are you going?"

I took off at a run toward the house, my heart pounding in my chest. *Oh, no you don't.*

There was only one staircase up to the attic. If I could get there fast enough, I'd be able to see who came down. I threw open the kitchen door. It slammed shut behind me as I barreled through the kitchen, taking the shortcut through the servants' corridor to the main entrance hall. As I took the stairs two at a time, Heather's tinkling laugh floated up from the Blue Room, and the unmistakable flutter of notes that could have only been Elena. So it wasn't either of them – no way would they have been fast enough to get to those rooms without me seeing or hearing them.

I reached the second landing and glanced around. None of the bedrooms were open, and no one stood around in the hall. *Maybe they're still up there, trying to hide.* I jangled the keyring in my pocket. They weren't getting away this time.

"I know you're up there," I called, trying to keep my voice steady as I took the steps two at a time. On the top landing, I paused, my ears prickling. All was silent.

Too silent.

My heart plummeted in my chest as I realized there was no light shining through the crack under my door. I shoved my key into the brand new lock and slowly, cautiously, pushed it open.

The light in my room had been turned off.

22

FAYE

*S*hit.

I flicked the light on, stepping boldly into the room even though my heart hammered against my chest. "All right, you can come out now."

My eyes swept over my furniture. Had I left the books like that? Was my underwear drawer supposed to be half-open? What about that dent in the bed? Everything felt tainted, befouled, because I *knew* someone had been in here.

How did they get in? How could they have a key to my new lock?

I looked into every dark corner and in every conceivable hiding place, my ears pricked for the sound of someone fleeing back down the stairs. But there was nothing. The room was empty.

Of course, they wouldn't hide in here. They must be in the storage room. They know I don't have a key.

I held up my phone's flashlight to the storage room's large keyhole and tried to peer inside, but it was so dark all I could see was the pale silhouette of the moon through the window behind slacks of boxes and old furniture. If they were still inside, they weren't moving.

"I know you're in there." I hit the door with my fists. "Show yourself."

The fear tightening my chest turned to anger. *This is ridiculous. They're not in here. They must have slipped down while I was in my room. They're probably great at sneaking for all the nights they climb up here without me catching them. In fact, this is an old house – there's probably a secret passage or something. There's always a secret passage in the movies.*

I turned on my heel and stormed downstairs. I stormed toward Dorien's door, but his voice floated up from the Blue Room below. *It can't be him, then. But I know who it has to be.*

I grabbed the handle of Titus' room and turned, expecting it to be locked. The door flung open, and I stumbled through it, my foot catching on the edge of the rug and sending me spinning. My knee cracked against a metal bed-frame, and my hands skimmed something large and warm as I struggled for balance.

Sheets rustled. "What the fuck?" Titus' face appeared over the side of the bed as I rolled over, my knee throbbing.

"Don't you 'what the fuck' me." I got to my feet with as much dignity as I could muster and leaned over the bed, hands on hips, legs wide, making myself bigger the way a cat fluffed up their fur before they went into battle with a pitbull. "You were in my room just now. And you sneak into the storage room at night. I *heard* you—"

I'd intended to threaten Titus with the police, with anything I could to get him to stop breaking into my room and stomping around in the storage room. Now that I was in here, and he stared up at me with tangled eyelashes and a pillow crease across his cheekbone, his sheet slipping down over his gloriously tattooed torso, the words dried on my throat.

Titus rubbed his eyes. He certainly *seemed* like he'd been asleep. But I hadn't imagined the face or the light going off in my room. And he admitted to being there once before.

Before I could find the words, Titus' hand shot out, circling my wrist. He rose up from between the sheets, revealing tattoos of snakes twining over his dark skin and abs that belonged on a bodybuilder. How did a dude get that toned playing cello? My fingers itched to touch Titus' skin, to drag my nails over those snakes, to watch them dance as he rolled on top of me and…

Titus leaned so close his breath kissed my lips. The air between us sizzled with tension. I didn't know what would happen next, what I *wanted* to happen next.

"I didn't go near your room." Mmmmm, his New Orleans accent came out thicker when he was tired.

"Yes, you did," I managed to choke out. "I was outside and I saw a face at the window. I was outside and I saw the light in my room, and when I got back it was turned off."

"Not me." Titus grabbed the chain around his neck and dangled it in front of my face. *A key.* The exact type of key that opened the old lock on my bedroom door. "This doesn't work no more. I haven't been upstairs since that first night, when I watched you drool on your pillow."

"Where did you get that?" I lunged for the key, but Titus held it beyond my reach.

"Clare gave Dorien a copy so he could sneak up in the night. I could hear the bed creaking from down here. Friendly warning – Dorien's got a real thing about shagging the help. Must be something about this tight black dress." Titus rubbed his finger down the inside of my arm, and even through the thick wool fabric it sent a fire through my body.

I knew I was rapidly losing control of the situation and myself, but the anger and violation still surged in my veins. *I must have that key.* It was a symbol of claiming back my space. I lunged again, taking Titus by surprise. As I reached for the key, my chest brushed his, sending a jolt through me like I'd stuck my nipple in an electrical socket. Titus felt it too, because his eyes narrowed, the lashes tangling together.

Titus didn't flinch away. Instead, he leaned in closer, his

fingers dancing up my arm as I scrambled for the key. My breath came out in ragged gasps as I fought against my desire. His face hung inches from mine, so close his musk and myrrh swirled around me, and the notes of rose conjured a memory that seared my skin with pain. Roses sent to my mother's hospital room by her board members, back when she thought she'd be cured in a week, back before the coma and the poisoning and—

"You should stay away from me," Titus hissed. His deep voice reverberated through my entire body, bringing me back to myself, to the present moment, to the scant inch of air that was all that protected me from the most delicious mistake of my life.

"Or what?" I tried to issue it as a challenge, but the words came out husky, thick with desire.

"Or—" He chose to finish the thought with his eyes, the fire within them promising darkness and depravity and beautiful obsession. Tension crackled between us, a lightning storm flickering between our eyes. Why, *why* did I let Titus do this to me?

Titus' fingers walked over my wrist, trailing along the veins pulsing against my skin. The touch was featherlight, but it left a trail of fire against my skin that melted my insides into a wobbly mess. My breath hitched, and I dared myself to lean a little closer, a little... to feel the air shift as his lips brushed mine—

"Bro, you wouldn't believe—what the *fuck?*"

Dorien. His voice shattered the spell. I wrenched my arm from Titus' grip and turned to the doorway. Dorien stood in the hall, a storm in his grey eyes, tension tightening his shoulders to rock. Titus stared bug-eyed at his friend, his mouth moving but no sound emerging, while I staggered toward the door, shoving my way past Dorien.

Shame burned in my cheek as the fire in my veins cooled to ice. *What the fuck just happened? What am I doing? That guy openly admits to tormenting me, and I was about to... I wanted to...*

Sound the fucktrumpets, I want to shag my bullies.

23

TITUS

"What was that about?" Dorien demanded.

"She thinks I was in her room." I lifted my knees so Dorien didn't have to see the tent in the bedsheets. My veins throbbed with fire from Faye's presence. "You didn't go up there? Apparently, she was outside with Aroha and someone turned the light off in her bedroom."

"What's she doing outside with Aroha? Our no talking to the trash rule still applies." Dorien glared at me.

I shrugged. "You know Aroha likes to flaunt our rules."

"She's not the only one."

"So you weren't up there?"

Dorien shook his head. "No way to get in with that new lock Harrison installed."

I sank down on my bed, Faye's scent spinning me out. When she burst in, her hair wild around her face and that defiant look in her eyes, I was *so fucking close...*

The only thing that stopped me was Dorien. He was in the room, a ghost between us, before he appeared at the doorway.

"And the storage room? She seemed to think someone has been up there at night, moving around."

"Usher would never give up the key to that place, not even if it meant getting her out of here forever. Sprite probably heard rats or something. Why do you care?"

Sprite. Hearing that childhood nickname fly from his lips made my stomach twist up with envy. It could have just as easily been me who had a history with Faye, if my parents had sent me to a different New York school. I looked away so I wouldn't fall apart under Dorien's gaze. "I don't care. I just think it's a waste of energy to terrorize her. She's a shit musician and can't keep up with Madame's rules. She'll eliminate herself."

"What energy? The only thing you have to do is not talk to her, but apparently, that's too difficult. Heather and I are taking care of the rest." The petulant tone in Dorien's voice reminded me of the first time we met at a music camp in Colorado in our teens, and he complained to the staff because he didn't want to share a room with me. It was touch and go for a while as to whether we'd end up friends or bitter enemies, but Dorien had a magnetism that drew you in, and I was a kid desperate for anyone's approval. By the time that camp finished we were like an old married couple. The kind of married couple where Dorien was the alpha and I went along with everything he said.

"You made me go into her room with Heather. While she was asleep." A cold shudder ran through my body. I didn't like the way that made me feel – like a creepy stalker. That was why I told Faye, even though I disguised it as another part of her torture. She deserved to know the truth.

"It's fine. I won't ask you to do it again. From now on, consider yourself out of the loop."

I shook my head. "Don't be like that. I don't want to be out. I just…"

"What?" Dorien barked. He sounded pissed as fuck, but I knew what lurked beneath that annoyance was fear. I'd never seen Dorien afraid before, not the way he'd been since we returned to Manderley.

He's not the only one.

I rolled over, shoving my feet out of the bed and standing in front of him, bringing half the blankets with me. "I need to go to the woodshed."

"We're not done here."

"We're done." I dropped to my knees and reached under the bed, dragging a case out into the light.

Dorien stiffened when he saw what I was holding. "You shouldn't keep that in here. If *she* finds out—"

"What's the worst she can do to me?"

Dorien smirked at that. He picked up a black t-shirt from my bureau and tossed it at my chest. "True. But be careful, you're not the only one she has by the balls. I'm not sure I can protect you."

I straightened up, my eyes meeting his, and an unspoken message passed between us. People heard Dorien in concert and read about what he got up to in the tabloids and thought they knew him. They saw the bad boy, the deviant, the one making a mockery of serious classical music. But I saw something different – the only person who had my back even when I fucked up again and again. The guy who never told me I wasn't good enough. The friend who never put a price on his loyalty. "Thanks."

I pulled on the shirt and some jeans, and slipped down the stairs, wincing as I stepped on a loose board and a loud *CREAK* echoed in the dim house. Downstairs, I padded through the servant's hallway and across the kitchen. Faye's scent clung to every surface, hidden behind the wafting Mexican spices she used liberally in her cooking.

That scent did things to my head. I couldn't fucking *think*.

The case slapped against my leg as I stepped out into the frigid mountain air and hurried across the grass. Over the lawn, down the path, around the back of the woodshed to the locked door. I lied to Faye – Heather had the key to her old room. The one around my neck unlocked my secrets.

I unlocked the door and kicked it open, shuffling the heavy

case inside and locking it behind me. I shone my phone's flashlight around until I found what I was looking for – the small generator I set up out here to give me light and power. I flicked it on, and the low rumble sent a shiver of anticipation through me.

I unlatched the case. It swung open. My secret stared back at me, beautiful and deadly.

Images and sensations swirled in my mind – Faye's face drawing toward me, those sexy lips parted ever so slightly, the feel of her skin shuddering beneath my touch – as I reached inside and drew it out.

24

DORIEN

Sunlight streamed through the high windows of the twelfth-floor studio, casting golden ripples across the cascade of Faye's hair. She faced away from me, out at the toy city far below, the violin against her neck as she slashed the strings with the bow in her signature overwrought style. Today she played a haunting Bach piece that grabbed my heart and squeezed, so tight. Or maybe that was the reality of what I was about to do.

Faye finished the movement with a low, trembling note, stepping back and bowing to her imaginary audience. I clapped, the noise like gunshots in the vast, empty space.

"Dorien." Faye whirled around. The grin on her face wavered when she saw my face. "What's the matter?"

"I came to say goodbye."

"What do you mean?" Her hair bounced on her shoulders. "You just got here. Class starts in fifteen minutes—"

"I mean, this is the last time we'll see each other. Mom's transferred me to another music school."

"No, that sucks." But her face brightened. "I know! I'll ask Mom to transfer me too. I can't stand Madame Usher, anyway.

She doesn't seem to like me much. I think she only puts up with me because of Dad—"

I shook my head. She didn't get it.

Harden your heart.

"I don't want you to transfer. I'm leaving *because* of you. I don't want to see you again."

Faye's face froze in shock. "What is this? What do you mean? We're going to perform the Beethoven together and—"

"I don't want anything to do with you, Sprite."

Tears welled in the corners of her eyes. "Don't use that name when you're being horrible. Is this about me coming to your house last week? I'm sorry I pushed you into inviting me, but we had fun, didn't we? Dorien, please, explain this to me."

Please, please don't make this even harder.

"There's nothing to explain. I don't like you, Faye. I pretended to like you because my parents wanted me to get closer to your father. But it's not worth it anymore." I narrowed my eyes and conjured up the dark desires and seething hatred that burned inside me, and I threw them up between us like a Greek warrior raising his shield.

At the time I didn't entirely understand my action, but I did now. She had to see me as a bad person, as this selfish, self-centered asshole who wasn't worth her time. I had to give her all the ammo she needed to forget me.

It was the only way she'd be safe.

"Dorien, I..." Her words trailed off as the tears spilled over her eyes and rolled down her cheeks. Faye never cried, not even when Madame Usher yelled at her or her father went away on tour and forgot to call. I commanded my feet to move, to go to her so I could throw my arms around her and take her pain away. But I couldn't. Because I was the root of that pain, the cause of those tears.

"I don't understand." Faye slid onto an overstuffed ottoman, her violin falling across her lap. "I thought your parents liked me. At your house they said—"

"They were being polite. And so was I." I turned on my heel. If I had to look at her any longer, I'd lose my shit.

"Dorien, wait!" The crack in her voice sent a shudder through my body. I didn't turn around.

Every inch of my body wailed in protest, but I walked away.

Out the door.

Into the elevator.

Across the parking lot.

Away from her.

It wasn't so hard to pretend to be an asshole. Maybe I wasn't pretending. After all, I learned from the best.

My mother waited in the back of the car, her brown robe pulled high around her neck. As soon as I slid into the seat, she indicated for the driver to take us home.

Mom patted my leg. "It's not too late to change your mind, Dorien. She is a good match; Father Aaron says so."

I nodded. I couldn't speak, or I'd scream.

"Not to worry." She had that fake brightness in her voice, the tone she always took when Father Aaron wanted us to do something she didn't agree with. The tone had no power – she never contradicted him. "We've already found you someone even better, from a less volatile family. You'll meet her at your new school. Her name is Heather Danvers."

My phone beeped, startling me out of my dream. I rubbed my eyes, trying to smudge away that image of my mother's hopeful face and Faye's cheeks streaked with tears. As I scrambled for the phone, my eyes fell on the portrait Clare made me. *No. I don't want to think of her now.*

I turned the portrait away and grabbed my phone, my heart thumping as I saw it was a text from him.

Hey I hope I dont wake you but things are bad here Aaron hit mom hes angry all the time and he talks about this thing called ascension I wish you would come back.

That was the longest text he'd ever sent. It must've taken him a long time to write all the words. My parents never allowed him proper schooling, so he was slow to read and write.

My chest twisted with cold, ugly hate. How could they not see what they were doing to him? How could they believe that this life was better? My mother blamed me. "You turned out the way you did because we gave you everything on a silver platter. You have no discipline. You're corrupted by the world of material wealth. I'll not make the same mistakes twice."

No, I turned out the way I did because you never loved me unless it had conditions attached. Because I was never fucking good enough so I stopped trying. Because you keep calling me 'a mistake.'

They hadn't even let me see him when I visited the other week. Father Aaron ushered me into the room that had once been our breakfast nook, now emptied of all furniture except for a circle of lumpy pillows on the floor. Anger radiated off him in waves. He didn't want me there in my fancy clothes and expensive cologne, reminding the others about the temptations of the world outside.

More than anything, I wanted to escape this cage I'd made for myself the day I dropped Faye as a friend, but I was trapped. Madame Usher's words echoed in my ears. *A new student will be arriving soon. I need you to destroy her. Do as I say, or I'll cut you off. How long will you last when the world finds out the truth about your family?*

She thought that was all I cared about. *She doesn't know the half of it.*

Of course, Madame remembered Faye and I used to be friends. That was why she chose me – if anyone could burrow inside Faye's heart and rot her from the inside, it would be me. That was what I did – I turned everything I touched into ashes and dust.

I lay awake, imagining Faye in her bed above me, wearing those sexy as fuck Snoopy pajamas that clung to her curves, fuming because I'd interrupted whatever was going on with her and Titus. And even though the thought of them touching made my body burn with jealousy, I didn't care – Titus was a good dude, almost good enough for her. He wouldn't fuck her over… unless I commanded it.

But I did wish…

I imagined creeping upstairs, rolling in bed beside Faye, my fingers tangling in her hair as I trailed a path of kisses along her neck, across her collarbone, my lips closing over her nipple until she writhed and begged for more. Mmmmm. To hear Faye de Winter beg for me…

But I remained still, paralyzed even as my dick jerked with anticipation, turning over the situation in my mind, looking for a loophole, a solution.

There was none.

I couldn't help him without the Manderley Prize. And I couldn't get the prize unless Faye left Manderley. Unless I broke her. And my time was running out.

25

FAYE

hose face was it?

I bent over my laptop in my corner of the library. I was supposed to be working on an essay on Sibelius, but I couldn't focus. My fingers kept tracing the skin on my arm where Titus had touched me. My lips tingled with the memory of that sizzling tension drawing us together.

Stop it. Stop thinking about it.

Don't picture Titus naked under the sheets. Don't consider that he *couldn't* have been the one up in my room. He wouldn't have risked running down the stairs naked, which meant that in the time I'd made it to the second floor, he ran downstairs, and climbed into bed without being out of breath or smelling of sweat...

I just didn't believe it.

So who else could have done it? Harrison had gone down to the gatehouse, and Master Radcliffe's lights had been on in the stable house when I walked back to the house. So neither of them were inside. Madame Usher could barely fit up that staircase – no way would she have been dextrous enough to get back down so quickly, so it wasn't her, either. Aroha had been with me, and Elena, Dorien, and Heather had been in the Blue Room.

The only one I couldn't account for was Ivan. I'd assumed he was in the Blue Room because he never left Elena's side, but someone had to have been in my room… because the only other possibility was that a ghost did it, and that was ridiculous.

Ivan was the only one who could have done it. And I was sick to death of taking the Muses' shit. It was time to fight back.

~

It took me a couple of days to figure out how to get back at Ivan. He and Elena went everywhere together, and despite the fact she never said a word to me and looked like a stony-faced bitch, I didn't want to involve her. This wasn't her battle.

Then, one night over dinner, Madame Usher announced an upcoming visit from the conductor of the Berlin Philharmonic. He was in America recruiting students for a week-long intensive residency and requested a performance from each of us, so we'd be hosting him for a full-blown recital of our most polished work. Something my mother said flitted through my mind.

She'd been trying to land a contract with a celebrity actor who was launching a line of merchandise, but another PR company was angling for the deal. The guy who ran this company was famous for not disclosing sponsored content on social media – he built a couple of successful celebrity brands off the back of his "authentic" influencer marketing, while my mom did everything above board, which meant her campaigns had less reach. He badmouthed her all over the city, and I kept asking her why she didn't fight back. She'd smiled. "Don't you worry about me. I'm keeping my hands clean while he digs his own grave."

Sure enough, two weeks later, an investigative article in the New York Times exposed this guy's shady practices, and the FTC swooped in. No one wanted to touch him. De Winter PR got the celebrity deal.

Mom was clever. She knew that people who refuse to play by the rules eventually got caught out in their own lies. She'd given me all the tools I needed to show the Muses that they couldn't fuck with Faye de Winter.

26

FAYE

While the students sat through one of Madame Usher's history of music lectures, I had to clean the bathrooms, change the sheets, and vacuum any visible floor space in their bedrooms. Usually, I tried to hurry through it as quickly as possible, but today I hesitated at the door of Elena and Ivan's room.

Let him dig his own grave.

I whipped through the bathroom, cleaning as I went. It was Elena's domain – her cosmetics decorated the counter, and a pyramid of her dirty laundry wedged the door permanently open. More clothes and shoes obscured her bed – it was a miracle she slept at night without accidentally poking a Louboutin heel through her eye.

Ivan's things were much neater – his bed made with military precision, a small pile of dirty clothes placed in the hamper, a stack of music books arranged on his desk. That made it obvious where I needed to search. I pulled out drawer after drawer in his armoire, hunting for the skeletons I knew had to exist. I didn't find anything other than perfectly folded shirts and rolled socks. Marie Kondo would be so proud—

Hello, what's this?

At the back of his sock drawer, my fingers grazed a baggie. I pulled it out and held it up on the light, watching white crystals cascade through the plastic.

Jackpot.

I knew enough about drugs to know I was looking at a *serious* quantity of cocaine.

Apart from the occasional joint, I'd never even seen drugs up close before. But I *had* seen the effects at Mom's business events. Guys completely whacked out, chasing women who didn't want to be chased. Women believing they were invincible because they had money and a shield of drug haze. In our last apartment, I got to see another side – addicts on street corners, shop windows punched in. Once, a guy chased me four blocks while loudly declaring his desire to slit me open and eat my intestines.

This baggie of white gold was exactly what I'd been looking for – it was the shovel that Ivan would use to dig his grave. I just wasn't expecting quite such a large shovel.

This wasn't a personal stash – it was enough for a Robert Downey Jr. yoga retreat or a Hannaford Prep study party. And people who dealt drugs tended to be dangerous, or have dangerous friends.

But then I thought of how I struggled to sleep, of how I looked over my shoulder every time I walked into a room and had to check under my bed in case one of the guys was hiding there. I thought of my eroded sense of safety, of peace, and I squared my jaw. *This is the right thing—*

"What are you doing?"

I jumped at the voice, hitting my elbow on the open drawer. My hand flew behind my back, shoving the coke into the waistband of my skirt. I glared at Ivan, who leaned against the doorframe and looked me over with eyes of ice and sapphire. That impenetrable stare that would make any girl long to be the one to crack open his frosted heart.

I straightened up, trying to paint my face into a picture of innocence. "What does it look like? I'm dusting, like a good maid."

"You usually dust in underwear drawers?"

Heat burned in my cheeks. Ivan folded his arms, and something tugged at the edge of his mouth. On anyone else, I might have mistaken it for a smile, but Ivan Nicolescu didn't smile. He was a glacier – hard and cold, and if you dug beneath the surface, there was just more ice.

That was just the thing. I couldn't see Ivan as an addict or a dealer, but then… Manderley was a house of secrets. I couldn't back down now that I'd uncovered his.

"Fair's fair. You were in my room." I straightened up, trying to move my body without letting the bag slip out from my shirt.

He didn't deny it. Instead, he took a step toward me, his long legs stretching over a pile of his sister's junk. My heart hammered. "You believe this makes us even?"

Even his voice sounded glacial – slow and primal, that Romanian accent edged with ice. It vibrated through my body even as I took a step away from him. As Ivan picked his way closer, I noticed the way he moved – a tightness in his limbs, a tension in his step. He battled to maintain control.

We circled each other like two animals ready to pounce, but what would happen if one of us made the move – bloodbath or fuckfest? Both were equally likely outcomes, but only one made my body tingle with anticipation.

Ivan stepped toward the bed, and I circled around the wall until I had a clear run for the door. As I backed into the hall Ivan spoke again. "Faye?"

My name on his lips was fucking *poetry*. I raised an eyebrow.

Ivan's features didn't waver, but something flickered in his eyes – a hint of emotion, a clue that he wasn't entirely made of ice. "Be careful."

I opened my mouth to ask him what he meant, but he'd slammed the door in my face.

27

FAYE

The day of the conductor's visit arrived. I'd stayed up past midnight the night before, preparing the evening meal so that I would only be heating things up the next day. I polished the silver setting until it shone. When I'd finally crawled into bed, I longed for sleep, but the Muses had decided to step up their torture. Instead of the creaking footsteps in my room, the faintest sound of violin music scratched the air.

It had to be a recording – it was too quiet to be someone playing in the storage room, and no one would dare play downstairs this late at night for fear of Madame Usher's wrath. *This is their assault on me because they know I was snooping in Ivan's room. They probably know I've got the coke. They're trying to keep me awake so I play badly tomorrow. Well, bet they didn't know that after my father left the only way Mom could get me to sleep was to put on recordings of his concerts. I love falling asleep with music playing. So there.*

Only, it turns out, I wasn't a kid anymore, and violin music can be fucking annoying when you add it to a stuffy attic, performance nerves, and the plot to destroy a Muse. I tossed and turned all night, fighting for every snatch of sleep I wrestled from the disturbed darkness. When the alarm went off at 5:30, I threw it across the room.

I dragged myself downstairs, made grilled cheese for myself, set out granola and yogurt for the royal dickweasels, and loped back to the attic.

Back in my room, I began my daily inspection of the cupboards and corners for an intruder. I shoved aside the bed, bureau, and locked chest to stomp on the floorboards. Then, I pressed on every wood panel and clawed at every crack in the room, searching for a secret passage. I hated that I was letting the students get to me even after I had the lock changed, but knowing they could come into my room any time they wanted and touch my stuff had me permanently on edge. Every creak and groan of the old house had me sitting upright in bed, heart in my throat.

I didn't believe in ghosts, but I honestly *wished* I was being haunted. It would be easier to deal with.

I crawled out from under the bed, satisfied that no one was spying on me today. Moving to my clothing rack, I pulled my concert dress from its dry-cleaning bag and hung it over my chair. Mom brought me this dress for my audition for Juilliard last year, back before she got seriously sick, when both our futures looked bright. Bonus, it had a little secret pocket in the seam of the skirt – perfect for a cocaine stash.

I stripped off my scratchy black dress and stepped into the shower, lathering up and rinsing as quickly as I could, my heart in my throat. Usually, I liked to take my time, letting the heat of the water melt away any performance nerves, but I couldn't rid myself of the itchy sensation of someone watching me. The Muses had stripped away that simple pleasure, too.

I wrapped a towel around myself and padded back into my room. Nerves crawled between my shoulders. *I fucking hate this.* I tipped my chin defiantly. If one of the guys was watching, let them have a fucking show.

At the thought of their eyes on me, warmth flared between my legs. My body betrayed me, aching for something that didn't exist. *They're trying to destroy me, and all I can think about is how much I want them. Any of them. All of them. I'm sick. I need help.*

Fuck you, Dorien, Titus, Ivan. You're going down.

I dropped the towel to the floor.

In the storage room next door, something banged. I jumped ten feet in the air, my heart in my mouth.

It's just the pipes clanging. They always do that after you've had a shower. Calm down. There's no one here.

My fingers trembled as I unhooked the clasps and pulled the slinky material over my head. Crimson satin pooled over my legs, clinging to my hips and flaring out into a fishtail skirt that accentuated my hourglass shape. A panel of red lace between the sweetheart neckline tied in a halter round my neck, leaving my shoulders bare. I did a little twirl and smirked at my reflection.

I might not be a skinny rake like Heather, but I could still look *damn fine.*

I stuffed the cocaine into the secret pocket, picked up my violin case, and descended the staircase as the other students gathered in the entrance hall. Even though it was just 10AM, Heather and Elena clutched glasses of Champagne - Elena's pixieish beauty only enhanced by her sky-blue dress, while Heather looked like she was auditioning for season 1 of *My Big Fat Baroque Wedding* with an enormous, puffy-sleeved monstrosity. The Broken Muse boys could pull off pseudo-Baroque frippery because of their superhuman good looks, but Heather didn't have the same blessings.

As I descended the staircase, my leg rubbing against the cocaine with every step, three pairs of eyes followed my every move. The grey storm, the dark blaze, the sapphire shard – their collective gaze turned me about and did strange things to my insides. I didn't understand how this sexual tension had risen up between us in the midst of the power struggle we had going on.

But for today I was determined I wouldn't let the Muses see how they affected me. Tonight was my turn to fight back.

Madame Usher swept in, her black skirts trailing behind her. "You all look fantastic. If you haven't already, please go to the music room and tune your instruments."

"I tuned earlier, and so did Titus and Ivan," Heather said in that annoying trill of hers. "It's always good to be prepared and treat your instrument well."

Gag me.

I followed Aroha into the music room, setting down my violin case next to Ivan's. While she shut the door behind us and pulled the lock across, I flicked the latches on Ivan's case and shoved the bag of cocaine inside. I stood up just as she turned to me, a vicious smile playing across her lips.

It was a symptom of the Muses' bullying that my mind immediately jumped on the idea that she was going to do something to me.

"Why did you lock the door?" I tried to keep my voice even as I wiped my sweating palms on my dress.

"Chill out, trash. I just didn't want to share with the others." Aroha set down her violin case and withdrew something from the inside pocket. A tiny bag of white powder. "Want some? I always take it before a performance. Helps with the nerves."

Cocaine.

Blood rushed to my ears. After I'd spent the last twenty-four hours with Ivan's stash in my possession, I was being offered *more* drugs? *Is this some kind of test?*

When I'd reeled from the shock, I shook my head. I was held to a different standard than the others. If I was caught with illegal drugs in my system, it would give Madame Usher the excuse she needed to get rid of me.

Aroha smirked. "Suit yourself." She knelt down beside the coffee table and tapped out a line. My fingers shook as I unlocked my case and removed my instrument. *Don't think about what she's doing. It's not your concern. It doesn't matter.*

But it *did* matter. It mattered so much that my hands shook as I tried to tune. And I couldn't figure out why. Aroha wasn't really my friend. Why did I care what she did?

Is it because I know she didn't come from the kind of wealth the others enjoyed? That Ivan was a drug dealer taking advantage of her nerves to get her addicted to a habit that could cost her career?

Yep. That probably had something to do with it.

When she'd finished, Aroha wiped her nose and stood up. "That's better. Now I can face them."

"Was that from Ivan?" I tried to keep my voice casual.

"Ivan?" Aroha's giggle had a slightly manic quality to it. "Fuck no. That straight-edged posh pimp won't even let a sip of alcohol touch his precious lips, let alone evil drugs."

My stomach lurched. Had I made a big mistake? But no, the coke was in Ivan's drawer. It had to be his. Besides, it was too late to fix it now.

Let him dig his own grave.

We finished tuning and left our instruments ready on opposite corners of the room. I followed Aroha as she joined the others in the entrance hall. Dorien passed us on his way to the bathroom, and she grinned and sashayed her hips at him. Her behavior puzzled me – Aroha was a strong, sassy woman who never had any trouble speaking her mind or talking to the others – why did she need drugs to get her through an informal performance?

Dorien arrived back in the entrance hall just as Harrison pulled up in the limo. Madame Usher threw open the doors. "Hans," she threw out her arms as a lanky man picked his way up the steps. They did that air kissing thing people in music always did, the sloppy sound of saliva hitting flesh.

"Allow me to introduce this year's students." She swept him

into the hall, taking his coat and tossing it to me. I hung it over the hook that was right behind her.

"Ah, Dorien Valencourt needs no introduction." Dorien leaned forward to do the air-kissing thing with the conductor, who had shoulder-length grey hair swept back into a ponytail, and a hooked nose straight out of my fairy tale book. "And I see Titus and Ivan have joined you. It has been too long since you played for us in Berlin."

"Agreed. Broken Muse would love to return to Germany."

Boris tsked. "Last time we hosted you, you threw a TV into a swimming pool and caused the police to be called to your hotel."

"Three times," Titus piped up, a wicked grin spreading across his face.

Dorien glared at him.

Hans nodded. "Ja, three times. My orchestra cannot afford another scandal, or we'll lose funding."

Dorien made the sign of the cross. "I swear on the Almighty the three of us are on our very best behavior."

"I'll believe it when I see it. And Elena Nicolescu." Hans clasped her hand, his eyes drinking her in. "You're still as enchanting as ever."

"Thank you." Her waifish voice soared with pleasure.

Madame shoved Aroha forward. "This is Aroha Rawhiri, from New Zealand. And this is Heather Danvers, of the New Jersey Danvers."

"And who is this crimson beauty in the corner?" Hans' eyes swept over me like he was the Big Bad Wolf and I'd just showed up at the door with a red hood and a basket of blackberry tarts.

Seven pairs of eyes flew to me, most of them flaring with annoyance.

"That's... Faye." Madame Usher answered stiffly. "She was a student of my New York school before moving to the public school system. I'm afraid her technique won't ever recover."

I love the way she says 'public school' like it's a disease.

"Faye *de Winter*," Aroha piped up from the back. I glared at her, and she gave me a sly wave.

At the mention of my last name, Hans' eyes widened with interest. "As in, Donovan de Winter?"

"He was my father," I said through gritted teeth.

"Astounding. That man had a *spiccato* technique that has never been replicated. The entire Classical world was devastated when he disappeared. I had no idea he had a *protégé*. You must share with me all you know of his whereabouts."

Yes, if I had information about my missing cockpoodle of a father, I'd totally be willing to reveal it to a complete stranger with an obnoxious ponytail.

Hans clasped his hands together. I could practically see him salivating. "Madame Usher, you never told me I was to expect such a star-studded lineup."

"Save your praise until after the recital." She led Hans into the Blue Room, the rest of us shuffling behind.

As Hans settled himself into the chair by the window, usually reserved for Master Radcliffe, I poured him a glass of Champagne. As I handed it to him, my gaze caught my music stand near the window.

My violin wasn't there.

Panic seized me.

There was Ivan's violin exactly where I left it, the case still locked tight. On the other side of the room, by the piano, was Aroha's piece. Heather's violin and Titus' cello sat together in the corner. But my instrument was nowhere to be seen. "Where's my violin?"

"Shhhh." Heather glared at me, obviously forgetting about the no-talking-to-Faye rule. "Don't make us look bad."

I snorted. "Sure, wouldn't want to put your *neck ruffs* to shame, Marie Antoinette. I left my violin set up by the window, but it's missing."

Madame's eyes flashed. "You're accusing another student of taking your violin?"

"No." My cheeks burned with heat. *This can't be happening.* "I'm just saying that it's gone—"

"I certainly didn't move your violin. None of my other students would have moved your violin. The only conclusion is that you forgot your instrument after I *specifically* said to have everything prepared for Mr. Brandt's visit."

Behind me, Heather stifled a giggle.

"Go." Madame Usher snapped, waving her hand at the door. "Bring your instrument. We will have words tomorrow."

I tore from the room, my heart in a panic. I knew I didn't leave my violin in my room – not fifteen minutes ago, I tuned it while Aroha snorted coke. The only way it could have moved was if someone *took* it.

Aroha? Possible. She left the room after me, but I looked back at her and I would've seen it in her. Or Dorien? He'd gone back to the bathroom—

Of course. I shoved open the door of the men's bathroom. Sure enough, there was my violin on top of the sink.

Smashed to a thousand pieces.

The aftermath of Paik's *One for Violin Solo.*

My worst fucking nightmare.

Splinters of wood decorated the marble tiles, unrecognizable as once belonging to a beautiful instrument. Strings curled into springs that bounced in the air, mocking me.

No.

Please, no.

Tears pricked in the corners of my eyes. That violin was a gift from my mother for my sixteenth birthday. It came from an artisan luthier in upstate New York and was a work of art in its own right.

It was *mine.*

How *dare* they ruin this for me?

Panic shot through me. They were all expecting me back, Hans eager to hear the daughter of Donovan de Winter strut her stuff. I still had to witness Ivan's downfall. I had to get back in that room now and deal with this later. If I couldn't use my instrument, *any* violin would do.

I raced through the foyer, taking the stairs two at a time. When I reached my bedroom, I grabbed the thick ring of keys from my bed and jogged back down to the first floor. At the end of the hall, just before Madame Usher's private chambers, was a small storage room housing a variety of instruments gifted to the school over the years.

I stepped inside and flicked on the light, illuminating immaculate rows of glass cases and racks of instruments standing silent and sentinel. My fingers traced a rack of violins, passing over a Sanctus Seraphin with the distinctive reddish varnish before picking up a beautiful, simple instrument that could have only come from the workshop of Carl Becker, the greatest luthier of the 20th century.

As soon as my fingers touched the neck, I knew this was the instrument I had to play. A tingle of fire ran down my hand – the same sensation I got when I touched Titus or stared into Ivan's eyes or traded barbs with Dorien: giddiness tinged with fear. I grabbed the instrument and the bow and flicked off the lights.

As I shoved the key in the lock and turned back toward the staircase, I noticed that the door to Madame Usher's private quarters was open a crack. I jolted.

She never leaves this open. Never.

Unable to stop myself, I crept forward, my chest prickling. I shoved the door open a crack, and peered inside.

The door opened into a receiving room, empty of furniture, with heavy drapes blocking the light from the windows. The fire looked as though it hadn't been lit for some years, and the floor was caked with dust save for a path of footsteps leading through to an inner door. Beyond that, I could just make out the shapes of furniture in a sitting room beyond.

My ears caught something else. The faintest snatches of a familiar melody. The same mournful song that I heard late at night – the mysterious music that seemed to flow from the walls of my room, that was familiar to me even though I couldn't place it.

It was coming from *inside* Madame Usher's chambers.

I knew it wasn't noise traveling from the ballroom downstairs because I could *also* hear the pounding of keys as Dorien and Heather performed their concerto.

I stepped forward, drawn by that music, by my desperate need to get to the bottom of who was haunting me, and *how*. I knew now it had to be Madame Usher, but why would she leave the recording running in here when she knew I'd be downstairs?

As soon as my foot fell inside the room, I realized my mistake. My heel made a loud clack on the marble. The violin stopped. I looked down and realized my print stood out amongst the jumble of others at the threshold. Madame Usher didn't wear heels.

Shit. *Shit.*

I reached down and smudged the print with my hand, but that only made *more* obvious. It was too late to do anything. I backed out and shut the door behind me.

Heather and Dorien were finishing when I entered the room. Dorien's eyes flicked to mine, and he raised an eyebrow at the violin in my hands. Hans stood and clapped, his eyes shining.

"Beautiful and enchanting. Dorien, you were adequate, as usual." But he said it with a twinkle in his eye, because obviously Dorien was the superior of the two. "I'd like to hear from the Nicolescu twins next."

Dorien slid out from behind the piano and inclined his head to Elena. Ivan picked up his violin case and opened the latch. As he took out his violin, the bag slid out onto the rug at Hans' feet.

Ivan's eyes bugged out when he saw it. It took everything I had not to burst out laughing to see stoic, buttoned-up Ivan Nicolescu look so completely shocked.

But this was no laughing matter.

The entire room fell silent as Hans bent down and picked up the bag, holding it up to the light and inspecting it as if hoping the substance inside might magically transform into table salt.

"Well, Ivan," he said mildly. A vein throbbed on his temple. "What do you have to say about this?"

Ivan said nothing. He masked his face with ice, even as his shoulders sagged. Dorien and Titus rose to stand behind him – silently throwing their towel in with their friend's crimes.

Hans dumped the bag into Madame Usher's claws. "This is your mess to deal with. I won't say a word about what I saw here today, but you must know I cannot host any of the Broken Muses for our residency."

"What?" Titus' deep voice rose at least two octaves. Dorien looked like he was ready to cut someone. Ivan stared at a spot on the wall behind Boris' head. I recognized the vacancy in his eyes – it was the same way I felt when the doctors talked about my mother's chances of recovery. I left my body and floated some-where behind my shoulders, watching the scene unfold before me with cool detachment. It was a survival mechanism – if I didn't detach and become Faye the floating ghost-girl, I'd go postal, and hospitals tended to frown on displays of Keith Moon-esque destruction.

That was what Ivan had done – he'd floated away so he could deal. Knowing I had something in common with him made my stomach church with a sensation I didn't like – sympathy.

Nope. Not gonna feel that shit. This is my revenge, and I'm going to enjoy it. I deserve *to enjoy it.*

Madame Usher glared at the three boys. "Ivan, leave. Now. The rest of you, either you go with Ivan or *sit down*. I don't want to hear another word about this."

Dorien stepped forward. "But it's not—"

"I said, *not another word.*" The two of them glared at each other, a battle of wills playing out on an invisible chessboard stretched between them. Dorien might have been a raging storm trapped in the body of the Prince of Darkness, but Madame Usher was like some ancient fucking demon goddess. She held dominion over storms. Hell, she could castrate the Devil himself with that glare.

Dorien backed away, lowering his eyes. Ivan swirled on his heel and left the room, the door clicking shut behind him. Elena didn't move a muscle, but a single tear rolled down her cheek.

It was that tear more than anything that shattered my triumph. In getting back at Ivan, I'd cost all three of the Muses their chance of the residency, and ruined Elena and Ivan's performance.

Then I remembered my beautiful violin smashed to pieces, and I shoved down that rotten feeling of regret. I *basked* in Hans' tight face and Dorien and Titus exchanging worried looks while Elena played through a solo piece – her notes all the more heart-wrenching because of the silent tears cascading down her cheeks.

"*Brava*, Elena, you were fantastic." Hans rose to kiss her damp cheeks when she was done. "Who is next?"

"I see Miss de Winter has returned, so perhaps— What are you doing?" As Madame Usher turned to me, she shrieked. "That's not your violin."

"*Someone* destroyed mine." I glared at Dorien as I held the Becker in front of me, like a shield. "I took this from the instrument room to play for tonight, until I can get a replacement—"

"That's not yours!"

For the second time that night, the room fell deadly silent. Madame Usher strode forward and tore the instrument from my hands. Beneath her caked-on makeup, her face had gone as white as a sheet.

Any other night I might have been able to calm myself enough to find a way out of this, but between my terrible sleep and Ivan's revenge and seeing my instrument bashed to fucking pieces, something had broken inside me. I leaned right in Madame's face and screamed, "What am I supposed to do, then? My violin is gone, and I need to *play*."

Madame Usher tapped her foot. "I'm disappointed. This isn't the behavior of a professional musician. Master Brandt, please don't accept Faye's attitude as a representation of our students. You will not perform. Dorien, you will go next – perform one of your solo pieces."

I headed for the door, but Madame grabbed my arm, her nails digging into my skin.

"You stay," she hissed. "For your insolence, you will suffer through his perfection."

Bitch.

I froze, my body riveted in the spot by Dorien. He played *A Graveside Story*, his most famous composition, the piece that made his career with Broken Muse. It was everything he was – dark and seductive, dragging you under a fierce and choppy ocean and holding you until the water closed your throat and you couldn't breathe for the beauty of it. For he was perfection. Every note was a blade slicing through my skin, baring my soul for him to devour with those slate eyes.

Why couldn't he have been my friend? I hadn't had a real friend since he dropped me. Except for my mom. She'd attended every one of my recitals, even skipping out on important meetings to be front row center. She went out to the store for snacks when I was in the middle of my Juilliard audition prep. She curled my hair and gossiped about boys and celebrities like we were BFFs instead of mother and daughter. And above all, she showed me by example what a woman had to do to succeed, for in business as in life she was fierce and unapologetic and impossibly kind.

Now she was in a coma.

And poison put her there.

Now I cried for real – fat, silent tears rolling down my cheeks like Elena's had moments before, smearing my perfect makeup. I didn't dare wipe them away and draw attention to myself.

Dorien finished and stood to take his bow. He returned to the piano to accompany Heather for some Vivaldi. He was faultless, of course, but her notes were flat and lifeless – or perhaps that was because I heard them through a lens of my own silent screams. After Heather, Aroha wowed with a performance of Turkish composer Fazil Say's sultry *Cleopatra*. Her cheeks glowed with pleasure as Hans praised her treatment of the unique piece. Looking at her, it was hard to believe she needed drugs to step into her power.

Madame Usher clapped her hands and signaled for us to leave. Numb, I followed her from the room, peeling off into the men's bathroom to collect the broken pieces of my violin. When I emerged clutching the remains of my instrument in my trembling hands, Dorien and Heather were just leaving the ballroom. Heather looped her arm in his and leaned into him as they passed me.

Dorien's eyes fell on the pieces in my hands. He stopped in his tracks, wrenching Heather's arm. She yelped in surprise, then she tried to pretend it was intentional.

"Dorien, you are *vicious*," she purred, gazing up at him with adoration. "I thought you were going to hide her instrument. This was so much better."

"I didn't destroy it," Dorien's voice coursed through my body. "I hid it in the bathroom. That's all."

What a fucktrumpet filled with shit. We were all together in the ballroom. Who else could have destroyed it? Harrison? The manor ghost?

"I didn't do this." Dorien looked up at me. A different sort of storm flashed in his eyes, dragging me back out to sea, to a recital when we were eight years old where he missed a note and his mother yelled at him in front of everyone. "Faye, I *swear*. I knew how much this violin meant to you."

He did. He *did* know. He'd been there – the three of us having a fancy birthday dinner at Denny's (all we could afford after my tuition and Dad's career) when Mom presented me with the box.

He knows exactly how to cut me to make me bleed.

I shook my head. If I opened my mouth to speak, I'd scream. Heather broke down into a fit of laughter, her singsong voice peeling along the vaulted hallway. "Oh, the poor little charity girl. Are you going to cry, Faye? Are you going to blubber like a baby? Look at you, all dressed up like you think you're one of us. Your fat rolls are spilling out of that dress. You're disgusting."

I'd been called fat and ugly my whole life. The words rolled off my skin, unable to penetrate because I didn't care what people thought of me. But tonight I held the remnants of my violin in my hands, and I stood in front of a boy who'd once been my friend, and I *broke*.

I slammed my fist into Heather's face. My knuckles connected with a *CRACK*. Heather cried and reeled back. Blood slattered along the wall and across the front of her designer dress. Triumph surged through me as I drew back my fist and felt the bruise blooming across my knuckles. Heather dropped to her knees, clutching her face, as more blood spurted betwee her fingers.

"You broke my nose, you *bitch*."

"Sprite—" Dorien stepped forward, but I jerked away, spinning on my heel and fleeing to the not-safety of my attic room, Heather's screams chasing me the whole way.

28

IVAN

I slammed the door so hard the entire wall rattled. A cascade of Elena's lipsticks toppled from the over-stuffed shelf and skittered across the floor. My whole body trembled. Fuck. *Fuck.*

I knew I should have gotten rid of that coke. I *knew* it. But I kept it because… because I was a *bou* of the first order.

Across the room, Elena curled up on her bed, like a dragon queen guarding her gaudy treasures. My own eyes peered back at me from behind her long, tangled lashes, wide and frightened.

"What's going to happen to us now?" she asked in a small voice.

I shook my head. I had no idea. Neither of us stuck around after the recital to find out what Madame Usher had in store for us. That Sword of Damocles would dangle over us for a bit longer.

Would she wash her hands of us? Send us back to Romania? Cold dread washed over me as the options lined themselves up in front of me, each bleaker than the last. Would she hush it up and add more to our sentence?

Elena's lip trembled. I knew she was thinking the same things

– what would this mistake cost us, for we both knew everything we did came with a price. I crossed the room in three strides and dropped beside her, sweeping her into my arms. Cosmetic tubes and handbags jabbed into my spine as I lay beside her. Elena rested her head on my chest, her fingers tracing the filigree patterns on my shirt. She waited for me to speak, to announce my grand plan. I was the older by two minutes – all our lives Elena had looked to me to be the responsible one, to find a way out of any mess.

But I could see no way out – only darkness, only the gilded bars of our cage closing in on us. We were in too deep.

"Ivan, open up." Dorien hammered his fists against the door.

"Dorien, what the fuck—" I jerked upright just as he rammed the door with his shoulder, tearing the lock from its screws. The door banged open and Dorien barged past, moving to the window to pull the curtains shut. He turned to Elena, his voice a maelstrom of barely-restrained rage.

"Get out."

"Don't talk to her like that." I threw myself in front of my sister, hands balled into fists. "This is her life, too."

Dorien's face softened, just a fraction. "Ease off, mate. You know I love Elena like my own sister, but we need to talk. *Alone.* Aroha's in the bathroom helping Heather plaster up her nose. They might want company."

Elena wiped her eyes and rolled off the bed. She leaned in and kissed my cheek. "We'll be fine. We'll find a way."

I wasn't so sure about that, but I kissed her back.

Titus stepped out of the way to allow her past. "Don't snort anything I wouldn't snort, Little Sis." They all called her that, and it usually warmed me, but not today. Elena swatted him in the arm, and then she was gone, hair flying behind her.

I loved that my friends cared for her like she was their own. They were the only real family we'd ever had.

Titus had to turn sideways to move his shoulders through the doorway. He locked the door and leaned against the frame, while Dorien paced across the floor. I shoved my hands in my pockets so I wouldn't do anything stupid.

"What happened to Heather's face?" I asked.

Titus laughed. "Faye punched her. It was glorious."

Dorien whirled to face me. "I need to know, did you smash Faye's violin?"

His words only made Titus laugh harder. "That's the most important thing here? Not that brick of coke in Ivan's violin case? What the fuck, man?"

Dorien glared at Titus. "That's not a brick, and we'll get to the drugs. First, Faye's violin."

"*You* did that." I glared at him.

"I didn't. I took it after she left the room with Aroha, sure. I hid it in the guys' bathroom. But I didn't smash it. That's *fucked.*"

Agreed. I recalled Faye's face as she'd returned to the room, her chin held high but quivering, her voice rasping as she told Madame her violin had been destroyed. She hadn't panicked – she'd gone to collect another instrument. She was stronger than any of us would have been under those circumstances. A swell of admiration rose in my chest. I spent all my life being strong for other people – for our mother, for Elena, for Dorien and Titus. I saw something of myself in her. Maybe that was why I felt…

No. Feelings are pointless here.

But I knew what Faye had done, stealing that cocaine and planting it in my violin case – and that wasn't like me at all. Her wrath was pure Dorien. That explained why the two of them raged against each other. When they finally broke down and fucked, it would tear a hole in the universe. I knew she'd choose him over me – women always did. *I just wished…*

But wishing wouldn't shove the coke back into the violin case. Faye had royally fucked me, and I couldn't even blame her.

Dorien kicked the dresser, splintering the wood. "Answer me, you fuckhead."

Titus and I exchanged a glance. This wasn't the Dorien we knew – those frantic eyes, that clenched jaw. I couldn't tell if he was going to break down or punch someone. I'd never seen him like this before. Even when he'd handed Elena and I those fake passports in Prague, he'd been calm. Determined. When Clare had been found dead, he'd held on to himself. But this...

Ever since Faye came to Manderley, Dorien had been pulled deeper into his madness. But how deep did that go?

Titus shook his head. "Why are you questioning us, man? We were all in the ballroom. No one left until Madame Usher sent Faye to find her instrument."

"If someone else in this house is out to get Faye, I want to know about it. There are too many fucking secrets around here."

"You can say that again." Titus stared at his shoes.

"Heather? I wouldn't put it past her to do it, but she would have owned it. Aroha was high as a kite again, or..." Dorien almost smiled. "Did Faye destroy her own instrument in the hopes of somehow framing me? She could have done it when she found the violin in the bathroom. I hadn't considered that before – how amusing."

"Dorien." Titus didn't yell. With that deep voice of his, he didn't need to. Just by opening his mouth he could cut through Dorien's bullshit.

"I know, I know. *Fuck.*" Dorien dragged his fingers through his hair. He swirled to meet me, collecting himself, pushing down whatever it was that agitated him so much. "You. Coke? I can't believe this shit. You won't even take a sip of wine."

"It wasn't mine," I mumbled.

Big fucking mistake.

Dorien grabbed my collar and threw me against the wall. My back slammed into the stone, my bones cracking from the force. His face, inches from mine, twisted as he struggled to control the demon that threatened to overwhelm him. "I am *this* close to putting your head through a wall. It was in your violin case. What the fuck is going on?"

I screwed up my face. In all the years we'd known each other, all the world tours and trashed hotel rooms and stupid fights and dark shit, we made a pact to be truthful with each other at all costs. I had no secrets from these two. *Until now*. I had to take this secret to my grave – I was going down, and I wouldn't drag them or Faye or Elena with me.

"It belongs to Aroha. I was keeping it so she wouldn't... so she'd sober up. I hid it in my drawer, but I'm pretty sure Faye found it and slipped it into my violin case."

"Faye wouldn't do that," Dorien growled, his fingers tightening around my collar.

"Oh, yeah? She wouldn't try to get us back for bullying her?" I choked out.

"Heather's ruined nose suggests otherwise. Maybe Faye thinks Ivan was the one in her room the other night," Titus said from the door. "She had this logic all worked out when she thought it was me, but it didn't make sense because I didn't do it. Dorien, let him down. You're not helping."

Dorien's eyes flashed, but he let go of my collar. I sank to the floor, pulling my knees up to my chest, sucking in deep breaths to try and get my racing heart under control. Titus crossed to my bed, dropping a bag of weed on the coverlet and rolling a joint.

"You've both got to chill out." He held out a joint to me. I shook my head.

"Don't do that in here. Elena—"

"—is the least of your problems, bro." Dorien accepted the joint, pulling a lighter from his pocket. He didn't even bother to move to the window, just letting the smoke curl around his face. Titus rolled another, and soon the two of them were puffing away, tendrils of smoke curling around their faces. The tension in the room dropped.

"We can't blame Faye for standing up for herself." Titus leaned against the wall, puckering his lips as he exhaled. "But we've got to do damage control. She'll be gunning for one of us next, probably Dorien, after he destroyed her—"

"I didn't do it," Dorien growled.

Titus shrugged. "Why do you care? You wanted to hurt her. Looks like mission accomplished. So why aren't we celebrating?"

Dorien's expression twisted, and I felt a familiar, jealous stab in my gut. Dorien thought he had it so hard, but he was the kind of guy who would always land on his feet, always find a solution, always get the girl. If he could pull his head out of his ass he'd see how he felt about Faye, and then they'd have loud kinky sex I'd be able to hear all the way from jail.

Faye and Dorien were written in the stars. And that left me down below with the weeds and monsters.

Dorien snorted. "We're not celebrating, because Ivan is about to go to jail. Or get kicked back to Romania, which is worse."

"Right. Fuck. What do we do?"

No one answered him. We all knew what had to happen next. There was one person at Manderley who had the power to make this go away, but she would demand a price. There was always a price. She'd already taken her pound of flesh from each of us. What else did I have to give?

29

DORIEN

Titus and I waited with Ivan all night. I spooned him in Elena's bed while Titus twisted his bulk to fit on Ivan's bed, the way we used to sleep in the early days of Broken Muse when we could only afford cheap twin rooms. Not that I slept – dark thoughts kept my eyes open, fixed on the door of Ivan's room, on a tiny shaft of light from the curtains that almost looked like a face leering back at me—

Madame Usher didn't come for Ivan. The police didn't bang down the door. But that didn't mean he was safe.

No one was safe at Manderley.

The next morning at breakfast, Madame Usher gushed over my performance. "Hans was so taken with your mastery and presence, Dorien." She ruffled my hair like I was a favored son. "I believe he will get over his reluctance to deal with an ex-Muse and invite to you the summer residency in Berlin."

Those words should have given me a thrill. Berlin was one of my favorite cities – to return there to perform and learn from a world-class orchestra would be a big deal for my career. Not to mention bringing me a step closer to what I'd come to Manderley to do. But the triumph felt hollow, meaningless.

I earned it off the back of Faye's misery.

Because even if I hadn't ruined her violin, everyone believed I did. I knew the truth that hid in Madame's words. *This is your reward for ruining her.*

But who had done it? And why didn't they come forward to claim their reward?

Faye pushed through the dining room door, but Madame Usher swept in her path. "You're not welcome today. The Master has not forgiven you for taking his violin."

That was a lie. Master Radcliffe hadn't been the one to react when Faye showed up with that Becker – but Madame Usher had. She *screamed* at Faye – in all the years I'd known her, I'd never, ever seen her lose it like that.

What was it about that violin? I had to know. We needed something, anything we could use against Madame Usher.

Faye's eyes leaped with fire as she stared down her foe. She looked like she was about to argue. Instead, she shoved a tray of scrambled eggs and bacon into Madame's hands, turned on her heel and stormed away.

After breakfast was composition. Madame Usher smiled at Ivan as he slunk into the room – a smile that said she would keep his secret along with all the others she hoarded like a mouse stockpiling cheese, but her silence would come at a price to be paid in the future. I shuddered to think of what the price might be.

Faye didn't show up for composition class, either. I couldn't focus with her gone. When I paired up with Heather to tackle her composition, my fingers were all over the place. Finally, she put her instrument down and glared at me, touching the dressing on her nose with annoyance. "If you're not going to take this seriously, I'll partner with Titus instead."

"Fine." I slid my fingers off the keys. "Be my guest."

"Don't be silly. You know we're perfect together." Heather raised her bow. "Do it again."

This is stupid. I shouldn't feel bad for Faye. I was getting exactly what I wanted – she'd have to leave soon. She would no longer be in danger, or a threat to my plan. I'd win the Manderley Prize, and everything would be okay.

But I didn't feel okay. I felt like a complete shit.

When we emerged from class, the dining room table was already set with platters of cold sandwiches. Faye was nowhere to be seen. Heather wrinkled her nose as she picked up the bread, but the movement made her flinch with pain. "Canned tuna? What is this shit?"

While the others bickered and gossiped about Faye, I pushed my food around on my plate. *This is stupid. I can't leave things like this. I can't have her believe I destroyed her violin.*

It shouldn't matter, but it did.

I shoved my plate aside and stood up. "I'm not hungry."

Heather searched my face, her eyes widening with annoyance. "Dorien—"

But I was already bounding up the stairs. Before I knew it, I stood on the narrow attic landing, my back stooped and the one dim lightbulb swinging against my cheek. I shuttered myself against the wave of memories – of Clare's excited face in the dark when I came to visit her, of all the things she said in the dim morning hours that I ignored, too lost in my own bullshit—

I knocked on Faye's door.

Nothing. No sound. Not even the string of profanity I deserved. I knocked again, and was just about to call out when the door swung open.

My breath caught in my throat. Faye opened her mouth to speak, but no sound came out. She looked... well, she was fucking gorgeous. But today it was a beauty borne of fragility – of red-rimmed eyes and tousled hair and a pillow crease along her cheek – not the strength that carried her. She clutched a battered old book in her hands. The fire in her eyes had gone out, and her chin quivered when she raised her face to meet me.

Her eyes, her face… it broke me.

"You happy?" she hissed, grabbing the door and slamming it behind her.

I stood in the hall, frozen and mute.

Fuck. *Fuck.*

That haunted look in her eyes. I'd done that. I'd *broken* her.

It was my job. I couldn't defy Madame Usher. Not without putting my entire future – *his* future – at risk.

Unless…

I slumped on the top step, my head in my hands, my mind whirring with possibilities. This blackmail thing could work two ways. There was some reason Madame Usher wanted Faye to leave Manderley. It didn't make any sense, because she didn't have to offer Faye a spot in the first place. But Faye was here, and Madame wanted her gone, but she refused to get her hands dirty. That was where Broken Muse came in – Madame had all three of us over a barrel, and she relished it.

She traded in secrets. But she had secrets of her own. If I could find out why she wanted me to destroy Faye so badly, then I might have a chance to set all of us free of her web.

FAYE

I hate you, Dorien Valencourt.
You're next.

DORIEN

"**W**anna jam some Bach?" Titus leaned over my desk, his cornrows falling over his ears. His deep voice echoed across the library.

I slammed my laptop screen shut and glared at my friend. "Can't. I've got to finish that essay on Baroque compositional structures. Go bother Ivan. He looks like he could use a break from perfection."

Titus punched me in the shoulder and slid off the corner of my desk to head for the twins, who sat together in the window seat. A set of old scorebooks lay open between them, ignored. Elena had some bright new idea, for her face was luminous with joy as she talked a mile a minute at Ivan. I knew from that strained look on his face that even patient Ivan was reaching peak Elena overdose. He looked relieved when Titus inserted himself between them.

Satisfied I was alone again, I flipped up my laptop screen, where I'd opened a new file titled "Concerning the Fall of the House of Usher." If anyone found it I could claim it was song inspiration. Underneath I'd written everything I knew, which wasn't much – Madame Usher invited Faye to the school, but she told me it had been Master Radcliffe's decision. He'd never corrected her lie. She blackmailed me into bullying Faye, and into pulling Titus and Ivan into it.

And then, there were these strange happenings – things done to Faye I couldn't explain. The ruined violin. The face at the window. Faye saying something about music playing at night. All things we weren't responsible for.

We weren't the only ones haunting Faye. That knowledge chilled my blood like nothing else.

I added to the list Madame's crazed reaction when Faye brought in that violin from the instrument room. At the time, I assumed Faye had picked up some particularly rare piece, but although it was a Carl Becker, it was on the low end of value for her collection. I'd never heard Madame screech like that – losing grip of her tightly bound control. For whatever reason, that violin was *personal*.

I just didn't know why. The instrument room was locked, and I didn't have a key. This would be easier if I could talk to Faye. But then if I was allowed to talk to her, I wouldn't be in this mess.

One thing was clear – Faye was the center of this. I realized just how little I knew about her life since we stopped being friends. Curious, I switched to the browser and Googled her name. I expected to see the usual news stories about the disappearance of her father, the ones I'd scoured for months after I'd left the music school, desperate to see a glimpse of her in the images, to know she was okay.

Instead, what came up were stories from the last eighteen months. PR LEGEND STRUCK DOWN BY MYSTERY ILLNESS, one headline read. I clicked on it and pulled up the article.

"Marguerite de Winter, the East Village It girl who built a PR empire from the ground up, was struck down this week with a mysterious illness. Her company, De Winter PR, will continue to operate with

executive assistant Natalie Baker keeping De Winter advised in her hospital room.

De Winter is familiar in certain classical music circles not as the PR giant but as the wife of famed virtuoso Donovan de Winter, who disappeared without a trace a decade ago. She has no family in America, apart from her daughter Faye, who has declined to comment to media on her mother's condition. Ms. Baker has explained that de Winter's condition is critical, with doctors having no clue as to the origin of her ailment—

I clicked on another link from six months ago: DE WINTER PR DECLARES BANKRUPTCY.

"De Winter PR announced its bankruptcy this week after the CEO's daughter Faye de Winter drained its coffers to pay her mother's medical bills. The firm will cease operations at the end of the week and vacate its trendy East Village office.

Faye declined to comment, but sources within the company explain how this tragedy came to pass. "We understand Faye's position, of course. Marguerite's health must take priority. But we're shocked and saddened that everything Marguerite built has now been torn apart."

How did such a successful businesswoman end up in this position? Of course, Marguerite de Winter couldn't have predicted her illness, but she could have protected her business. Chief Operations Officer Natalie Baker explained, "Marguerite was a force of nature – she tore through life like a hurricane, and that was how she built such a successful business. She kept a big, beautiful vision in her head and relied on those around her to fill in the details. She was a total scatterbrain – constantly forgetting things, leaving her keys behind, dropping important documents at the cafe. I'm not surprised she struggled to remember to pay insurance bills."

According to Baker, De Winter's tragic story should be a warning to all business owners. "It's a powerful message that even those who are successful should take care of the little things. If Marguerite had paid her bills on time, her insurance wouldn't have lapsed and her legacy wouldn't have been dismantled."

Interesting that this Natalie was previously an assistant and was now promoted to COO. My heart pounding, I kept clicking. A short piece on an industry blog from a week before Faye arrived at Manderley noted that Marguerite De Winter had fallen into a coma.

Shit.

I knew Faye was visiting someone at the hospital because Harrison picked her up there, but I had no idea... Faye's mom was on life-support, with *no insurance*. She had no money to her name.

She was alone.

I knew what that felt like.

Shit.

No wonder Faye was so determined to stay at Manderley no matter what I did to her. She needed the prize money just as much as I did. *More.* And that was saying something.

Madame Usher knew that. She dangled the Manderley Prize over Faye's head, making Faye dance like a puppet for her own amusement. Surely, Faye could see Madame would never reward her the prize even though – and it burned in my throat to admit it – she probably deserved it for her composition talents alone.

Madame Usher pulls the strings, and we both dance.

But why?

My mind flashed back to the nightmare I relived every night as I lay down to sleep.

Clare lying at the bottom of the staircase, her neck bent at an impossible angle.

Her words, shouted at me seconds before she fell to her death.

Dorien, listen to me! I have to tell you something about Madame Usher. About the noises in the walls.

I squeezed my eyes shut. I told myself it was an accident.

Clare was running after me, trying to get my attention, and she tripped on the stairs and fell. That was what I had to believe. For his sake.

My eyes flew open. *I can't ignore the truth.* Clare's death. Faye's mother's illness. Madame Usher's strange behavior. It all came back to one question – why?

Madame Usher usually handled her own dirty work, but this time she'd entrusted three broken muses. I'd make her regret that decision.

FAYE

*A*fter the disastrous recital for Hans and my confrontation with Dorien and Heather, no one in the house spoke to me for a week. Good. I didn't want to speak to them either.

To punish me for punching Heather, Madame docked my pay. It was worth it to see the bitch walking around with a giant plaster over her nose. Every time I looked down at my bruised knuckles, I smiled.

The eyes of the Muses followed me everywhere I went – itching across my shoulders, boring into my soul. Perhaps they suspected I was responsible for putting Ivan's coke in his violin case. Not that he got any kind of punishment for it. I refused to acknowledge them in any way – if they wanted to treat me like a ghost, I'd become one.

I gathered the pieces of my ruined violin. In my room, I laid them out under the window on top of my father's fairy tale book. As the moonlight cast its glow over the shards and splinters, I cried all the tears I'd held inside ever since Mom went into hospital. It was a bloodletting, and afterward, I felt better. I wrapped the remains in a scarf my mother gave me and took them outside.

I found a shovel in the woodshed and dug a hole in the dirt behind the gazebo.

I opened my door on Monday morning to find a brand new violin on the landing – a beautiful Venetian instrument in the style of Sanctus Seraphin. I dragged it inside and turned it every which way, hunting for a label that might say who it was from, but there was nothing. My mind flickered to the three Muses, but that was ridiculous. They were the ones who destroyed my violin, so why would they replace it?

I didn't want to accept the gift without knowing who it was from, or why they'd given it. But I wouldn't get far at Manderley without an instrument, and Madame made it clear that the pieces in the school's collection were off-limits to me. So I held the instrument to my chin and played until my fingers bled, until the music had seared determination for revenge into my soul.

I refused to eat in the dining room with the other students. Instead, I'd set the table and retreat to the kitchen. At least there I could cling to the belief that the silence was of my own choosing.

No one acknowledged me or the new instrument when I walked into class on Monday morning. I held my head high as I took my seat in the corner. I channeled my mother. I wouldn't let their scorn get to me.

I held that new violin to my chin, and I played every note flawlessly.

But it wasn't enough to repair what had shifted when I picked up that Becker violin. Even Master Radcliffe seemed at a loss for what to do with me. Although he was cordial in our lessons, a tension tugged between us that had never existed before. After Monday's lesson, I decided to save us both the agony and skip classes to practice my Sibelius and Paganini alone in my room.

Someone got to Harrison, because instead of his usual jovial greeting when he brought the wood in, all I got was silence and a pitying stare. I didn't realize how much I desperately needed his kindness until it had been taken from me.

The Muses did this.

They hate me this much. All because I... what? Existed?

Their ghosting shit was getting insane. My senses worked overtime. I fancied I heard footsteps following me as I moved around the house. Groans and creaks followed me inside the walls. Yet every time I turned around, the hallway would be empty.

Eerie violin music wafted into my room at night, keeping me awake. Hiding under the sheets from a resident ghost was not as fun as the movies made out. Even through my noise-canceling headphones I caught snatches of the same haunting tune, played over and over.

By the end of the week, I was a zombie. I dropped a glass at dinner and Madame Usher screamed that my mother raised me as an animal. I sat at the kitchen table, fighting back tears as I devoured an entire package of Red Vines.

As I stacked the dishwasher, I noticed a figure moving across the back porch. Odd. Titus couldn't have come through the kitchen, because I would have seen him. I cupped my hands over the window and squinted into the gloom. The window to the Yellow Room was pushed all the way up, the curtains flapping in the wind. He must have slipped out there. But what was one of the Muses doing sneaking around in the dark? They usually stomped about like they owned the place. Titus jogged down the path toward the woodshed, looking over his shoulder at the house as if he didn't want anyone to follow him. A large, rectangular case slapped against his leg.

Hmmmm.

He hadn't come back to the house by the time I finished the dishes. Curious now, I peered at the clock above the fridge. Nearly 8PM. I could hear the others laughing and playing music in the Blue Room. Why wasn't Titus hanging out with them?

Come to think of it, I wasn't sure I'd ever seen Titus wandering around the house in the evenings. Was he sneaking out to the woodshed every night? If so, what was he doing out there?

A rising rage seethed inside me. Thanks to those guys, I'd lived through a hellish week. They took pleasure in making me look like I flouted Madame Usher's authority at every step, when really *they* were the ones running circles around her.

Maybe it was time I turned their cruelty back on them. *I bet Madame Usher would be interested to know where Titus goes at night.*

I grabbed my coat from the hook by the kitchen door and pushed it open as silently as I could. The wind was up tonight, howling down the valley and scraping the branches across the walls.

I closed the door as silently as I could and darted through the kitchen garden, pausing at the gate to check no one was coming from the main house. The coast was clear. I unlocked the gate, wincing as the creaking hinges pierced the night. The wind whipped the sound against the house. If Titus knew I was coming after him, it wouldn't be because of that sound.

I slipped through and crept down the path, keeping close to the house. I reached the woodshed with its open bay where Harrison stacked firewood to dry and stored his rusting garden machinery. I couldn't see Titus anywhere.

Behind the woodshed was another outbuilding – I'd never noticed it before, but then I didn't spend much time out here. It was long and low and made of brick, hidden by the overhanging trees. A faint light flickered at the dirt-smeared window.

Gotcha.

I crept over, pausing at the door to press my ear against the wood, struggling to hear.

There was a strange noise, like a… I couldn't explain it. A dull buzz. A flicking sound. Titus grunted. *Ah, he's got a girl in there. Some local woodcutter's daughter? A scandal worthy of a Broken Muse, for sure.*

I smiled to myself. I had him now.

Welcome to your worst nightmare, Titus Thibodeaux.

I shoved the door open and stepped inside.

It took a moment for my eyes to adjust. The buzzing came from a small generator in the corner, belching noxious fumes into a jerry-rigged chimney pointing out a window facing the forest. A pair of lanterns sat on crumbling wooden shelves, their light aimed like twin spotlights at the far wall.

And what they lit up... robbed my lungs of breath.

Titus stood in the lanternlight, legs spread-eagled, flinging his head around in frantic circles so his cornrows flew about like plumage. Headphones covered his ears, and their cord snaked across the floor to a small amplifier and head unit plugged into the generator.

Slung low across his hips, his fingers flying over the strings so fast they were a blur, was a battered Gibson Flying-V electric guitar.

33

FAYE

I stood, frozen by the sight in front of me, my mind casting back to the hours of video I'd seen of Titus on stage, the ferocity of which he stabbed at the cello, that unwieldy instrument putty in his hands.

His eyes flickered open. He saw me standing there, and he leaped so high in the air he smashed his head into the low ceiling of the shack.

"What the fuck?" Titus tore off his headphones and marched toward me, tearing the headphone cable from the socket. His guitar slapping against his naked chest, and the amp emitted a loud buzz.

I swallowed hard. He looked angry as fuck – angry enough to do something…

Well, fuck him. I had a few things to be angry about myself.

"What's this about, Titus?" I angled my phone toward him, snapping a couple of pictures I could use as security. Because he clearly wanted this a secret, otherwise he wouldn't be hiding out in a shack in the freezing wind. I hoped the bright flashlight would slow him down if he lunged at me.

"None of your business." Titus tore the guitar from around his neck and dropped it into a case covered with band stickers, his eyes never leaving my face. His shoulders trembled with rage, and I realized how stupid it was to walk into this remote shack to face off against this guy.

"Wrong." With more bravado than I felt, I slid my phone into my pocket and patted it with satisfaction. A stack of old tools stood against the wall. I grabbed up a shovel and held it in front of me. "Broken Muse has been trying to ruin my life ever since I arrived at Manderley. After Dorien destroyed my violin, I thought you'd won. But with these photos, I've got something on you."

"What are you going to do?" He narrowed those sinful eyes at me.

"Nothing. For now." I let a slow smile play across my face. "But if you or your friends do anything else to me, these photographs go straight to Madame Usher. And maybe a few of my friends in the music media."

"You wouldn't," he growled.

"Don't presume what I would or wouldn't do."

I whirled around and flounced away before he could think to come after me.

Outside, my bravado broke down, and my legs shook so badly I had to lean against the woodshed to catch my breath. I dropped the shovel in the dirt and dug out my phone, flicking through the photographs again.

I finally had something on the guys. I held my freedom from their bullying in my hands. But all I could think about was the fear flickering in Titus' eyes. He was the most intimidating person I'd ever met, so what could make a guy like that so afraid? And why was he playing guitar in secret in an abandoned shack in the first place?

And why did I *care?* It couldn't have been because of that time in his room, when I *swear* his lips brushed mine, where I'd wanted so badly to fall into him and lose myself.

How fucked up did I have to be to crave my bully when I finally had power over him?

34

TITUS

"I'm fucked." I buried my head in my hands.

"You're not fucked." Dorien leaned out his window, sucking the last pleasure from a joint. He'd offered me a toke, but I was way too agitated. I didn't need to calm down. I needed…

Fuck. I needed to get those photographs back from Faye. I needed to see her again. I needed her lips on mine, to feel her body succumb beneath me as she gave in to the insane chemistry between us.

But while she had those photos, she might as well have my cock in a vise.

"Sprite won't talk." Dorien closed the window and crossed the room to face me. He looked far too calm considering the situation.

"She's got no reason to stay quiet," I shot back. "She's still upset about me being in her room. You saw what she did to Ivan. I'm next. She's got all the ammo she needs to get me out of the picture."

"I'll talk to her," Dorien growled. "I'll make her see reason."

I didn't like that tone in his voice, the way he said *make her* with a dangerous inflection. I knew all about Dorien's powers of persuasion. I'd seen him work them on hundreds of girls on tour. The idea of Faye being another notch on his bedpost when she meant so much… "No, I should do it. I dug the hole, I should be the one to fill it in again."

"To her, you're just a pervert stalker. Faye and I have history. She trusts me, even though she won't admit it. I'll talk to her."

There was a gleam in his grey eyes that I didn't think even he understood. Dorien wanted Faye, and he wanted to keep me away from her.

And Dorien always got what he wanted.

35

DORIEN

I set my alarm for 5AM and snuck downstairs before Faye snagged her morning practice room. She'd been practicing early in the day so she could fit her chores in around us without having to see us. I hid in the corner so she wouldn't have the opportunity to shut the door on my face, and waited.

At 5:30AM, Faye unlocked the door with her house key and let herself in, flicking on the lights. For the briefest moment, I thought I saw a white face with a gaping mouth staring at me from the china cabinet, but it was just an illusion formed by reflections on the glass. Faye set up her music stand and was mid-scale when I stepped out from behind the sideboard.

"*Shit.*" She dropped her bow. "Dorien, you twatface."

Real fear darkened her eyes. Fear that I'd hurt her. And why shouldn't she be afraid? I'd done nothing but hurt her, and now I was hiding in the corner. I hated seeing my cruelty reflected back at me.

It made me feel unfamiliar things. Hurt. Regret. Self-loathing.

I held up my hand. "This isn't about you and me. It's about Titus. You can't tell anyone what you saw last night."

Faye narrowed her eyes. For someone afraid, she stood her

ground, moving her feet apart in a power stance, making herself bigger. Faye de Winter never backed down. "Why not?"

"Titus hasn't done anything to hurt you. Except for that one time he was in your room with Heather, and he *hated* it. He told me he wouldn't do anything else to you, Sprite. So just pretend you never saw him out there."

"Don't use that nickname. You lost your right to it a long time ago. I can't just pretend I never saw Titus, because it doesn't make any sense. Why is he out in the cold with a guitar? Why is that such a secret?"

I sighed. It wasn't my secret to tell, but Faye wasn't going to drop this. I had to make her understand. "Titus' parents... you know they're quite famous—"

"Amos and Delphine Thibodeaux. I'm not stupid."

"Right. Well, they want him to follow in their footsteps, carry on their legacy. That's been his destiny since the moment he was conceived. But it's not what he wants."

Faye snorted. "Titus wants to give up his Classical career to join Iron Maiden?"

"Yes. Titus has been secretly playing guitar for most of his life. He hid an ax at my house. He used to stay with me whenever his parents were on tour and play in our ballroom. Until that... wasn't an option anymore. He's *good*. He could be fantastic, but his parents refuse to hear of it. If he came out as a heavy metal guitarist, they'd disown him, cut him off."

"Titus is legally an adult. He can do what he wants."

"I've told him that a hundred times, but you don't know Titus like I do. He can't stand the idea of his parents hating him. Their approval and love are everything to him. That's why you have to keep his secret. No one else knows – not Madame Usher, not Heather or Aroha, *no one*. If anyone finds out and the media gets hold of the story, or if the others find out about it, they'll tell his parents, and it's all over for him."

"Why haven't you used it against him? Get him out of the way for a clear shot at the Manderley Prize." Her eyes flashed. "Or is it only me you're hellbent on destroying?"

"Titus has had my back more times than I can count. I'll kick his ass in the competition, but I'm not going to sabotage him. You may not believe this, but I take friendship seriously."

"You're right." She grabbed her bow and held it across her chest like a medieval knight. A memory flashed in my mind – Faye and I collapsing into giggles as we had a swashbuckling sword fight with our bows. "I *don't* believe it. Now get out, I've reserved this room."

"So you won't—"

"*Get out.*"

36

FAYE

I can't believe him.

I dragged the bolt across the door and shoved a chair under the lock for good measure. My hands flew to my violin, the agitation and fear in my body desperate for release. I drew the bow across the strings, launching first into Paganini's caprices and then divulging off along an unknown path, following the music where it led.

I wasn't even thinking – this was pure improvisation, conjuring images from my past that meshed with the present. I craved Dorien. I hated him. I wanted to crawl inside his spice and violet scent and live there forever.

Three Broken Muses. All I smelled, all I could feel, were Dorien, Titus, and Ivan. They flowed in my veins, inseparable from their music – the magic that stirred my soul and made me feel things I didn't understand.

With a cry of frustration, I tore the violin from my chin, spinning across the room in a reckless dance. From the corner of the room, a faint scratching sound echoed from the wall, followed by the creak of receding footsteps.

"You're the most useless fucking ghost I've ever met!" I yelled at the wall.

37

FAYE

That Sunday, I had a spare block of time I'd set aside to visit my mother. But Harrison was conspicuously absent when I went to find him. Tears pricked in my eyes. I knew it wasn't that he'd forgotten. Someone was deliberately keeping me from her.

I called a taxi company to see if I could get someone to pick me up – it would cost every cent of Madame's allowance that I'd saved, but it was worth it. Suddenly I wanted nothing more in the world than to be in Mom's presence, even if she was asleep. But when I called to order a taxi to Manderley, the guy on the end of the phone laughed at me.

"You'll never get anyone to make the trip out there. Even if they were willing to travel that far, they wouldn't do it because that place is haunted."

"That's ridiculous. It's just an old house owned by an eccentric lady."

"Eccentric? Hah. We all know the stories – footsteps in the night, noises in the walls, music playing when no one's sitting at the keys. And that girl died there not two months ago, all mysterious like. Manderley is haunted, you mark my words."

My heart leaped into my throat. Those were the exact same things that were happening to me. But ghosts? *Really?* Manderley was old and creepy, sure, but I was fairly certain its creep-factor was entirely down to the dickweasels who inhabited it.

What about Dorien's face when you confronted him with the violin?

He looked horrified. Completely taken aback. He insisted he only *moved* my violin. Every other awful thing he'd done to me he freely admitted. He reveled in his cruelty – that was part of the torture. He wanted me to know he was out to bring me down. But he refused to admit he destroyed my violin.

And none of the guys admitted to being that face in my window, or breaking into my room to switch off the light. I remembered how I'd checked every corner of my room, how I'd never heard anyone creep down the stairs, how my fancy new lock hadn't been disturbed and I found no trace of a hidden panel. It seemed impossible that anyone could have been there and yet, I *knew* what I saw.

Unless it was a ghost—

Stop it. I shook my head. *You're being ridiculous. Don't let Manderley get to you. There's no such thing as ghosts.*

The urge to throw myself down on my bed and sob into my father's book threatened to overwhelm me, but I squared my shoulders and put on my war face. If I couldn't see Mom, I'd at least make sure my day was productive.

All the practice rooms were taken, but I still had an essay to finish. It wasn't due for months, but it wouldn't hurt to get a head start. Perhaps if I handed it in early I could claw back some of Master Radcliffe's respect. I wasn't ready to give up on the Manderley Prize just yet. I headed toward the library.

Dorien glanced up from a table by the window as I pushed open the door. *Great.* I shot him a 'don't fuck with me' look and pointedly sat down as far from him as possible, pulling books from the shelves with venom. *THUMP THUMP THUMP.* I slammed volume after volume on the table, relishing the loud noise echoing throughout the high-ceilinged room.

I slumped down in a cubby and got to work on the essay, but it was impossible to concentrate with Dorien in the same room being all Dorien-like. I read the same page on Paganini's performance techniques five times before I gave up. I let my hair curtain over my face, and I dared a glance through the strands across the room.

From over his laptop, Dorien's grey eyes peered back at me.

Fuck.

I glared at him and returned my eyes to my books, but the sensation of being watched didn't leave me. Unlike the crawling in my skin that usually beset me at night, this felt different – I welcomed it. I *craved* it. And I couldn't understand why. Of all the Muses, I hated Dorien the most.

He destroyed my violin – the most precious thing I owned.

What I'd done to Ivan was *nothing* on the hell I was going to rain down on Dorien... just as soon as I worked up the nerve.

I dared another look across at the Bad Boy of Baroque. He didn't even try to hide that he was watching me. He leaned back in his chair, a smirk playing across his lips.

Dickweasel.

Those perfect lips parted. "Sprite, I—"

BANG.

I leaped out of my skin. My books clattered across the floor as the door banged against the wall. Heather strode across the room. She still wore the plaster over her nose, and somehow it made her look even more beautiful – like a valkyrie returning from the battlefield.

Heather planted both hands on either side of Dorien's desk. "There you are. I've been looking everywhere for you. We're supposed to practice together."

"I'm not dueting with you." The smirk never left Dorien's face, but when he turned it toward Heather, it took on that cruel quality he'd hitherto reserved only for me.

"Dorien, don't be silly. We have a month of recitals coming up. You know we play perfectly together, inside a concert hall and other places..." she trailed her fingers across his arm.

He shoved her hand away. "Heather, I've tried being nice, but you don't seem to be getting the message. I'm not playing with you anymore. We're over."

"Don't be so stupid." Her voice took on a shrill tone, all the musicality sucked away. "You know I am your destiny, Dorien. You don't screw with destiny."

That's kind of a weird thing to say.

"I screw whoever I choose, and it's not you."

"You'll regret this." Heather's fingers curled into fists at her side. The vintage fur she wore slipped down over her shoulder. "You still think you're so important, Mr. Bad Boy of Baroque. But you've slashed and burned your European career, and if you have any hopes of reaching the top again, you need me – and you know it."

"I've never needed anyone, and that hasn't changed. *If* I decided to bring someone else to the top with me, it wouldn't be five feet of spoiled bitch and weak fingering wrapped in dead animal skins. You're not even interesting enough to string along anymore."

"You'll regret that. Call me when you come to your senses," Heather hissed through gritted teeth. The door slammed behind her.

Interesting.

Nope. I reached for a book that had slid right to the back of the shelf. *Not interesting. So two horrible people decided to be horrible separately. That is no concern of mine. I have an essay to write—*

Dorien slid his chair out, the legs squeaking against the parquet floor. I went back to picking up my scattered books, crawling under my desk on my hands to reach a volume that had slid under the shelf.

"Faye."

I jumped at my name on his lips, the word churning up a storm on my insides. My head hit the underside of my desk, sending my drink bottle flying off the end to bounce off my tailbone. *Fucktrumpets. Ow.*

I dared a peek over my shoulder. There was Dorien, in all his dark and brooding glory, leaning against the stacks with that smirk on his face as he stared at the most unflattering view of my ass I could have possibly presented him.

Dear Manderley ghost, if you really do exist, I'd appreciate you rattling some chains or splashing some ectoplasm around right now, or just opening the floor so I can fall in, please and thank you.

"Go away." I slid out of the desk, my skirt riding high on my thighs. Color blazed in my cheeks, and I hated myself for it. I had no reason to feel embarrassed in front of Dorien, especially not after what he did.

"I want to talk about your mother."

"Maybe I don't want to talk to you."

"Faye…" Dorien threw a glance over his shoulder, his eyes darting around the room. He was nervous, but why would he be? Dorien Valencourt had never been nervous a day in his life. "I don't know if you know this, but we used to have a maid before you. Her name was Clare. She fell down the stairs and broke her neck."

"Harrison thinks you pushed her," I shot back.

I regretted it instantly. Even on his cruelest days, I couldn't believe Dorien capable of such an act. But that was before my violin. I dared a glance into those limitless eyes, and what I saw there grabbed my heart and squeezed. His grey eyes swirled with pain and regret – not the look of a cold-blooded killer, but something much more human and un-Dorien-like.

Dorien sighed. "Of course he does. The police had their suspicions, too. I was an asshole to Clare, no argument. She liked me, and I strung her along. But I couldn't have pushed her. I was already on the staircase ahead of her. I'd just reached the bottom when she fell. Clare was running after me. She wanted to tell me something about Madame Usher."

"I don't care. Go away."

"You should care. Because I think you're in danger. Madame Usher..." Dorien looked away. "She doesn't want you here."

"*You* don't want me here. And so far you and Titus and Ivan are the only ones tormenting me, destroying my—" I choked on the word. I couldn't even talk about my violin around him; it still cut too deep.

This time, Dorien didn't look away. A storm made of torment swelled in his eyes. "I did those things on her orders. I didn't have a choice. And I swear on my brother's life that I never smashed your violin and none of us was the face at your window. You have to believe me—"

I didn't know Dorien had a brother.

"Why should I believe you? You've done everything in your power to make me miserable, and what did I ever do to you except be your friend? Now you want me to talk about my mom – the most horrific experience that's ever happened to me? Why do you think I owe you?"

"You owe me nothing." Dorien stepped toward me, his eyes hardening to stone. "I owe you, Sprite. I owe *everything* to you."

I opened my mouth to ask what the fuck he meant by that, but then Dorien mashed his lips on mine.

The kiss drove all rational thought from my head. Dorien's hot, demanding lips dragged me under, sweeping me up in the storm of his need. All those nights I'd huddled over my computer watching videos of Dorien on stage – those cruel lips pouting as he caressed the piano keys like a lover – touching myself as I imagined what it would be like to have the attention of a guy like that. Now I knew, now I fucking knew – it was *everything*.

Music danced over my skin as Dorien wrapped his fingers around my neck, tugging me closer, his lips devouring mine. The song of our lives played out in a tangle of tongue and lips and sinful touches. A moan escaped my throat that made Dorien's body shudder. He swallowed my gasp as his fingers tightened on my neck, and a deep growl rumbled in his throat – raw and primal and *so fucking hot*.

The fingers of Dorien's other hand curled in mine, pressing my palm back against the shelves. Books toppled around us as he ground against me, playing my body the way he played piano – hard and relentless and wickedly delicious. I felt like my skin would melt away from the heat searing through my body.

The image of my violin in pieces flickered in my mind, and all the heat drained from my skin. I tore myself away from him.

"Sprite?" The eyebrow cocking, that cruel mouth turning up in a question. Dorien still had no fucking *clue*.

I can't believe I'm kissing him. Sound the fucktrumpets, because this is messed up.

I needed space. I needed to *think*.

"Get off me."

I drew back my foot and slammed my knee between his legs, feeling a satisfying jolt as it connected with its target. Dorien's smirk collapsed into a grimace of pain. He doubled over, crashing into the opposite stack and sending an avalanche of books down on himself as he writhed in agony, gasping for air.

"You break off our friendship without explanation, you act like I've deliberately come here to ruin your fun, you *destroy my violin*, and then you use that nickname you made for me like nothing has changed, and then you *kiss* me? I don't care if you're the Bad Boy of Baroque and every girl wants you. I'm not your plaything."

"I never..." The storm in Dorien's eyes raged against my fire.

His chin quivered as he fought against the pain. I wanted to look away, but the magic he conjured in his eyes held me trapped. "Faye, I wasn't trying to...fuck, this hurts...I don't even know what I was doing. But you have to believe I didn't—"

I refused to let him finish. I tore myself away and fled the library.

38

DORIEN

I watched her flee through a haze of pain, black hair weaving around her, hot ass sashaying through the stacks. I wanted to go after her, but I knew it was pointless. Besides, I couldn't exactly move at the moment.

I leaned back against the shelf and fought for breath. My lunch was in serious danger of being spread across the rug. My balls were on *fire*. I doubted I'd walk right for a week, and I deserved it.

Faye had every right to hate my guts. I'd been horrible.

But now that I'd tasted her, no fucking way was I letting her go.

Faye was right about one thing – she wasn't like other girls. Classical musicians didn't have groupies like rockstars, but when the tabloids named you 'The Bad Boy of Baroque,' it carried with it a certain mystique. I had enough girls falling at my feet in every city that my bed never went cold. I learned tricks from the whores of Amsterdam that were whispered in reverent tones between Maestra in green rooms across the Continent. But no matter who I conquered – how rich or beautiful or talented they were – they all blended together in the end. Willing vessels into which I poured my sorrows, vices in which to numb myself, a parade of nameless pleasures to distract myself from the gaping hole of misery that was my life.

None of them had ever kneed me in the nuts before.

Only one face stood out to me. Only one. Faye – the only person who cared about me enough for me to scar.

Faye wanted me. The desperate way she sucked my lip, that gorgeous growl she made when I brushed my hand over her nipple, the way her body bent toward me, every curve yielding.

Before the ruination of my testicles, that is.

I winced as I rolled on my side and tried to stand. They were still tender.

Faye wants me, and she hates herself for it. I know that fucked-up dance well.

Yet she could bite down on that want and ignore the sparks between us through sheer force of will. If I wanted her, I had to earn her.

Luckily, I knew her well enough to understand exactly how to touch her heart. There were two things Faye loved more than anything in the world – her mother, and music.

As soon as Master Radcliffe entered composition class the next morning, I pounced on him. "Master, I'd like to ask that I work together with Faye on a joint composition. I've heard the piece she's working on, and I believe turning it from a sonata into a duet between piano and violin would give it a depth it's currently lacking."

Master Radcliffe raised an eyebrow in surprise, but he knew better than to question me. "Certainly, Dorien. I think that's a wonderful idea. Faye would benefit from working alongside a musician with more... *traditional* training."

Just then, Faye walked in, her cheeks flushed from rushing through her chores, the black dress clinging to her curves in a delectable way. Her eyes narrowed as I walked over to her, blocking her way to her usual spot in the shadowed corner of the room.

"Out of my way." She held her violin case like a Roman shield and barged at me. My testicles shrunk inside me at the memory of their cruel treatment, but instead of fighting against her, I stepped out of the way. I wasn't fast enough to avoid a violin case in the ribs, but I caught Faye's arm as she stumbled forward.

"Of course." I gestured to the piano. "Do you want to work in here, or in the ballroom?"

She wrenched her arm away. "What are you talking about?"

"Master Radcliffe paired us together to work on a composition."

Faye's already stormy eyes churned into maelstroms. "He didn't."

"He did." I flashed her the smirk that turned most girls to butter. Most girls, but not Faye. "Lucky me."

Master Radcliffe stood from where he was sitting next to Elena and came over. "Ah, Faye. I've told Dorien he should work with you on your composition. Your piece is extremely accomplished, and I believe adding the piano will give it the depth it needs to be truly exceptional."

Faye's face did this twisting thing as she fought against her dueling urges to please Master Radcliffe and strangle me until I turned blue. I knew a little about how she felt – at that moment I wanted to crack up laughing and throw her up against the wall and kiss her at the same time. I opted for neither, instead offering my hand. "Ballroom, then. Shall we?"

Faye shot me a filthy look, lifted her violin, and shoved her way past me and out the door. I grinned as I followed her, watching that gorgeous ass swinging down the hall, while Heather jabbed daggers into my back with her eyes.

BANG. Faye threw open the ballroom door so hard it slammed against the wall, rattling a dresser filled with china plates. She stomped across the room and threw down her violin case on a velvet ottoman. A shaft of diffused light beamed from the window and fell across her face.

"I don't know what your game is," she snapped. "But you can stop right now. That kiss was a mistake. You took advantage of me, caught me off-guard, and I—"

"You, Faye Winter, taken advantage of? My nuts remember things differently."

She smirked, and that satisfied smile was worth all the tenderness in my crotch area.

I dared a smile back. "I still remember how you used to yell and kick and scream when Madame Usher paired you up with other students until she'd cave and let you work with me. You never did anything unless it was *exactly* what you wanted. The way your body curled around mine, you wanted me." I slid onto the piano stool, lifting the lid. "You *still* want me, Sprite."

Using my old nickname for her was a gamble, but it paid off. Faye snorted, but I noticed her chest heave as she took a position in the middle of the floor, facing me. The shaft of light cut across her chest, highlighting the curve of her breasts even through that severe black dress. I wet my lower lip.

"What game are you playing now?" she demanded. "Is this a distraction while Titus and Ivan destroy my room? Are you planning to dump a bucket of pig's blood on my head?"

"No pig's blood. We're going to make beautiful music together." My mouth turned up as I reached out to touch my fingers to her wrist, to feel the pulse of her blood in her veins. "Maybe I'll bend you over this piano and make you scream my name as you come."

Faye jerked her arm away, and a wall of shame hit me. After everything I'd done to hurt her, I didn't blame her for being suspicious.

But that kiss gave me hope. Faye had melted into my body like she was made for me. She wanted this as much as I did. She just had to forgive me first. My balls could attest that forgiveness wouldn't come easy, but I knew what I had to do to earn it.

I had to figure out what Madame Usher wanted from her.

"You make one wrong move, Dorien Valencourt, and I will murder you. I just want to get through this composition without doing that. The last thing I need is to be thrown in jail for homicide."

I settled down. "Then we'll work. Play for me."

Faye closed her eyes and raised the violin to her chin. She sucked in a shuddering breath, and I wondered if she was trying to rid the scent of me from her body, erase me so that I didn't infect her music.

Too late.

She struck the first note. It was the piece she'd been playing in the garden that night, only she'd refined it, drawing out the theme, turning it over itself to create a melody so achingly haunting that it stole my breath.

Her music held me mesmerized, but it was *Faye* that sent me reeling. The way she immersed herself fully in the moment, giving body and heart and soul to the song. That was my Faye, my sprite – she lived for the here and now. Although she played with the grace of a seasoned performer, she eschewed the stoic stillness of traditional posture for passion, her body moving as she played through the sweeping arpeggios that were part of her signature style.

I was back in the drafty classroom of Madame Usher's old school, the two of us giggling as we made a classical arrangement for the Muppets Mahna Mahna song, which we played at a recital to rapturous applause even though Madame Usher frowned at us the whole time.

I remembered Faye as the bright, happy-go-lucky child, the antidote to my dark moods. Father Aaron hadn't walked into our lives and burned everything to the ground yet, but my parents only noticed me when I did something wrong. As soon as I walked through the doors of Madame's studio and Faye's bright eyes lit up to see me, the world seemed happier.

She needed me, and I abandoned her.

Even though I saw her fallen face in my dreams, I'd been too selfish, too mired in my own shit to think about how that must have hurt her. I'd spent the last few weeks rubbing salt in her wound.

She set down her violin, inclining her head. To clap now would be to break the moment.

Instead, I turned to the piano and started to play.

I hadn't prepared anything, but it was as if her composition was perfectly designed for me, for my style. I picked up on the theme of her piece, expanding and deepening it, giving it more emotional punch at just the right moments. I wanted to look, to see her reaction, but I knew that if I broke my focus, I'd lose the magic that wrapped around my fingers.

I gave her this music, this piece of me. With every note, I tried to say words that had never fallen from my tongue before.

I'm sorry. I miss you.

I need you.

I finished with a flourish, my fingers sweeping the air. I dared to look up. Faye stood in place, her fingers clutching the neck of her violin like she was about to break it in two.

I raised an eyebrow. "You like it?"

She nodded.

I patted the stool. "Come sit beside me."

Faye hesitated, a million arguments playing out in her eyes. Her shadow side won, because she walked across the room like she was in a trance and sank onto the cushion beside me.

Where our knees touched, heat flared through my skin, leaping between us. I debated my options.

She'd look amazing bent over the piano, her dark hair spread out across the keys as she writhed in ecstasy—

No. I tried to ignore the throbbing in my cock. In the library, I broke through her defenses. I'd seen her stripped bare, vulnerable. She hated me for it because she believed she'd shown weakness, given ground to me that she couldn't take back. That was what the kneeing was about.

I had to show Faye that her arrival at Manderley had shaken me.

I took a deep breath. My fingers touched the keys. The back of my shoulders itched, as though someone watched me from behind, but I knew the room was empty. Manderley did that to you after awhile, made you imagine all kinds of ghosts. I thought of that pale face I imagined I'd seen – a face that looked far too much like Clare – and had to supress a shudder.

With a single hand, I played a little ditty, the kind of thing we used to invent together all the time when we were kids.

"Do you remember that day you came over to my house?" She nodded. "I didn't tell you, but it was the last time I ever celebrated my birthday. That guy who interrogated you – Father Aaron – he's not my uncle. He's a… he used to be a priest, but he was kicked out of the church for his extremist views, so he formed his own religion. My mother was his first and most loyal convert."

Faye looked surprised. I think of all the things she expected me to say, this wasn't it. "She wore this long robe…" she remembered.

"Yes. All Aaron's disciples wear those robes unless they are in public. They weave and sew the cloth themselves. Aaron believes that humans have become disconnected from nature and the heartbeat of Mother Earth, so his cult is all about returning to that. At first, he spent a lot of time at our house, then he seemed to have an opinion on everything my parents did, then I got back from a residency in London and he'd moved in permanently.

"Aaron only targets the super-rich. When he discovered my musical talents, I became a key part of his plan. He saw a way to get his message out to many wealthy people – through my music. He took over decisions about my career. He uses my parents to control me, and me to control them. And that's where you come in."

Faye looked shocked. "Me?"

"At first, my parents were happy that we were friends. They approved of your father's rising career. They saw you as part of the plan. They actually went to your mother and offered her money if she would promise you'd marry me."

Faye's eyebrows shot up. "She never told me that."

"She probably forgot about it. According to my mother, Marguerite de Winter laughed in their faces and told them where they could shove their money."

"That sounds like her." A smile tugged at the corner of Faye's mouth, but it was quickly snatched away by that melancholy. "I can't believe your parents tried to arrange your marriage. That's barbaric."

"That's Father Aaron's influence. That's why I told you we couldn't be friends anymore. I had to do it, or—" I caught myself in time.

"Or what?" Faye jabbed her fingers into the keys. "Dorien, or what?"

I opened my mouth and shut it again. I couldn't. All these years of silence and indoctrination. I couldn't break the bonds of my cage, not even for Faye, not even when I desperately wanted to.

Instead, I laid my hand over hers, my fingers pressing down on the keys, playing the notes of the Mahna Mahna song. Faye's lips parted in a silent O of surprise and delight. She let her left hand wander down the keys, playing the chords that must have come to her like muscle memory.

"I can't believe you remember this," she whispered.

"I remember you," I whispered.

This time when I kissed her, I took it slow. My lips lingered on hers for a moment, giving her the chance to pull away. I needed her to feel in control, to take this moment.

I needed to protect my balls.

Faye's eyes widened, but she didn't pull away. I could see the decision burning inside her, before a decisive moment where she gave way to her shadow side and collapsed into my arms.

Yes. Yes...

Her pocket vibrated, breaking the spell of lust and fury that locked us together.

"That's my phone."

"Leave it," I growled. My heart ached with a need to have her, to taste all of her.

"I can't. It could be the hospital."

Faye's eyes never left mine as she dragged the phone from her pocket. The call ended. The name DOC NELSON flashed across the screen. Faye punched the button to call back, pressing the phone to her ear so hard I worried she'd embed it into her skull.

"Faye? I'm so glad I caught you." Doctor Nelson's voice sounded far away – something that didn't belong in our moment. "Come quickly. There's been an incident."

39

FAYE

"Faye, you can talk to me." Dorien's fingers drummed on the wheel of his Porsche as he waited for the lights to turn green.

I didn't say anything. I couldn't. If I opened my mouth now, I'd scream.

My fingers clawed the edge of the leather seat as I stared straight ahead. When the lights changed and Dorien hit the gas, my stomach lurched. I'd spent the last hour tying it up in knots, and the insane speed he drove didn't help.

Not that I was complaining. As much as I hated his guts, Dorien was my savior today. When I remembered in a panic that Harrison was AWOL, Dorien offered to drive me to the hospital. I was in no state to refuse.

He tore out of Manderley's drive and careened around the forest trails like we were on a racetrack. On the freeway he ducked and weaved between cars, reaching the city in record time. I would have voiced my appreciation if I wasn't such a fucking emotional wreck.

Dorien hadn't even pulled to a stop outside the hospital when

I was out of the car and running for the doors, my heart clenched, my eyes stinging with unshed tears.

Doctor Nelson met me at the nurse's station. "We've conducted a thorough check of all the equipment – she's fine, nothing was tampered with. I know this is distressing to you, but I want to assure you we take this extremely seriously. We have our hospital security combing through the CCTV footage right now. We'll catch the creep who did it."

I shook my head. "I doubt it. The only people who'd do this wouldn't get their hands dirty. They'd hire someone and make sure it's untraceable."

The doctor looked skeptical. "I think this might just be a random attack. They happen from time to time. People are upset at the healthcare system in this country, and they act out their personal aggressions on strangers."

I shook my head, too enraged to speak. Doctor Nelson must've noticed the smoke coming out my ears because she leaned forward and squeezed my shoulder, leading me down the hall to my mother's room.

As soon as I laid eyes on her, the tears spilled over.

I rushed to Mom's bed and bent over her, crushing her body with the force of my one-sided embrace. The nurses had done a good job of scrubbing her forehead, but the word scrawled across her skin still remained visible.

The handwriting was appalling, but I understood it clear enough.

LEAVE

To do this to a person who couldn't fight back, who was fighting for her life in a hospital bed... my stomach turned. I clamped my hand over my mouth, fighting to keep my lunch.

Doctor Nelson nudged a tissue box toward me. "I can go if you want to be alone—"

"No." I swallowed hard, rallying myself. I lay my head on Mom's chest the way I did as a child, listening to the slow beat of her heart, feeling the rise of her chest – an ocean tide, sweeping me home. Behind me, the machines beeped their constant, steady rhythm.

She's still alive. That's what matters. At least the bastards didn't tamper with her machines.

"You called the police?"

Doctor Nelson nodded. "They're with the security team right now. I've told them you're here. If you're up to it, they'd like to speak to you as well."

"I can do that."

Doctor Nelson shifted on her feet, flipping through pages on her clipboard. "Faye, I don't know if you want to talk about this now, but I prepared it for your visit." She unclipped some papers and handed them to me. "Your mother's lab reports have come back. I've made you copies. It's definitely chronic poisoning from *Aristolochia clematitis* – a plant commonly known as birthwort."

I sat up, taking the papers from her in shaking hands. "What?"

"It was commonly used by the Ancient Egyptians and in the Classical World to ease pain during childbirth. There was this pervasive belief that if a plant looked like a certain part of the anatomy, it would help with ailments of that area. The flowers are shaped like a uterus, hence… birthwort. By the Victorian era, it was a known poison, but the plants were still sometimes culti-vated in manor gardens for their beauty. It's not a common plant now, and your doctors didn't spot it in previous tox screens because no one thought to look. I never would have thought of it either, if you hadn't told me about your mother's herbal teas. That gave me the idea to investigate poisonous ingredients in natural medicine. Birthwort is still used in some herbal medi-cines despite FDA warnings, and this might have been how your mother ended up ingesting such a large amount."

I sank back against the bed, struggling to process this new

information. After all these months of hospital visits and my mother begging doctors to take her pain seriously, even as her kidneys shut down, we *finally* had a name for what was killing her.

Naming the enemy was one thing, but could it be fought?

Doctor Nelson anticipated my questions. "The good news is, now that we understand what happened, we believe we can help her."

My heart pattered against my chest. "You can?"

She smiled. "It's involved a lot of digging through old Victorian poison books and some lab experiments, but we think we can halt the poison's progress on her body. Once this treatment is administered, as long as she doesn't ingest any more and we monitor her kidneys for complications, she should be able to live a normal life. We'd like your permission to proceed with treatment."

"What does that mean, exactly?"

"First, we'll administer a small amount of antidote and monitor changes. If that goes well – and we expect it to, as her body would have processed much of the poison in her system by now – we can attempt to wake your mother from her coma."

Those words… those magic words I'd been wanting to hear for weeks rushed at me. My head spun, and I gasped for breath. This was too much. It was amazing. It was the hope I hadn't dared to feel in so long.

"If she's…" I swallowed the lump rising in my throat. "Best case scenario, what will happen when she wakes up?"

"She'll still have organ damage, and she'll likely need dialysis. But many people live full and happy lives with greater damage than she's taken. The wildcard is her brain. There's just no way of knowing what damage has been done by the prolonged coma."

I nodded, not trusting myself to speak.

"If you're okay with it, we'll start the initial tests immediately. If they go well, we can discuss the next steps. I don't want to leave her under any longer than necessary now that I know we can help her. How does that sound?"

I nodded again. "Th—thank you."

The police came shortly after, and I answered their questions and stumbled out of the hospital in a daze. Dorien slouched on the hood of his car, sipping from a cardboard coffee cup.

"The hospital cafeteria food was shit, so I went out for the real deal." He shoved a coffee cup and paper bag filled with doughnuts into my hands. "I remembered you liked these."

I stared down into the bag, hesitating before peeping inside, half expecting some enormous spider to crawl out and go for my face. Instead, a heavenly smell greeted me. Four doughnuts heaped with Oreo cookie crumbs. They looked and smelled just like…

A memory assailed me. I was eight years old. That day at school Rebecca Marshell and her posse of mean girls stole my clothes from the gym changing rooms and pinned them to the noticeboard under a sign that read WHALE NETS. I went straight from school to practice in tears. Dorien ran away as soon as he saw me, and I thought my life couldn't get any worse. But he came back ten minutes later with a bulging bag of peanut-butter Oreo doughnuts from a little shop around the corner called Nothing But the Dough. We hid in a storage room and ate them all, and in minutes he had me laughing. I forgot about those stupid girls. Ever since then, peanut butter Oreo doughnuts had been our go-to whenever something bad happened, whenever we needed cheering up. Until Dorien became the bad thing in my life, and I hadn't touched them since.

Nothing But the Dough was all the way in the East Village, if it even still existed. *Dorien can't have—*

"Go on. Try one."

I pulled a doughnut out of the bag, scattering Oreo crumbs down the side of the car. I bit into it. Chocolate dough and peanut-butter frosting exploded in my mouth. A rush of emotion slammed into me – all the horror of seeing my mother with that word scrawled across her forehead crashed into the memory of the doughnuts and what they meant. For what felt like the first time since my mother's nightmare began, I wasn't entirely alone. *Dorien's here.*

My chest tightened. Fuck, I didn't want to have to do this alone anymore.

I stared up at him with wide eyes. "How did you—"

Dorien flashed me his signature smirk, the one that promised mischief. "I'm rich as fuck, remember? It cost a fortune to get a delivery person to drive them out here on a motorcycle, and I wasn't even sure they'd arrive in time. But it was worth it to see your face."

I wiped frosting off my chin. "To see me covered in peanut butter?"

Dorien stepped close. The doughnut bag was the only thing that stood between us, and suddenly I found it very hard to breathe. "To see you smile, Sprite. You don't know how much I've missed your smile."

The tears I'd been holding back spilled over, rolling down my cheeks and dropping on the bag. I wanted so badly to fall forward into Dorien's arms, to let him hold me, to give myself over to the idea that someone fucking cared about me.

But doubt scratched at the back of my neck. *That's exactly what he wants you to do.*

Getting me to trust him again was all part of his plan. That was why he got the doughnuts and told me that story about his parents being in a cult. Dorien knew how to manipulate a situation for his own gain, and he was playing me like a sonata right now. This was deception with doughnuts.

He guessed that I didn't believe he killed Clare. Now he knew about my mother too, so he could also guess at how much I needed the Manderley Prize. He knew I wouldn't give that up without a fight. Now he was trying to convince me that

Madame Usher was behind all this, that he had no choice, but the bullying was over because he kissed me and brought me doughnuts.

But I couldn't believe it. I couldn't be that gullible. *How far will he go to get what he wants?*

LEAVE MANDERLEY was written on my mirror in lipstick, and then someone writes LEAVE on Mom's forehead? Obviously, they were connected. It had nothing to do with Mom – it was a message for *me*.

The ghosting, the stupid messages, the sounds that kept me up at night – it was all juvenile stuff. Trying to convince me it wasn't him… that took some doing. But breaking my violin? Hurting my mother just to affect my performance?

What a sick, horrible thing to do.

Is it him? Is it?

My fingers tightened around the doughnut bag. I pulled one out and slammed it into Dorien's face.

"Ow, what the fuck?" Dorien staggered back, peanut frosting dripping down his cheek. Oreo flakes peppered the front of his shirt. I wanted to burst out laughing, but the rage burned too raw inside me.

Without another word I whirled around and stormed out of the parking lot, dragging my phone from my pocket. No way was I driving back in the same car as him, even if that meant I had to walk all the way back to Manderley.

"Sprite, wait!"

"Go away!" I screamed.

"Sprite… please." Dorien's voice broke, and it took all my self-control not to turn around to him. "At least it wasn't my nuts this time. I'm calling Harrison. He'll come and collect you. Don't run off by yourself. I'll go. Sprite, I'm sorry."

I'm sorry. I never imagined I'd hear those words from the lips of Dorien Valencourt. Too bad they were a fucking joke. I swiped angrily at the tears falling down my cheeks, refusing to turn around until I heard the Porsche's wheels spin as Dorien sped away.

My mouth still tasted of peanut butter frosting – one of the few happy memories of him that he'd destroyed. My jaw set in a hard line.

It's time.

I'd been holding back on retaliation, unsure if I was ready for what I planned to do. I wouldn't be letting Dorien dig his own grave – this plan meant breaking a few laws. It meant doing something I could never turn back from. But it was the only way.

Dorien had seen right into my heart, into the music of my soul, and he'd smothered the notes with his cruelty. If I wanted Dorien Valencourt to pay, I would have to hit him where it hurt.

His wallet.

40

FAYE

"Thank you, Harrison." My legs wobbled as I climbed into the back of the limo. "I'm sorry you had to come all this way..."

"Any time, my pet. I am just sorry I couldn't have brought you here in the first place." His face shifted uncomfortably. "She gets these ideas in her head, the Madame—"

"I know. Don't worry about it." I knew now how much power Dorien truly had in that house – Madame Usher had given Harrison an order to ignore me, but one call from Dorien and here was my limousine. Everything he told me in the library was a lie. His lips devouring mine, his fingers on the back of my neck, that growl he made as he sucked my lip...

All lies.

"I hope your mom's okay. I hope they get the bastard who did this. Dorien said that something happened."

"*Dorien* happened," I muttered, my hands curling into fists.

"You think Dorien—"

I didn't say anything. I *couldn't*. If I opened my mouth, I'd explode.

Harrison swore, something I'd never before heard him do.

"He won't get away with this, love." He jerked the car out of the hospital lot. "You make him pay."

Oh, I planned on it. Sound the fucktrumpets, Dorien Valencourt was going down.

~

"Hey, Cory," I whispered, cupping my hand around the receiver.

"Faye?" Creepy Cory – the mouth-breather who worked across the bar from me sounded surprised and fucking *delighted* to hear from me. Gag. "They told me you weren't coming into work anymore. I was so worried. I even went around to your house to see you, but the place is empty."

Obviously, you creepy stalker. Cory was half the reason I was so glad to leave that place. He was always leaning too close, always asking me out and trying to walk me home, always staring at me like he was wondering what my organs would look like splayed across his bed. "Yeah. I've enrolled in a fancy music school. I won a scholarship."

"That's amazing. Can I come and see you perform?"

"It's not really that kind of a school. The thing is, there's this guy who's being horrible to me." I let my voice simper, giving Cory something to latch onto – the chance to be my hero. "I'm... scared. He's a bully, and he's turned all the other students against me. It would usually be the kind of thing a swift throat punch would handle but..."

"But?" Cory's voice sounded kind of choked-up. I bet he was remembering that time he tried it on with me after closing and I throat punched him. He couldn't talk for a week.

"But... this guy has resources. He's a rich dickweasel, and I need him not to be able to destroy me. I was hoping you'd be able to help."

"You want me to teach this guy a lesson?"

"Something like that. I want him to know that this kitten has claws."

"I can help. Give me ten minutes. You'll have to friend me on Facebook again if you want to see. What's his name?"

"Dorien Valencourt." I hung up the phone, flipped open my laptop and logged into Facebook. I'd blocked Cory months ago because ick, so I went into my settings to unblock him. He popped up instantly with a link. 'Click that.'

I clicked the link. A window popped up, showing a login for a managed fund account. A cursor moved across the screen of its own accord and a line of asterisks appeared as Cory typed in a password.

"Your creep isn't very bright. I broke his password in seconds," Cory messaged. A moment later, a list of accounts and transactions popped up on the screen. The banner across the top of the screen read, "Welcome, Dorien."

I can't believe I'm doing this.

Cody passed control over to me, and I clicked on the first account. Dorien used his money to wield control over not just me but everyone at Manderley. The only way to show him that he couldn't control me was to take that money away.

My finger hovered over the mouse. What I was about to do was hella illegal. I was *stealing* money. A lot of money. Not for myself – I'd chosen the perfect charity to receive Dorien's generous donation. They offered music tuition to underprivileged inner-city children, sending the best and brightest to conservatories all over the world on scholarships. Just the sort of thing Dorien would be behind one hundred percent.

Yes. I'm doing this.

I exhaled sharply as I clicked Dorien's main account, bringing up a list of transactions. My finger hovered over the Make a Transaction button when I noticed something odd.

Huh?

His account held only $224.67.

That can't be right. That's probably his last withdrawal or something. A guy like Dorien spends that much on luxury silk boxers.

I clicked through to his statements, searching for the honey pot. I didn't find it. What I *did* find was a steadily dwindling total. Three years ago, Dorien had over half a million dollars in the fund. Month by month, that money had been withdrawn and never replaced.

Where's all his money?

I rang Cory again. "Does Dorien have any other funds? We must've made a mistake. There's no money in this account."

"Not that I can see. He's got a checking account with his bank, but I already hacked that and it only contains $23. Plus three credit cards, all practically maxed out. The last transaction was yesterday, for a little over $400 to NOTHING BUT THE DOUGH in the East Village. $400 on doughnuts, can you believe it? He must rack up tens of thousands of dollars each month then get Mommy and Daddy to pay them off. Rich bastards, right?"

"Right." Curiouser and curiouser. "Thanks anyway, Cory. Listen, could you keep looking into Dorien? I'd love to know where all the money is going."

"Sure thing. But you're going to have to keep me unblocked on Facebook." Cory sounded like a hopeful puppy. I'd feel sorry for him if not for the fact I remembered what his unwanted hand felt like cupping my tits.

I sighed. "I suppose so. Bye, Cory."

"But wait. Shouldn't we meet up and strategize? Maybe I could take you on a date Friday night—"

I stabbed my finger on the END CALL button and flung the phone on the bed. My skin crawled. *I can't believe I just did that. I tried to steal Dorien's money.*

I can't believe Dorien doesn't have *any money.*

I turned back to the computer. My hand hovered over the mouse. I'd steeled myself for this revenge plan. I'd justified it with the fact that Dorien was a rich bastard sitting on a big stash. His parents owned that enormous estate, after all. They were old money. They'd never run out.

But $225? Maxed-out credit cards? What was going on with Dorien? Could I really take his last penny?

Grinning, I slid my finger over the trackball, typing out the information to send every last cent of Dorien's money to the charity.

Dorien had made it his business to learn my secrets and use them to hurt me. But it turned out the biggest Bad Boy of Baroque hid a secret of his own.

Dorien Valencourt was dirt broke.

41

FAYE

I turned over this new knowledge in my head for the next few days, unsure of what to do with it. The police called to tell me they had identified a man on the security footage, and were chasing down a number of leads to identify him. The detective in charge was interested in hearing about Doctor Nelson's discovery of the poison and my mother's herbal teas. I gave her the name of my mother's old assistant. If anyone could remember the name of that tea company, it would be Natalie.

Dorien hadn't spoken to me since I got back from the hospital, but his stormy eyes followed my every movement. Unlike with Cory, it didn't make my skin crawl but instead sent sparks of electricity through my veins. I hated myself every time I felt his gaze sweeping my body and I lapsed into a memory of his lips on mine.

I'm supposed to hate him, not want him.

And he's not even the only one I want. There's Titus with the eyes of fire and huge hands. I bet he knows exactly how to use them. And Ivan, who didn't even come undone when he got caught with those drugs. What would it be like to see him lose control...

I'm sick. I should be in that hospital bed beside Mom.

Mom. Fuck, I wished I could talk to her. She'd know exactly what to do. With her successful business and wild personality, Mom had a constant string of powerful men vying for her affections. Once, she even dated a semi-famous rapper for a few months, and his paparazzi followed us to the dry cleaners. She'd know exactly how to handle Dorien and Titus and Ivan.

But she wasn't here. I had to deal with all this on my own.

Despite Dorien's gaze and the looks I was getting from Titus and Ivan, no one else talked to me. Heather glared at me like I'd grown a third head. Tension crackled whenever I walked into a room, and I had this creeping sense of foreboding that soon everything would boil over into a big mess.

When Dorien discovers what I've done...

I couldn't face composition class with the others, so I skipped it and headed to the library to work on my final essay. I'd chosen to write about Paganini – he was this amazing violin virtuoso in the nineteenth century. Paganini had all these stage tricks he liked to play – he'd tamper with his violin strings before a performance so they'd break during the night. By the end of his performance, he'd be playing an entire caprice on one string. Some of his lost compositions were rumored to be so impossible to play that it was said Paganini made a pact with the devil in exchange for his talent. He was the original bad boy of classical music, and so obviously I adored him.

I told you I had a thing for the bad boys.

I shoved my earbuds in my ears and put on my indie rock playlist (a girl can't live on Paganini alone). My phone beeped with a message from Doctor Nelson. She'd been amazing, updating me every day about the progress with Mom's illness, offering to text me instead of calling in case I couldn't handle a phone conversation.

"Hi, Faye. I suspect you'll get a call from the police soon, as I've just got off the phone with them. They have good news and bad news, I'm afraid. The good news is, they caught the guy who assaulted your mother. The bad news is, he's a homeless man who did it for cash. He doesn't have a name or description of the person who hired him."

I'd suspected as much, but seeing it written in black and white made my blood seethe. At first, I assumed someone from the PR world had done it – Mom made a lot of enemies when she clawed her way to the top, and I'd already given the police a long list. But when I'd made the connection between the word LEAVE and the message on my mirror, I knew who did it. I told the police that, too, but they said it would be tough to prove. They didn't want to go after a powerful family like the Valencourts. Cowards.

I tapped my fingernails against the desk.

When I walked around the mezzanine level to collect a volume on Paganini's life, I noticed Dorien hunched over a cubby in the corner, frowning at his laptop. He slammed it shut as I walked past, and he glanced up at me, the slash of his smirk lacked its usual venom.

"What's wrong, Dorien?" I cooed. "Poor baby in trouble again?"

Dorien made a growling noise low in his throat, like a cornered lion preparing to lash out. That growl sank through my body, pooling between my legs, spreading warmth to dark and hidden places inside me.

"What are you smiling about?" he rasped.

I lifted a hand to touch my face. He was right – I *was* smiling. It had been so long since I had something to smile about that I forgot what it felt like.

"Nothing," I said sweetly. "I'm just reading a really funny book."

"'*Translations and Annotation of Choral Repertoire*' is a funny book?" Dorien narrowed his eyes at the title in my hand.

"Oh yes." The heat in my body bubbled through my veins,

turning to a giddy mirth that warmed my skin. "It's fucking *hilarious.*"

As I walked out of the room, I burst out laughing. And I *know* I imagined it, but I fancied I heard the faintest chuckle in the air, as if somewhere in the house the ghost was laughing, too.

42

DORIEN

I slammed the door to my room so hard the wall shuddered. Faye's gleeful face as she stood over my computer played over in my mind, imprinted on top of her vicious scowl as she smashed the doughnut into my face.

She did it.

How she did it wasn't important, and the why was obvious. Revenge for the shit I'd put her through since she came to Manderley. She was working her way through all of us – first Ivan, then Titus, now me. She thought I had something to do with her mother's assault.

What rattled my bones more than anything was what this meant.

She knows your secret.

I grabbed my phone off the bed, my fingers flying over the keys to text him, but I deleted all the words before I hit send. What could I say that would make a difference?

Calm down. Don't lose your shit. She doesn't know everything. She knows about the money... or lack thereof. But she can't know where it's gone, or why.

She'll figure it out. And you only have yourself to blame. You mentioned your brother. You poked the bear, and now the bear's not going to rest until she's clawed out your guts.

And this secret… it could cost the life of the one person in the world I cared about more than Faye.

"Fuck. Fuck. Fuck." I grabbed a pillow off my bed. That was the annoying thing about being stuck at this school in the middle of nowhere. There was no one to punch. I could punch Titus, I supposed, but since he was lending me money and he was the size of a freight train, all that would achieve was breaking my knuckles.

Ivan? I could punch him. That would be kind of satisfying – I'd at least get a reaction out of him. But he'd punch me back, and Ivan might be small, but behind that icy facade lurked decades of repressed Romanian fury. I was quite fond of the shape of my nose as it was.

I'd happily punch Master Radcliffe until his face was a bloody pulp, but that would make things worse for Ivan and Elena, and I couldn't do that.

With nowhere to direct my anger, I slammed my fist into the pillow. Feathers flew everywhere, blanketing my room in a soft, yellow snowstorm.

I flung the pillow away in disgust. It hit the photo frame on my bedside table, sending it flying. Glass shattered across the floor.

Faye. I bet she was loving this. Those red lips of hers had tugged back into a genuine smile because she bested me. I imagined those lips slipping around my cock, her tongue flicking over the tip as she took me deep. I moaned at the thought of surrendering to her.

With trembling fingers, I tapped a message into my phone on the Broken Muse private chat. We needed to sort this shit out, once and for all. We were dancing too close to the flames – one of us, or all of us, were going to get burned.

43

TITUS

I was chilling in the Blue Room, drinking wine and watching reality TV shows on Aroha's laptop, when my phone vibrated.

"Ooooh, I'll have some of that." Aroha wriggled her ass in the chair, shooting me her wicked grin. Her pupils were wide, dilated. *She's on something. Shit.*

We all knew Aroha had a crippling fear of performing, one she hid with cocaine and cigarettes and her fuck-off attitude. But we were just hanging out, no pretense, no performance, so why was she snorting now?

As if we didn't have enough to worry about. I opened my mouth to ask her about it, but then my phone buzzed again.

Across the room, on the sofa he shared with his sister, Ivan was frowning at his screen. That could only mean one thing.

Dorien.

"I have to go." I stood up, untangling Aroha's arm from around my shoulders and handing her back her computer. She flashed me a megawatt grin.

"When the Prince of Darkness calls, his little minions go running." She rolled her eyes.

"I'll watch TV with you, Aroha." Elena slid in beside her, tucking the bottle of wine into her lap. Aroha grabbed the laptop and started scrolling through the selection. I met Elena's eyes and she nodded. She'd seen the haze in Aroha's eyes, too. She wouldn't leave Aroha alone.

In the hallway, Ivan and I exchanged a look. "Faye?" he whispered. I nodded. It had to be. She was the only thing that could twist Dorien up in knots like this.

Faye de Winter.

Her scent followed me everywhere, seeping from the wallpaper, curling from the stuffy furnishings and threadbare carpets, filling my nostrils with the promise of more.

But there could never be more, because Dorien had already stamped his claim. And what Dorien wanted, he got.

Faye was proving a formidable opponent. She'd gone after Ivan and nearly got him kicked out of Manderley. If anyone else had done that, Dorien would tear them to pieces, but he never even considered it. He went to Madame Usher and smoothed things over. Ivan remained at school and we would never speak of the incident again. I hadn't the courage to ask what Dorien bargained to get that, but I know it had to have hurt him. Bad.

Although we were still ghosting Faye, he seemed to have given up on the plot to destroy her. He drove her to the hospital the other day, and then called to have Harrison pick her up. He snapped at me when I asked what happened, and Faye had been avoiding him and glaring at him across the room. I'd never seen him spun out on a girl before – it was weird. A little scary.

And it sucked, because I wanted her. But Dorien had first dibs, as he always did. Broken Muse was supposed to be a democracy, but we all knew that was bullshit. Dorien called the shots, and Faye was his the moment she walked through the doors of Manderley.

He'll tear her apart like he does everything in his life, like he did with our band. If Faye thinks being hated by Dorien was hell on earth, then she should try having his love.

As we ascended the stairs, Ivan cleared his throat. I turned to him, but he crumpled under my gaze, swallowing down whatever he'd been about to say. We reached Dorien's room in silence. I shoved open his door.

"What happened in here? Faye finally give you the tar and feathering you deserve?"

Feathers flew in all directions, spinning in lazy circles through the air to settle on Dorien's stuff. He lay on the bed with his knees in the air, picking at the down sticking to his trousers. A dusting of duck-down snow clung to his hair, his shirt, even his cheeks. In the corner of the room, the feathers swirled in the air, forming a shape that at first glance looked like a pale face with a wide, black mouth. I blinked, and the unsettling image disappeared. *It's just feathers. My imagination is going wild in this stupid house.*

Beside me, Ivan covered his mouth with his hand, stifling a laugh.

"You're fucking hilarious." Dorien glared at me. A yellow feather stuck to his eyebrow. "Faye knows about my money."

That stopped me short. I slammed the door shut and folded my arms. "How?"

"She hacked my account and cleared out everything that was left, not that there was much. She donated it all to some charity for underprivileged musicians."

I couldn't help it. Laughter burst out of me like fireworks on the Fourth of July.

Dorien glared at me. "Chortle away. She'll be coming for you next, Van Halen."

I shrugged. "Let her. Maybe I *want* her to come after me."

"What does that mean?"

"I want to ask her out."

I hadn't intended to say those words. They'd burst out along with the laughter, and I couldn't stuff them back in. Ivan glanced between us, pressing his back against the wall and moving his feet into a position to run if things got violent.

Dorien tossed back his head. The laughter started deep in his stomach and bubbled out of him like a volcano starting to erupt. He kicked his legs in the air and caught a floating feather in his hand, crushing it between his fingers.

"I can't believe this shit. Good fucking luck, bro. We've spent the semester bullying her. She thinks you snuck into her room while she was sleeping. If you think you can charm her into overlooking that and giving you a chance, you're welcome to try. You don't need my permission – but I recommend packing some groin protection."

"So you don't care if I ask her?"

Dorien shrugged. "I didn't say that. I just said it's pointless."

My fingers curled into fists. "You can't lay claim over her just because you knew her before. You fucked that up, and she's made it pretty clear she can't stand you. Give someone else a chance."

Dorien sat up, his feet slamming on the floor. When his eyes met mine, the storms threatened to blow me over. "She kissed me back in the library. Fuck, she made this delicious moaning sound… you should have heard it, it'll turn your dick stone hard."

"Don't be a *bou*, Dorien," Ivan warned. "She kicked up in the nuts, also."

"That she did," he grinned. "It was hot as fuck."

My fingers tightened, nails digging into my skin.

Dorien spread his arms wide. "Go on, Titus. Lay me out. You know you want to."

"Fuck off." I turned to his bureau and tipped a stack of music books to the floor. *Thump, thump, thump.* They bounced on the rug. That didn't make me feel better, but it did break the hypnotic hold he had over me.

Dorien laughed again, and the sound was hysterical and a little bit terrifying. "You're right, bro. Faye can't stand me. She thinks I hired some bum to break into her mother's hospital room and write on her face. But that doesn't mean there isn't something there. Trust me, one thing I know *for a fact* is that I don't own Faye de Winter. But you know I will tame her. So why are we fighting over this? It's not like the two of us haven't been into the same girl before. Remember Cherie in Paris? We found a way to—"

"Three," Ivan said from the door.

I whirled around. "Excuse me?"

Ivan swallowed. "I said, the three of us had the same girl before. And we want the same girl now."

I lifted an eyebrow. "You too?"

Interesting. I wasn't sure if Ivan had ever liked a girl. I was the one who fell hard for every chick who batted her eyes at me or complimented my playing. Dorien was a force of nature, and he sucked everything and everyone in his path. But Ivan... he had only one love, and that was Elena.

Until now, apparently.

Ivan nodded as he stepped forward. "I don't want us to fight over her."

Dorien flopped back on the bed, sending up a flurry of feathers. "Who's fighting? Here's the thing – as far as us three and our cocks are concerned, it's Faye's choice. One of us, two of us, all three of us, we can give her the option, but it's her call, right?"

"Right..." I said slowly, not sure where he was going with this.

"So there's nothing to argue about. We simply present Faye with a buffet of options – the best Broken Muse has to offer. No sabotage, no playing each other off to win, no jealousy. Faye chooses, and we accept her choice. Fair?"

Ivan and I glanced at each other. On the surface, everything Dorien said was perfectly reasonable. And it wasn't unusual for us. We'd shared girls before. Things got pretty wild on tour, especially when we hit Amsterdam. Or Berlin. *Oh, Berlin... how could I forget the jelly, and the things Fraulein Ana did with giant pickles...*

But this wasn't just some Broken Muse groupie. This was *Faye*. Dorien's Faye. And just because he agreed to this didn't mean he intended to fight fair.

But fair or not fair, I wasn't going to miss my chance.

"Deal." I stepped forward, offering my fist.

"I agree." Ivan placed his fist on mine.

Dorien thrust his fist on top, the treble clef tattoos dancing over his knuckles. "Good. Because we have something bigger to deal with then your overeager cocks. Someone who isn't us is after Faye. Someone is trying to get to her through her mother. And we need to focus all our resources on bringing that person down, even if it means Manderley falls with it."

44

FAYE

The three boys disappeared into the city for a recital, and Madame Usher ordered me to clean the rooms while they were away. As soon as I opened Dorien's door, I was greeted with a fluffy, downy mess.

Feathers. *What?*

I assumed this was some new way to torture me until I found the source of the down – a pillow torn through the middle. My shoe crunched on something – a broken photo frame lying amongst scattered books and other things. The room looked like a war zone, with duck casualties and Dorien's intoxicating scent laid out like barbed wire ready to trip me up.

As I carefully packed the glass into a trash bag, I slid out the photograph to place it on Dorien's bureau. It was a picture of Dorien – his slate-grey eyes glaring defiantly at the camera, accentuated with dark, smudged eyeliner, arresting any viewer who dared gaze upon him. He wore a black shirt with a ruffled collar and stage makeup that gave him the appearance of a mesmerizing vampire – timeless and breathtakingly beautiful. He had his arm around a smiling girl, pulling her against his chest, his body language possessive.

Beside the photograph, someone had used lace and diamantes to create a collage, with a handwritten note in the center. "Dorien. Thank you for the greatest night of my life. Love, Clare."

Clare.

My finger traced over her face. This was the dead maid. Seeing her face – young and fresh and happy, with a slightly-turned up nose and friendly green eyes and brown hair swept up into a high bun – made her real to me for the first time. She lived in this house, slept in my room, died on the hallway carpet. The loopy handwriting on the note matched that I'd rubbed off the old whiteboard in the pantry. And she had been with Dorien. He'd taken her on a date. *The best night of my life.* I squinted harder at the lights in the background. *Are they in New York City—*

Creeeak. Creak.

I whirled around, my heart in my throat. "Who's there?"

No one answered. Obviously they didn't. Because it was just the house settling. But my nerves were already shot. I dropped the photograph onto the bureau and cleaned up the room as quickly as I could, all the while feeling the scratch of invisible eyes on the back of my neck.

Being around Dorien's scent like that... touching his things, stroking my fingers along the raw silk of his comforter... it did things to me. It made me doubt my earlier conviction that he'd been behind Mom's attack. It made me wish for things that could never be.

I needed to let the tension from my body. If I couldn't fuck, then I needed to play.

Luckily, with three students still away at the recital, the practice rooms were empty. I scrawled my name down on the whiteboard for the Yellow Room and slipped inside. I remembered the last time I'd been in here, when I found my father's book, and my shoulders tightened with tension. My fingers buzzed with pent-up energy as I removed my violin from its case and rested it against my chin.

I drew the bow over the strings, and in that first lingering note I transported myself out of my body and into the music. I played through *Nigun* as a warm-up, letting the mournful notes conjure images of my mother that made my chest ache, before launching into Paganini's explosive caprices.

My fingers flew along the strings, and my mind became a mess of color and light and sensation. The caprices aren't so much musical movements as they are exercises in madness – it took every ounce of concentration I possessed to keep my fingers on the strings as I executed the double-stop trills and impossible jumps. No memory could push through the wall of music, not even Dorien's scent.

In some faraway corner of my mind, I became dimly aware of the door creaking open. Elena appeared at the edge of my vision. She hovered in the doorway a moment, casting a glance over her shoulder, before slipping inside and locking the door behind her.

Instantly, the hairs on my neck stood up. My finger slipped on the string. *Why is she here? What fresh torture have the Muses cooked up for me?*

I didn't stop playing, but I tracked Elena as she crossed the room and perched on the end of the velvet chaise under the window. Sunlight peeked through the lace curtains, dappling her golden hair. She watched me, her expression serene. I waited for Elena to speak, or for *something* to happen. But she said nothing, so I kept playing.

I didn't dare close my eyes, the way I usually did when I played for myself. Instead, I focused on the new techniques Master Radcliffe taught me – resting my hand against the body of the violin so I could use my thumb as a pivot to accomplish the stretches. A cramp ran down the side of my index finger, but I ignored it.

As the last notes of the caprice trembled from the strings, Elena rose. Her eyes met mine – that frozen pixie stare that lured men like the Titanic attracted icebergs. I was surprised to see a tear fall down her cheek. She acknowledged me with a nod as she left the room, a trail of exotic perfume wafting after her.

What the fuck was that about?

I nestled my violin back in its case, unable to control my pounding heart. Did Elena come in here to spy on me? Was it the first stage of some new torture the Muses dreamed up? But that tear... it seemed impossible, but I couldn't help but wonder if Elena came to *listen to me play.*

The gong sounded through the house as the Muses arrived home. A commotion in the hallway drew my attention. I clipped the case shut and crept to the door, pulling it open a crack to peer outside. Ivan and Elena stood at the foot of the staircase. Elena's fingers curled around the carved banister, while Ivan tugged on her free wrist, trying to draw her back to face him.

"Where were you?" Ivan managed to spin her, wrapping his arms around her waist, holding her in place against his body. I tightened my grip on the door, debating interfering, but it didn't look like he was trying to dominate her. More... that he was desperate. Afraid. "I could not find you when we left. I was worried. I thought—"

She shook her head, pressing her hands to his back, letting her cheek fall against his shoulder. "I wasn't with him. I wanted to see Faye. I had to make sure she is worthy of you, and I believe she is."

Wait, what?

Ivan frowned. "You can't disappear like that."

"Please, Ivan. Drop it."

"I can't drop it. What he's doing to you... it's wrong. It's all so wrong." Ivan's voice trembled with rage. He let out a string of words in his native Romanian.

Elena replied to him in the same language, her shoulders sagging with defeat. I was just about to close the door again when she switched back to English. "There's nothing we can do. We are prisoners here. But he will help us be free. That is the only reason

I let him near me, and that is my promise, Ivan. It will all be worth it."

Ivan spat a reply, his hands curled into fists against his back. I didn't have to understand Romanian to know he threatened violence against someone. But who was the *he* she referred to? Was it Dorien?

I drew back and tapped the door shut with my foot, leaning my ass against it. Why had Elena come to watch me play? Why didn't she want Ivan to know where she was? And what did she mean when she said that they were prisoners?

Was this another secret lurking in the walls of Manderley?

45

FAYE

"Students, as a special treat, Master Radcliffe and I would like to invite you to attend the gala performance of the New York Philharmonic this weekend as our guests, as well as the ball afterward."

My ears perked up. Mom and I used to attend performances all the time. When we were well-off she was a patron of the orchestra, and I danced with her at many a gala ball under glittering chandeliers. Even in a room filled with stuffy rich dick-weasels, my mother wasn't afraid to scorch the floorboards and draw the eye of every man in the room. A Wall Street banker once interrupted us mid tango to propose marriage to her.

Going without her would feel... about as shit as everything else I had to do without her, but it would be wonderful to be immersed in the music and remind myself what I was fighting for.

"As punishment for certain misdeeds, Ivan and Dorien will stay behind." Madame raised her nose in the air. "And, of course, Faye is much too busy with her chores to attend."

Ivan shot a glance at Elena, his fork clattering out of his hand. Elena placed her fingers over his. "I can't go without Ivan," she said, eyes meeting Madame's in a showdown of wills. Her wispy voice robbed her of the power in her sapphire gaze, and she quickly gave in, dropping her eyes to her plate.

"Don't be daft. You're a grown woman who can live without your brother for a night. What will happen when you're touring solo?" Ivan was shaking. Madame glared around the table, daring someone to challenge her. "The rest of you, be ready to depart at 10AM sharp Saturday morning. I've already booked hotel rooms in the city."

Not getting to go to the gala didn't bother me nearly as much as an entire weekend alone with Dorien and Ivan. I took an armload of plates into the kitchen, and when I returned to finish clearing the table, I noticed Dorien and Heather whispering together at the other end of the hall. Heather no longer had a plaster on her nose, but it still looked bruised, even through her makeup. She jerked her thumb in my direction, her voice dripping with venom. I stopped in my tracks.

They're talking about me. What the fuck?

Dorien whirled on his heel and strode away. Heather screamed after him, "If you don't have the stomach to finish what we started, I'll do it myself."

"Do that, and I'll ruin you." Dorien didn't yell, but the threat was clear in his voice.

Heather slammed the Red Room door in his face. Dorien stared at it for a few moments, his chest rising and falling, his hands balled into fists. He stalked down the hall toward me; the storm in his eyes could sink a battleship.

Dorien's step wavered as he spotted me, then he narrowed those slate orbs at me and quickened his pace. His boots thudded on the thick rug. He made his intention clear. If I didn't get out of his way, he'd mow me down and feel no remorse for it.

He must've discovered his charitable donation.

A strain. A break. Even a bruising could impact my playing. I couldn't afford to get hurt.

But I also knew I couldn't let Dorien win. If I gave this dick-head an inch, he'd destroy me.

I stepped toward Dorien, squaring my shoulders, making it clear that I wasn't budging.

Dorien kept coming, that beautiful jaw set in grim determination. The space closed between us, bringing a wave of his intoxicating scent that almost knocked me back. But I didn't stop, didn't slow down.

At the last possible second, I slammed my body against the wall and stuck out my foot. Dorien's heavy boot slid beneath it, and he dropped like a log.

"What the fuck?" he groaned as he rolled over to kneel on the rug. He clutched his hand, which had slammed against the dado rail.

"It speaks." I stood over him with arms folded. A smile crept across my face, and I let it linger. I liked this view of him, groveling beneath me with a bewildered expression on his face.

"You… tripped me." Dorien raised his arm. It had sliced down the hook on the wall, opening a small cut along the side of his forearm. "I'm bleeding."

"Don't sound so surprised." A twinge of guilt wriggled in my gut, but I pushed it down. "You intended to hurt me just now, *and* you tripped me twice. You hurt my mother. All's fair in war and prize money."

Dorien pulled himself to his feet, using the arm that wasn't bleeding to flick dark curls of hair from his eyes. "I never touched your mother, and if you thought about it for a moment, you'd realize you know that. Even if you were the best musician in this school, which you're not, Madame Usher will never give you the Manderley Prize."

"Maybe not, but I can stop it going to any member of Broken Muse." I shrugged. "I get it. You hate me. But I'm not going anywhere, so you're wasting your energy tormenting me."

"It's not a waste." Dorien dusted off his trousers. "I enjoy it."

"There are so many *more* enjoyable ways to spend your time."

The words flew out of my mouth before I could stop them. A flush formed on my cheeks, and I resisted the urge to bash my head against the wall until I wiped all memory of Dorien's raised eyebrow and shocked expression from existence.

Dorien pushed past me, leaving a trail of frankincense and violets and a fluttering in my chest in his wake.

Did I imagine it, or did Dorien Valencourt just flash me a *smile?*

46

FAYE

The weekend rolled around. Heather, Aroha, Elena, and Titus went off in the limo with Madame Usher and Master Radcliffe, which meant it was just Dorien, Ivan, and me for dinner.

While I was chopping vegetables I got a call from the police about Mom's case. They had security footage of the homeless guy standing with someone at an ATM two hours after the incident. They couldn't see the figure's face or even if they were male or female. It couldn't be Dorien, because he'd been with me.

He could have hired someone, or it could have been one of the others, but... I just didn't believe it. And then there was all that stuff Dorien was trying to say in the library, about Madame Usher and... the $400 doughnut delivery didn't lie. Just like I didn't believe Dorien capable of murdering Clare in cold blood, I couldn't see Broken Muse orchestrating this.

But if not them, who?

Feeling villainous, I cooked the hottest, spiciest chili I knew how to make – with my mom's classic *mole* sauce – and piled spoonfuls on top of two heaped mounds of rice. I took their mounds out to the dining room, dumped them on the table, and returned to the kitchen to serve a more reasonable portion to myself.

A few minutes later, a creak sounded by the door. I looked up from my book, a knot of fear twisting in my stomach. But instead of a ghost, two muses leaned against the frame, holding their plates.

"What's this?" Dorien stared at his mountain in unveiled disgust.

"You're talking to me now?" I winked at him from the table.

They crossed the room and slid onto the wooden bench opposite me. Dorien jabbed his chili with a fork. "Only to tell you that this food looks like dog shit. It's inedible. Get me something else."

Ivan was already eating, his eyes flicking between Dorien and I. He made no reaction as the chili hit his mouth. *Is that guy made of stone or something?*

"This is what I cooked," I said. "If you don't want to eat it, you're welcome to make yourself something. Otherwise, eat up."

Dorien picked up his fork, letting chili and guacamole splatter on the table. "It looks like someone already did."

"It's nice." Ivan shoveled in another mouthful. My mouth burned just *watching* him.

"It's not even proper Mexican food. It's an abomination. I've eaten at Aarón Sánchez's restaurant, and he wouldn't deem this fit to feed the peasants who shine his shoes."

"You wouldn't know proper Mexican food if it bit you on the ass, and you're not getting anything else, so eat up." I crunched a corn chip extra loudly. "You could have gone to the fancy gala dinner with the others if you'd begged Madame. You're not in the dog house with her like me and Ivan."

"You know I couldn't."

I choked on my chili. "What do you mean?"

The room sizzled with tension.

"I opened my account to find the last of my money has been donated to a charity." Dorien shoved back his chair. "I don't know how you did it, but that's harsh."

Ivan set down his fork and glared at his friend, but Dorien ignored him. As I watched his face for a reaction, I realized what he meant when we confronted each other in the hallway. He didn't have the money to pay anyone to hurt my mother. I'd have seen it when I was trawling through his funds. Relief washed over me with a force I wasn't prepared for. *Why did I want Dorien to be innocent so badly?*

"I would never do such a thing," I said sweetly. "But *if* I did, I might've been surprised to discover just how little money was there. Seems at odds with the rich asshole image you've created for yourself. I wonder how the press would feel if they knew the Bad Boy of Baroque was really the Bad Boy of Broke?"

Dorien stiffened. Something in his eyes glinted at me. Something like… admiration.

"Well played." Dorien drummed his fingers on the table. "Ivan, you got plans tonight?"

Although he spoke to his friend, his eyes never left my face. Ivan answered with the same intense attention – those sapphire shards cutting slivers from my skin. Once again, I longed to know what Ivan was thinking behind that icy stare.

"We've got this whole house to ourselves," he answered without emotion.

"And I have a key to the liquor cabinet," Dorien grinned. "What do you say, Faye? Titus isn't here, but that doesn't mean we can't have a proper Muse party."

For a moment I didn't register what they were getting at. "You're asking me to hang out with you?"

"C'mon. It's Friday night, and Ivan needs a distraction from worrying about his sister. You should let your hair down, Sprite."

Dorien reached across the table, his fingers brushing my cheek as he curled a strand of my hair around his fingers.

For a moment, time stopped. All that existed was the warmth of Dorien's fingers on my cheek, and the slight tug on my hair that made fire plunge through my body to pool between my legs, and Ivan's eyes tugging at me, a flicker on the edges of his ice that promised *something...*

I collected myself, just barely, and slapped his hand away. I slid the bench back, doing my best to ignore the crackle of fire across my skin from where he touched me.

"I've got dishes to do."

"We'll help." Dorien gave a bitter laugh. "After all, servitude might be in my future."

~

*D*orien and Ivan carried the plates to the dishwasher while I wiped down the table. When I turned around, they'd both tied frilly embroidered aprons over their dress shirts. Ivan filled the sink with hot water while Dorien tried to flick his ass with the tea towel.

"If you're here to help, you need to actually help." I pointed to the dishwasher. "Finish filling that, and give everything that doesn't fit to Ivan."

"Aye, aye, Kitchen Mussolini. And while we're slaving away, what will you be doing?"

Pinching myself to make sure I'm not hallucinating this madness. "I've got to tidy the spice rack and fold the laundry."

Having them in the kitchen was odd. A memory flashed in my mind – of a different kitchen, and a different boy. Dorien's eyes widening as he took in the tiny confines of our shitty walk-up the first time he came over after music lessons. "Wow," he bounded over to look at the colorful Mexican tiles my mother used to decorate the wall. "This place is *so cool*."

I'd never thought of our little apartment as cool, especially not when I compared it to Dorien's penthouse. I only went there once for his birthday, and it looked more like a Star Trek set than a home – everything glistening so white it hurt my eyes, his mother hovering over us in a floor-length brown robe with this creepy smile on her face, and that guy Dorien called Uncle Aaron grilling me about my father's career while we ate a gross buckwheat birthday cake.

And Ivan… that guy looked like he was made to put on a pedestal to be worshipped in a pagan temple – hella distracting when one was trying to clean the counters. He moved around the kitchen with such quiet grace that I kept stopping to watch him and forgot what I was doing. He followed me into the laundry as I pulled the sheets out of the dryer and silently picked up the corners to help fold them. I worked hospitality jobs for long enough that I was pretty neat and tidy, but his military-straight corners fascinated me.

"I folded a lot of laundry as a boy," he volunteered. "Lots of tourists visit our city because of its medieval buildings. Our mother would do laundry for the hotels for extra money. Elena and I had to go around to collect the dirty sheets, and return the clean linens." That was the most words he ever said to me. Actually, the most words I heard him say to *anyone*.

"When did you come to the States?" I asked.

"We were eight years old. We played a recital in Bucharest. Elena… even then she played like no one else. Master and Madame Usher approached my parents afterward and offered to bring us both to the United States. They would act as our guardians and ensure we had the best education. They named a figure that had my father's eyes bugging out of his head, and my parents agreed right there. They did not ask us what we wanted." His eyes flashed with resentment. "We have been at Manderley now fifteen years."

I knew we were skating around the crux of why he worried

about Elena off on her own, but he wouldn't reveal more. The words were out of my mouth before I could stop them. "How can you *stand* it?"

Ivan dropped his eyes to the sheet, which slid through his deft fingers as he folded it with precision. "It is not a matter of choice."

I was puzzling over those words when Dorien poked his head around the corner. "Dishwasher is on. Is it time to play yet?"

"What's the sudden interest in me?" The memory of our kiss scorched through my body. My toes curled into the floor. And then I flashed back to the weeks of ghosting, the rotten pranks, my violin in pieces on the bathroom sink, and I wanted to kick myself.

"Relax, Sprite. We're just hanging out." Dorien's lips curled back into his signature smirk. "Unless you have a standing engagement with the resident ghost."

At the word *ghost,* a flicker of panic crept up my spine. All the things I'd seen and heard and felt at Manderley that I couldn't explain, that were connected to the Bad Boys of Baroque in some way… and here I was agreeing to spend time with them, *alone.*

I could just say no and return to my room and read a book or practice my Paganini.

I *could* say no…

But standing between Ivan and Dorien, with their eyes locked on mine, no was not an option. I thought of my mother in her hospital bed, and her lifelong resolve to take every opportunity and seize the days while she still had them. I shrugged, hoping they couldn't hear my heart pounding against my chest. "Sure."

I followed the Muses down the hall. Dorien ducked into the Blue Room and pulled a bottle of Scotch from the cabinet. Tucking it under his arm, he led the way to the ballroom, shoving the double doors open to reveal the vast space, shrouded in cool, dappled light that peeked through the trees.

Ivan moved to light the silver candlesticks on the sideboard. I noticed someone had moved my violin case from the practice room to under the window, next to Ivan's. Dorien sat down at the piano, his fingers sweeping over the keys as he pulled the stopper and took a swig straight from the bottle. "Play with us."

The way he said it, with the corner of his mouth twisted up, purred through my body. I knew he wasn't just talking about music. I held my hand out for the bottle. When Dorien pressed it into my fingers, his touch lingered on mine, and the pounding in my heart ratcheted up a notch.

I yanked the bottle away and took a deep swig. The alcohol burned the back of my throat and pooled warmth in my belly. The tiniest bit of my nerves slipped away. I slapped the bottle into Ivan's outstretched hand and picked up my bow. "What are we playing?"

"Ladies' choice," Ivan said.

"What about the Broken Muses piece, 'Confessions of an Opium Eater'?" All their pieces had weird titles like that, many referencing old gothic literature. I loved this piece because it was a perfect example of what Classical music could do – it transported you as the listener into a darkened corner of an opium den and sent you on a dizzying high before crashing you through the despair of addiction.

Dorien tapped the opening bar. "It's not written for two violins."

"I might have a few ideas about that." I didn't tell them that the notes haunted my dreams so much that I'd toyed with the composition.

Ivan nodded to Dorien and lifted his violin to his neck. Dorien's part was low, the notes long, the sound reaching me deep in my belly. Ivan's eyes locked on mine as he came in with the melody. He conjured the sweet scent of the drug, the air heady with smoke, the seductive promise of unexplored parts of the mind...

I came in on the third bar, layering my melody over his,

adding a melancholy that hinted at the future turmoil of the third movement, where the pleasure of opium has morphed into the pain.

I turned toward Ivan as I played, and as the music took me over my body moved, swaying and dipping with the music. Ivan's gaze followed me, that ice burning my skin like fire. A laugh escaped my throat as the music lifted away my fears, my inhibitions. I felt like I was sinking under opium's spell.

Or perhaps that was the spell cast by the two beautiful, broken muses who played for me, toyed with me, their eyes raking my skin even as their fingers called forth more old and reckless magic.

Ivan moved closer, his eyes never leaving mine as he faced me, bow to bow, our fingers and wrists working in unison – an evenly-matched duel where the winner would take away… what? The tension between us pulled taut, like a cord that would either crush us against each other or snap apart and fling us across the room. We hung there, suspended inside the music, our bows casting magic into the air.

Dorien's fingers slid from the keys, leaving me and Ivan on our own. Violins screeched through the cavernous space as we descended into the dark euphoria of the second movement. I didn't stop playing as Dorien moved behind me, his presence dancing across my skin. I couldn't stop. The music had taken hold of me.

Dorien's hand slid up my thigh.

His touch was pure sin and fire. Ivan's eyes captured me, trapped me between them. Every inch of my skin sizzled with heat.

Fingers touched my hair, trailing through the strands as Dorien pushed it aside. Warm lips grazed my neck as the hand slid further around me. His fingers splayed across my stomach, pressing me back against him, grinding my ass against his jeans until I could feel his hard cock.

Hard for *me*.

Ivan's bow squealed on the strings. My mouth opened as Dorien kissed a trail of fire along my neck.

"Fuck this," Ivan groaned. He tossed his violin onto the chair, not caring that the instrument slid off and bounced on the rug. He closed the space between us, pressing his body against mine, trapping my hands so I could no longer play.

His lips met mine with a longing that knocked my breath away. Ivan clung to me like he was drowning and I was his life-line. I sank into him, reveling in the joy of being wanted.

Ivan's fingers wrapped around my neck, pulling me closer, crushing my instrument between us. Dorien grabbed the neck, and I released my grip so he could tug it away. Now nothing separated us but the promise hanging in the air.

Dorien's finger slipped under the hem of my t-shirt. I gasped into Ivan's mouth as warm fingers touched the bare skin of my stomach. Ivan made this growling noise that was so fucking delectable.

Dorien tugged at my shirt, dragging his hands over my flesh as he rolled it up. His hands grasped my breasts through my bra, and his teeth dragged over my neck.

Fingers circled my nipples through the sheer fabric of my bra, and I thought my pounding heart would burst from my chest. I'd lost all sense of whose hands were where; all I knew was how amazing I felt.

I had so many questions, but if I asked, we'd have to stop. And I didn't want to stop. Not when their hands were everywhere and their lips and tongues…

"Piano bench," Dorien rasped, his voice tight with need.

Ivan looped his fingers in mine and led me to the bench. He splayed his fingers across my shoulder, pressing me back until I lay down against the floral fabric. The filigree moldings on the ceiling framed Ivan's face like a halo as he dragged me into another of his intense kisses.

"No hogging the prize, Nicolescu."

With a grunt of protest, Ivan rolled off me. I whimpered with need of him, but Dorien's fingers were on my fly, unbuttoning my jeans and pulling them off my hips, and the kiss of the air against my skin and the prickle of their eyes on me sent a wild ache deep into my core. Ivan reached around and flicked off my bra, tossing it across the room. The boy who had been in my dreams since I was eight years old and the sapphire beauty who stole my breath stared down at my body covered only in a scrap of black fabric. I reveled in their gaze. Here, I was the one in power.

A wicked smirk crept over Dorien's face. He bent in front of me, nudging my legs open. His hand brushed over the fabric of my panties. I gripped the edges of the stool. "You're soaked," he whispered, his tone reverent.

Ivan bent down at the other end of the bench, beside me. I thought he'd lean in to kiss me, but instead, his lips closed over my nipple. The sensation of his hot tongue flicking over that sensitive nub sent molten lava flowing through my veins.

With one swipe, Dorien tore my panties off, tossing the ruined fabric aside. He bent over me, and as Ivan sucked my nipple into his mouth, Dorien's tongue circled my clit.

Holy fucktrumpets, that's amazinggggggggg...

Dorien's tongue worked in slow circles, taking his time, teasing out the heat inside me. Ivan moved to my neglected nipple and gave it the attention it deserved.

I writhed between them, knowing I was making a wet spot on the bench and not caring one bit. Dorien worked a finger inside me as he licked at my wetness, and I was gone gone gone.

Fire crashed over me in waves, like a tsunami of heat pulling me under, tossing my body on an ocean of ecstasy. I lost myself to the fire and the warmth and the pleasure, surfacing moments later to see the two Muses leaning back, their arms around each other as they stared down at me like I was some treasure they'd just uncovered.

Ivan's sapphire eyes twinkled with delight, and Dorien's smug expression begged to be slapped.

As the heady warmth in my veins subsided, I became aware of the tension hanging in the air again. We weren't finished yet.

Dorien turned to his friend, tugging on the edge of Ivan's shirt. "I'm not sure it's fair that Sprite's the only one naked."

Wordlessly, Ivan tugged off his shirt. My eyes widened as I took in the ethereal beauty of his alabaster skin and perfect form, and the disfigurement that marred it. I reached out to touch the lattice of scars covering his back. "What are these?"

Ice coated Ivan's eyes. He flinched away for a moment before turning to me again. He'd pulled up a facade, locking away his secret in a dark corner of his mind so I couldn't get to them. "They are not important, not when I am looking at a beautiful woman."

He means me. I'm the beautiful woman. No one had ever called me that before. Fatty, lardass, hippo – those were the names I was used to hearing yelled at me across campus by guys. Lecherous drunks drooling over the counter about how much they loved my curves and Creepy Cory following me after work was not the same thing as two members of Broken Muse looking at me like I was a goddess deserving of worship.

Dorien flung off his shirt and stepped out of his jeans. The candlelight flickered over his tattoos, illuminating the Latin script across his chest, the phrase *In Cauda Venenum*. I had to ask him about it, but not now.

Now I had other things on my mind.

Dorien gripped my hips and flipped me over like I weighed nothing. Honestly, that was the sexiest thing he'd done up until this point, which considering the shudders of pleasure still coursing through me from the orgasm, was saying something.

He trailed a finger over my ass cheeks. "Such a beautiful derriere," he murmured. "I'd love to turn it red with a whip one day."

Fuck. Why did that suggestion make my stomach pool with warmth?

Ivan's fingers knitted in mine, and he planted a gentle kiss on my forehead. I heard the tear of a condom wrapper, and then Dorien's hands were on my hips again. My whole body ached with a need I couldn't express. I tipped my hips back, inviting him, begging him, *commanding* him.

With a single motion, Dorien bent over and plunged into me, burying himself as deep as he could go. Balls to the wall, that was Dorien's style. I felt a sharp pain as his size stretched me, pushing me to the limit of what I could take. Once all of him was inside me, he held still, his forearms bracing against the piano bench, his body raised above mine as his ragged breath seared my skin.

"I never thought I'd get to be inside you," he whispered, his breath against my ear sending a shudder of delight through my already quivering body. While my body opened for him, warming to his presence, Dorien remained hard, tight, rigid, a coiled snake ready to strike.

His hand snaked around my throat, tugging my head up and back, attacking my mouth with his as he started to move. Slow at first, and then he was bucking against me, losing himself in the wildness of it, in the release of all the tension that had stretched between us for so long.

Ivan knelt down beside me, his fingers tangling in my hair as he tore my lips from Dorien's to devour me in his. I reached out and pulled Ivan toward me, dragging him up so my lips could close around his cock. He tasted amazing, hot and tart and uniquely Ivan, and his cock twitched against my lips as I took him in as deep as I could.

Two cocks inside me. Two broken muses all to myself.

I can't believe I'm doing this.
It feels so good.
So right.

Dorien's finger plunged between my legs, rubbing my clit as he slammed into me, pushing Ivan deeper. I moaned around Ivan's cock, and that might've been too much for him. He fisted a handful of my hair in his hand, his eyes never leaving my face as his jaw clenched. For the briefest moment, as he surrendered to his primal self, that tightly wound control slipped from his eyes, and I glimpsed the *real* Ivan. The proud and kind and scared guy who would do anything to protect the people he loved.

Ivan's body jerked. Hot, salty cum hit the back of my throat at the same time Dorien thrust deeper than ever and his finger slammed into my clit, and a second orgasm exploded through me.

My whole body came alive, my veins humming with the same magic I felt when I played music, only amplified times a million. The melody of our bodies meeting conjured a rush of sensory detail – the smell of my mother's home-cooked food, the taste of peanut-butter oreo doughnuts melting on my tongue, the ache in my shoulder after playing a difficult concerto, the swell in my chest whenever Mom told me she was proud of me. All of those bright moments and perfect details converged inside me in a single moment of rapture.

I saw stars and galaxies and the birth and death of the universe on the insides of my eyelids. I screamed as I came, my voice echoing through the cavernous room.

It was too much for Dorien. His body tensed, his muscles tightening. He fell over the edge with me, coming with a grunt before collapsing against me, skin on sweaty skin. His cock slid out.

Dorien pushed his hair out of his eyes. The gaze that met mine burned with something I'd never seen on him before –

contentment. "Well, well, Sprite. You certainly played all the right notes."

I laughed as I sat up, tossing tangled hair over my shoulder, and reached for the whisky bottle and took a long swig. I sought Ivan's icicle eyes and gave him a flirty wink. "Drink up, boys. We've got all night."

47

FAYE

Why is my brain on fire?

I rolled over, arms flailing, trying to pat out the flames engulfing my skull. But there were none. The searing pain came from inside. I tried to open one shaky eye to gaze upon the world, but at the sight of the bright light streaming through my open window, my eye rebelled and slammed shut again.

I'm in a hell of my own making.

Shaky memories flickered through the pain. Me, grabbing a whisky bottle from Dorien, giddily ballroom dancing with Ivan while Dorien thumped out a waltz on the piano, breaking onto the second-floor balcony to howl at the moon, running naked across the overgrown lawn to jump into the freezing mountain stream at the bottom of the garden, sitting on Dorien's shoulders while we drunkenly tried to untangle my torn panties from the chandelier, more whisky... so much whisky...

Oh shit.

I bolted upright, gasping for breath as the memories solidified into a disturbing, terrifying, and *very* naked picture.

What have I done?

I slept with two guys. *Two guys.*

Two guys who had bullied me ever since I arrived at Manderley.

They fucked me on the bench. And then... and then Ivan on the chaise lounge, and Dorien bending me over the piano keys, and again beside the stream...

My cheeks burned.

I had... a threesome. Like I was a porn star or one of their groupies instead of the dowdy and not-at-all-sexually-deviant Faye de Winter.

I mean, wasn't there supposed to be a step between losing your virginity and group sex? The first and only time I had sex was with a guy named Henry at music camp in southern Maine. I may have been a geek with no friends at school, but music camp was where geeks like me went to get laid. Stick a hundred ostracized teenagers in dorms together with minimal supervision, and you've got one long sex party.

Henry Oxshott traveled to camp every year from his British boarding school, and we always hung out together. He wore wool sweaters and had an adorable accent and a face full of zits. We bonded over our shared love of Mexican food and absent fathers. Two summers ago, we decided it was time. Neither of us knew what to do, but Henry held me and whispered sweet things into my hair and it was nice, if not underwhelming. I came back from camp feeling older and wiser. I told my mom what had happened and that I didn't get what all the fuss was about.

Now I got it.

Sound the fucktrumpets. Dorien Valencourt gave me my first orgasm, and Ivan Nicolescu could make me come practically just by whispering evil things in my ear.

I wanted many, many more.

All the orgasms for me.

Only, not now. I moaned, clutching my head in some vain attempt to stop my brain leaking out my eyeballs. *Now I wanted to die.*

Fuck, why did I drink so much Scotch?

Beside the bed, my phone beeped, reminding me it was time to get up and start my chores. After a few blind tries, my fingers circled the phone. My whole body screamed as I dragged my arm back and tossed it at the wall. *CRASH. THUMP.* It clattered to the floor. That seemed to shut it up.

Beside me, something moaned.

Fucking ghost.

Wait, hold the poltergeist. My brain fog parted just long enough for a sliver of fear to slice through my skull. *Seriously, what is that noise?*

The ghost moaned again. I sat up, fumbling for the lamp, my heart hammering so fast it churned up the bile in my delicate stomach. As I struggled to open my eyes, something moved in the bed beside me.

"Morning, Sprite," the ghost murmured from beneath the sheets.

"Fuck!" I leaped from the bed, tugging the sheets over my breasts. The ghost rolled over as I revealed it to the light, and Dorien's sleepy face peered up at me with wry amusement. "What are you doing in my bed?"

"You mean she's already forgotten us?" Ivan sat up, his white-blond hair piled on one side of his head.

"Arrrrgh!" I yanked the rest of the sheet off and staggered back until I crashed into the wall. My hand flew to my churning stomach – my weakened disposition couldn't deal with two very hot and *very* naked Muses entangled together in my bed.

I died in my sleep. That's the only logical explanation. I've died and gone to some weird version of heaven. Or hell.

Definitely hell. Because the fact they both look that good after how much whisky we drank is downright sinful.

"I can't deal with this right now." I slumped against the wall, pressing my fingers to my temples. "Why are you here? You have much larger and less crowded beds downstairs."

"The company down there wasn't as good." Ivan yawned. "Besides, you were the one who dragged us up here."

"You wouldn't take no for an answer." That dangerous smirk played across Dorien's face. "You kept yelling that if the ghost of Manderley came for you in the night, you needed some big strong men to sacrifice while you escaped out the window."

"You were quite forceful," Ivan added. "It was hot as fuck."

I moaned again, my cheeks burning with heat. "I thought that was a dream."

"The best kind of dream." Dorien sat up, sliding his legs off the bed. His rumpled curls flopped over his face, and I went weak at the knees… from the hangover or his hotness, I couldn't say. "Hey, so we need to talk. About serious stuff."

"No serious before coffee." I bent down to pick up my jeans from where I'd thrown them on the floor. Big mistake. My stomach did not approve of bending.

Dorien's fingers circled my wrist, and he pulled me into his lap, brushing my hair from my face. His fingers against my skin were like a healing balm. "This thing that we're doing, Sprite, it's not a one-time thing – not if you don't want it to be. You're a Muse girl now. *Our* Muse girl."

I lifted an eyebrow. "Wouldn't Titus have to agree to that?"

"Oh, Titus agrees. He's going to be pissed he wasn't here. He's been wanting to ask you out since the start of the year."

What? "He has not."

"Mmmhmmm. He didn't make a move because he thought I laid claim to you."

I slapped his hand from my cheek. "This isn't the Dark Ages. I make my own decisions, and I'm not some object to fight over."

"I never doubted it." Dorien's hands skimmed my thighs, drawing circles on my back. Even through the haze of my hangover, it felt so good to be touched by him. "That's why we're not fighting. The three of us share everything, so why not share our girl? You don't seem to mind – for a straight-laced music geek, you turn into a lioness in the sack."

Ivan shuffled over, taking my hand and knitting his fingers in mine. "What Dorien is trying to say in his usual dicksome way is that we never wanted to hurt you. We did horrible things because we didn't believe we had a choice."

"You still did them." I pressed my hand to my temple, trying to stop the rush of bad memories from flooding my head, in case they made my brain leak out my ears.

"Yes. And we know we have a ton of groveling to do before you forgive us." Dorien rolled my nipple between his fingers, and I bit my lip to stop the moan from escaping my lips. "How does a morning orgasm sound?"

"Dorien." Ivan frowned, his voice thick with warning.

Reluctantly, Dorien pulled his hand away. The storm crept in the edges of his eyes. "Right. Serious stuff first. You're our Muse girl, Sprite, and we'll protect you. But we've got to keep this secret. We have to continue to bully you."

I stiffened. "Why?"

"Back in the library, I was trying to tell you Madame Usher wants you gone from Manderley. She came to me before you arrived, and said that Master Radcliffe had insisted you become his student, but she felt your background would be too much of a handicap. She mentioned her affair with your father, and how chins would wag in the music community. She said she couldn't go against Master Radcliffe, but made it very clear you needed to be driven away. Since then, I've heard her change the story."

"That's… either she lied to you then, or you're lying to me now." My chest tightened. "Madame told me she kept an eye on my career since I left her school. My invitation came from her, not Master Radcliffe."

"She lied to one of us. That doesn't surprise me. I just don't know what that means."

I squeezed my eyes shut. This was too much to deal with right now. I couldn't process this with hangover brain. "Why did you agree? It can't be because of your family—"

"She holds the sword of Damocles over my head," Dorien growled. "Over all our heads."

"People we care about are in danger if we don't do as she says," Ivan added.

Like Elena, I guessed. But that made no sense. What could Madame Usher possibly do to Elena with Ivan always in her shadow? And what power did she have over Dorien? It had to do with what Dorien told me about his family, but that didn't make sense – beautiful, wild Dorien who never gave a fuck what anyone thought. He wouldn't let Madame own him over that secret.

"Are you going to tell me what she has on you?"

Dorien shook his head. "Greedy girl. You already have our hearts, don't make us give you our secrets, too."

"For now, it's safer for you to live in ignorance." Ivan squeezed my fingers.

"I think – although I can't prove it – that she's behind all the weird things we can't explain. None of us smashed your violin or paid that homeless guy to hurt your mom. But I can't figure out how she did those things, either."

"And there's this, too." I fumbled on the nightstand for the *Grimm's Fairy Tales* book. As Dorien frowned at the inscription, I explained about the night I found it.

"Something is going on in this house. And my bet is it has something to do with that Carl Becker violin you picked up. We're going to figure this out. We will deal with Madame Usher," Dorien vowed. "She expects us to follow her like little lambs to the slaughterhouse. She has secrets of her own, and we'll bury her with them. But if we have any hope of figuring out what's going on at Manderley, then Madame Usher needs to believe things are normal. That means, we hate each other and we're trying to force you to quit. Plus, it might be the best way to contend with Heather."

"Heather?"

"Turns out I did my job a little too well." Dorien leaned forward and tasted my lips with his tongue. "She hates you with the fire of a thousand suns – the trailer trash who's captured Master Radcliffe's attention and my heart. Punching her nose didn't help, either. Heather's got some nasty plans for you."

"Plans she intended to carry out with her future fiancé, before he dumped her," Ivan added.

"I didn't dump her," Dorien shot back. "It's impossible to dump someone when you were only together in their imagination."

"Am I in danger?" I whispered.

"Heather will be the one in danger if she touches you." Dorien tipped my chin up with his finger. His ragged breath sent heat coursing through my veins. "What do you say, Sprite? Let us pretend to hate you in front of Usher, and we'll keep blowing your mind in private. You're stronger than anyone I know. You can handle a few harsh words and stupid pranks."

"Mmmm." His lips met mine, and I lost myself in the kiss. Ivan's hands crept over my naked skin, his mouth trailing featherlight kisses along my neck, raising the hairs on my skin. I sank back onto the bed as the two of them pressed themselves against me, lips and hands roaming freely, exploring every hidden place inside me.

Through the haze of hungover orgasm, my mind whirred with everything Dorien and Ivan told me. Was Madame Usher really going to such lengths to get rid of me?

And, most importantly, have I seriously just agreed to let the Muses continue to torture me?

48

FAYE

By the time the others returned, I'd managed to kick the guys out of my room, put on my black dress, and guzzle a million gallons of coffee. Dorien and Ivan (who both barely seemed to feel the effects of last night's whisky, the dickweasels) helped me clean the mess we made in the ballroom, then disappeared to get some practice in while I continued with my chores. I was struggling my way through polishing the banister on the grand staircase and trying not to think about Clare's body lying at the bottom when Elena, Heather, and Aroha burst through the door, all smiles and laughter. At the back of the group, Titus looked up at me, his dark eyes burning with questions.

Dorien's words echoed in my head. *He's been wanting to ask you out since the start of the year. He didn't make a move because he thought I laid claim to you.*

Titus' lips turned up in a smile that twinkled with promise. I dropped to my knees, pretending to polish between the railings when really my legs wouldn't support my weight anymore.

Madame Usher bustled in last, frowning as she saw me on the stairs. "Have you prepared lunch for us?"

"Not yet. I wasn't certain what time you'd return—"

She huffed. "Hurry and set it out."

I dashed back to the kitchen and nearly threw up in the sink. I managed to pull myself together and find a selection of cold cuts and leftovers to lay out. All through the meal, I kept sneaking glances at the Muses. True to their word, they continued to ignore me. Dorien even whispered 'wide load' under his breath as I took my seat, and Heather giggled. The comment stung until I caught the storm in his eyes – part regret, part promise of how he'd make things up to me when we were alone. I was surprised the electricity crackling between us didn't set the table linen on fire.

After lunch, I took my violin to the Red Room to practice. Just as I played the final movement of my version of "Confessions of an Opium Eater," Elena slipped into the room. She took a seat in the darkest corner, pulling her legs to her chest and hiding behind a curtain of hair. I was practicing the Paganini again, and I had to keep going over the same tricky passage to make my fingers bend in an impossible way. It had to be tedious to watch and yet, she stayed almost to the end, slipping out just before I'd finished.

Weird.

I climbed the stairs two at a time, my stomach wrapped up in knots, hoping to pass one of the guys on the landing and yet dreading the encounter. Already it felt as though last night had been a dream. Had Dorien and Ivan really said all those things to me, about protecting me? About me being a 'Muse girl'? Or was this just some elaborate ruse so they could keep playing games with me?

I didn't meet anyone on the stairs. I dropped my violin in my room and lay down on my bed for an hour, staring at the ceiling and trying to slip into sleep. My ruined mind and pounding temples refused to cooperate.

I glanced at my watch. Time to head back downstairs to start dinner. I popped a couple of ibuprofen, ran a brush through my tangled hair, and splashed cold water on my face. *Hangovers suck.* The last thing I wanted to do was face cooking right now.

As I trudged back down the servants' staircase, a familiar song wafted through the house – another Broken Muse favorite, called 'Graveyard Shift.' *The guys must be practicing in the Red Room.* I paused, resting my back against the wall, letting that dark, seductive music fill me.

No matter what happened next, I would always have my memories of last night. Nothing could take that away from me.

I hummed the melody under my breath as I went straight to the pantry. I opened the chest freezer to inspect my options. Maybe a fried chicken salad? Or I could use that New Zealand lamb leg and—

Hands wrapped around me, pinning my arms around my back. I cried out, trying to twist my head to see who it was. The cool steel of a knife pressed against my throat.

49

FAYE

I let out a yelp of surprise. The lamb leg I was holding dropped from my hands and thumped on the floor.

"Quiet, trash bitch," Heather rasped in my ear. "Make another sound and I'll cut you. Don't think I won't."

Shit. *Shit.* My blood froze. All the self-defense moves I learned in a YMCA class with Mom flew from my head. All I could focus on was the blade kissing my skin and Heather's hot breath in my ear. *She's holding a knife. Blow the asswhistle, this is bad.*

"Hold her tight," Heather barked. Someone grabbed my hands, twisting them backward at an angle arms aren't supposed to twist. I yelped as my body jerked forward in protest, pressing me against the knife. Panic rose inside me as I struggled against the grip, trying not to slit my own throat.

"I'm trying." Aroha's voice reached my ears, and my panic ratcheted up a notch. Two against one, and they had me cornered in the pantry, where no one would hear me even if I did cry out. *The guys are in the practice room.*

I was on my own.

"Move!" Heather shoved me toward the door. The knife bit into my skin. I hated the whimper that rose from my lips. My legs wobbled and the blood rushed in my ears, but I somehow managed to shuffle into the hallway.

Heather and Aroha shoved me across the kitchen, pressing my stomach against the edge of the stove. Warmth from the wood burner seeped through my clothing, stoking my rising panic. "You've been forgetting your place," Heather hissed as she leaned her weight into my body, jamming me in tight. "Swanning about the house like you're the mistress of the Manor, trying to take what isn't yours. It's time you remembered your place, *servant*. Aroha, get the gas."

Heather dropped the knife and grabbed my wrist, wrenching my arm out from behind me. I was so relieved to have the blade away from my throat that I didn't realize what she planned until it was too late. Aroha twisted the knobs until a ring of fire circled the burner. I tried to wrench my arm back, but I was at the wrong angle. Pain radiated along my arm as I fought for control, but Heather had the advantage – she snarled with triumph as she shoved my hand toward the flames.

"Let's see you impress Master Radcliffe with a burned hand," she rasped.

As the heat kissed my fingers, the bubbling panic exploded inside me. I swore and cursed and bucked and thrashed, but I was one and they were two, and Heather was used to getting her way.

"No, please."

No.

My whole world shrunk to those orange flames looming closer and closer—

Aroha wrapped her arms around my shoulder to pin me in place. I slammed my foot down, grinding the heel of my boot into a soft sneaker. Heather yelped, and I gained back a couple of inches before Aroha forced my shoulder down. Heather dug her nails into my wrist, biting deep. The flame licked the tip of my pinkie and I screamed.

No no no no no, not my hand, please, no—

"Take your punishment, trash whore," Heather rasped, her voice reaching through my panic. "He'll never want you after this—"

Her words broke off into a scream as something slammed into her from behind. I yanked my hand back just as Aroha lunged in a last-ditch effort to shove me into the stove.

I ducked under her blow and whirled around. Ivan locked Aroha against him, her arms pinned. Titus held Heather by her blonde ponytail.

"Touch her again and I'll burn you." Titus held Heather's head an inch from his face, and his features twisted with barely-concealed rage.

"Oh, will you?" she shot back in a singsong voice, even as she clawed at his hand in a frantic attempt to free herself. "It seems to me that the three of you have forgotten why you're at Manderley."

Aroha looked from Heather to Titus in confusion. "What's she talking about?"

"None of your business, junkie." Titus yanked Heather's hair, dangling her feet off the ground. Heather's smugness turned into screeches. I reached over with shaking hands and turned off the stove.

"Let me go!"

"As you wish." Titus opened his hand. Heather collapsed in a heap on the wooden floor, clutching her skull and howling with pain.

"It's not just Dorien's who's under the harpy's spell. It's all of you," Heather cackled, her eyes wide with agony as she dragged herself to the door. "You're all fucking her trash pussy. Madame Usher will love to hear this."

Ivan dropped Aroha and shoved her toward the door. She glanced back over her shoulder at me. "I didn't mean—"

"Get out," Titus growled, his deep voice like a rumble from the heavens. Aroha ran for it.

Titus was on me in a moment, sweeping me into those enormous arms of his. Being held by him was like hiding in the trunk of a tree, or getting a hug from a grizzly bear. I felt as though I had this force of nature larger than myself who was looking after me. Titus pressed my head into his shoulder, his giant fingers tangling in my hair. I breathed deep his luscious scent – musk and myrrh, with the slightest hint of English rose garden – and it was like coming home to somewhere I'd never been before but instantly felt at peace. The trembling in my limbs faded, although the fear of what they'd almost done bit into my skin.

Ivan took my hand, turning it over, running his fingers over mine. "They didn't burn you? Have they hurt you?"

I shook my head. The relief washed over me, and tears flooded my eyes, spilling down my cheeks. I collapsed against Titus again and Ivan wrapped his arms around us both, pressing his chest into my back until I was cocooned in their warmth.

"How did you—hic—know to find me?"

"Elena heard Heather and Aroha sneak off to the kitchen," Ivan said. "She barged into our practice to tell us, and we ran straight here."

"Dorien's waiting in the hall for them," Titus added. "He'll make sure they don't run to Madame Usher."

From the doorway, a worried face peeked in. *Elena.* I gave her a weak smile as I drew back from Titus. "Thank you."

Her eyes widened, and she darted off.

I collapsed against Titus' chest again, relishing the warmth of both their arms around me. "The two of you popped up like guardian ghosts." A panicked giggle bubbled up from my throat.

Like ghosts.

I never thought I'd be so grateful for the Muses haunting me.

"They will never touch you again," Titus whispered, holding my head against his chest. "We'll make sure of it."

I sagged into him, and I thought about the Titus I'd seen hiding his true self in a tiny, damp shack on the edge of the wilderness. If he couldn't protect his own heart, how would he protect me?

So many secrets crowded the halls of Manderley, stacked one atop the other like a house of cards. One wrong move, one anxious breath, and the entire house would fall. I'd seen the hated flare in Heather's eyes – what lengths would she go to get what she wanted? She was ready to burn this bitch down, and me with it.

50

FAYE

I clung to Titus and Ivan as long as I dared. Dorien appeared at the doorway, his eyes raging. "Madame Usher wants to see both of you. She won't wait."

"We're busy," Titus glared at his friend. "What's it about?"

Dorien shook his head. "We all have to keep our secrets, remember?"

Titus pulled away, staring down at me with those dark eyes. "You will be okay on your own?"

I nodded. As if I had a choice.

Reluctantly, Titus drew away from me. He raised one of his huge hands to ruffle Ivan's hair. "Let's go see what the witch wants now."

~

A fter a tense dinner where no one said a word and all three Muses deliberately avoided meeting my eyes, I retreated to the kitchen to stack the dishwasher. As I made up a batch of pancake batter to sit in the fridge for the morning, my neck prickled with the sensation of being watched.

I grabbed the knife I kept on the counter beside me and whirled to face the door. Ivan leaned against the frame, his icy eyes flicking to the weapon. "I didn't mean to frighten you."

"Then you probably shouldn't lurk in doorways and sneak up on people," I shot back.

"That is fair." Mmmm, that Romanian accent did things to my insides. Ivan stepped forward and held out his hand. "It's a lovely night. Madame Usher has retired for the evening, and the others are in the Blue Room playing cards and drinking. Will you walk with me?"

It was on the tip of my tongue to say no, but his crystal eyes begged. I couldn't resolve Ivan's cool facade with his possessive adoration of his sister, or the cocaine-addicted junkie the evidence of his room suggested. Curiosity got the better of me. I nodded.

I followed Ivan out into the kitchen garden. He held the gate open for me. I sucked in a breath as the frigid air pummeled my skin. I should have thought to bring a coat.

Ivan was already shrugging off his leather jacket and holding it out to me. "You want it?"

"Let me guess, it's filled with bugs?" I cocked my head to the side. "No, wait, I put it on and some sensor inside electrocutes me?"

"Suit yourself." Ivan started to tug the sleeve back on, but I snatched it from his hands and pulled it over my shoulders. If I had to be out here with a Muse, I wasn't going to freeze my tits off.

Ivan's lip curled back in what might have been the start of a smile. "Looks good on you."

"Damn right." I twisted around to admire it. "Don't expect to get it back."

We wandered past the gazebo. In the moonlight, it took on a sinister air. I dared to look back at the house – the gables pierced the cloudless sky, teeth of a demon taking a bite from Heaven.

For some reason it made me think of my mother, all alone miles away in the hospital. My skin prickled from invisible eyes watching me. I shuddered and turned back to Ivan.

I'd been dying to get this guy alone, to peel back the layers of those icicle eyes, but now that it was just the two of us, I struggled to find something to say.

"Did you…" I tried again. "Is… I mean… sorry." I laughed, and then felt stupid. "I don't know what to say to my bully-turned-booty-call."

Ivan laughed. The sound was so rare, so unexpected, it caught me off guard. "Please, don't apologize. I thought you might want to talk about the cocaine."

The cocaine. That was right. I hadn't even stopped to consider the fact I was getting involved with someone who might not just be on drugs but dealing them.

"The drugs didn't belong to me. They're Aroha's. We all want to help her quit, and I was hiding them from her. It turns out to be pointless, as she's simply found another supplier." Ivan sighed. "I know you put that cocaine in my violin case. I wanted to say I understood why you did it."

"I did it because you went into my bedroom after I changed the lock. You've been trying to convince me there's a ghost."

"And if I told you I never set foot in your room until last night, would you believe me?"

I started at that. He sounded so earnest, but I knew how to math. That couldn't be true. "There's no one else it could have been, unless there's a secret passage between my room and some other place in the house, like the storage room."

"I have no key to the storage room. Madame Usher has never allowed any of us in there. She cites something called Health and Safety."

Mmmmm. Why did I never know I had a thing for Eastern European accents?

"But this is interesting." Ivan stared straight ahead. "A secret passage. We should all look for one."

"So if it wasn't you, who's been playing music through the wall and stomping around upstairs and turning my bedroom light on and off?"

Ivan raised an eyebrow in an expression that was far too much like Dorien. "Mice?"

I whacked him on the shoulder.

By now we had reached the poison garden. Whereas the path had been bright with forest noises – owls hooting, rodents skittering in the dirt, insects chirping – nothing stirred in this clearing at all. It was as if everything living knew to give the greenhouse a wide berth. Ivan stared straight ahead. "Did you know that Madame Usher is still my guardian?"

"That… doesn't make any sense." Why would he need a guardian? He was in his early twenties.

"I told you Elena and I did not grow up with money, but our house was filled with music. Our father played all kinds of instruments, mostly the fiddle – he would play Romanian folk songs for the tourists who visited our village every summer. We inherited our talents from him. I was always good, but Elena… she was touched by the gifts of the *zâne*."

"*Zâne?*"

"This is like a fairy godmother in Romanian stories. The *zâne* live in the woods and mountains, and they visit pregnant women to bestow their unborn children with the gifts of dancing, music, beauty, or luck. My mother believed she was visited by one of these sprites, and it is true that when Elena touches the keys, people sit up and listen. She conjures magic with her music."

"I know." I smiled, thinking of the first time I heard Elena play.

"My father never brought in much money, and what he did he spent on drink and cigarettes. That is why my mother worked several jobs and did laundry and scrimped and saved. She managed to purchase a house in our town with a spare room to rent to guests. Our government had announced plans to build a Dracula theme park near our home, and everyone was buying up property to cash in on the influx of tourists when the park opened."

"I remember reading about that theme park." I loved anything Dracula. It was the horror movie fan in me. Mom and I talked about going when it was finished. "Didn't it get canceled?"

Ivan nodded. "People complained. They said it was tacky and that it would be built on the ashes of an ancient oak forest. Historians noted that while our hero Vlad Tepes was born in my city, it had no link to the Dracula of fiction, and many Romanians do not like the confusion between the two. Prince Charles of Great Britain got involved, and the government decided it would not happen. But that left many of our people without hope for a brighter future from tourism, including my parents, who owed the bank a lot of money for this room they could not fill."

It was wonderful to hear Ivan talk. I nodded for him to continue.

"We had no choice – Elena and I had to work. My father pulled us from school and took us to Bucharest – more tourists equals more money. We stood on a corner by the Parliament Buildings and played for six hours a day. I noticed a woman who sat across the square, watching us. The same woman, day after day, wrapped in a fur even under the fierce sun. One day, my father came to collect us, and she approached him with her husband. She said she had a music school in the United States and that she would offer him a yearly payment if she could be allowed to take us with her and manage our career. She is like our manager. She pays my father the same paltry sum every year while she makes tens of thousands from our shows and recordings. We have toured Europe and Asia many times, yet we have not a dime to our names."

"I don't believe it."

"She says she has placed money in trust for us, but we cannot access it until we are twenty-five years old. That is two years away. Until then, she owns us. The only thing she cannot control is Broken Muse, and even then she exerts her influence in other ways. You may think you are the charity case at this school, but you are not the only one. I wanted you to know because... because it might be dangerous to be with me, and you should consider that before you choose to be with me."

Ivan shoved his hands deep in the pockets of his trousers, his face turned away from me, toward the moon. He looked kind of wiped out by speaking so much.

We stopped in front of the greenhouse. Ivan wrapped an arm around my shoulder and pulled me close. I stared up at the vines escaping from the broken glass, at the bulbous shapes that twisted in on themselves and bulged against the sides of the house. The moonlight hit a ball of plants and for a moment I saw a face – pale skin with violent eyes and a mouth that was a hole of darkness – but then I blinked, and it was gone. *Just a trick of the moonlight.*

A shiver ran through me as I thought again of my mother and the doctors working to rid her system of the poison.

"Why are we here?" I breathed.

In reply, Ivan turned to me. He reached up, his fingers brushing my cheek as he tucked a strand of my hair behind my ear. The world hung between us, suspended in a moment where everything was perfect.

"I wanted to be alone with you. I wanted to know that what I feel between us is more than just unfinished business between you and Dorien."

Those words ached with longing, with a desperate need that twisted in my heart. As Ivan's lips grazed mine, I let the bad thoughts go, releasing them into the crisp air. The mountains tore them from me as Ivan wrapped me in his warmth. Far from being ice, his kiss was sweet and light and breathtakingly beautiful.

A rustling in the trees startled me from my reverie. My eyes fluttered open. I caught movement behind Ivan's shoulder, and my breath hitched as I remembered that face I'd seen. I pulled back as Aroha stepped out of the shadows, a cigarette dangling from her lips.

"Just coming for a smoke," she sneered, patting her pockets for a lighter. I stiffened as she approached. I thought we were… not friends, exactly, but we had an understanding. That was before she tried to burn my hand.

Ivan narrowed his eyes. "Don't come near Faye again."

Aroha laughed, tossing her hair over her shoulder. She stepped into the shadow of the greenhouse and cupped her hand around her cigarette as she tried to light her smoke. "You think you have power here, Ivan?"

"I do not care what she does to me." Ivan's hands balled into fists, and he stepped toward Aroha. I grabbed his arm, and my touch seemed to steady him. Because I knew he spoke the truth – he didn't care about himself. But Madame Usher knew that – if he stepped out of line, she would go after Elena.

If she isn't already.

"Whatever." Aroha finally got her smoke to light. She took a long drag, tossing her head back. "It's nothing personal, Faye. I gotta survive here just like you, and sometimes that means aligning with a bitch like Heather. Little word of warning – I'd stay away from her. She's not done with you yet."

51

FAYE

"Students, we have a very special event to mark the end of the term."

My fork poised halfway to my mouth. I knew by now that Madame Usher saw her 'special events' as new ways to torment me. I didn't dare glance at any of the Muses – I was sure something in my face would give away the things we'd been doing together in secret.

"Is it another visit from one of your friends in Europe?" Heather asked, her voice high with excitement.

"It's even better." I watched through lowered lashes as Madame Usher passed a gold-lined envelope to Dorien. He flipped open the flap and drew out a fancy-looking invitation, his. "Harrison has left for the city to post a hundred of these invitations to my most influential friends in the business, including all your parents. We're to host a little party here at Manderley."

Dorien's fingers slipped, and the paper dropped into his soup. Madame Usher didn't seem to notice.

"I'm pleased with the progress you've made this year, and I want to show you all off. There will be many important people – conductors, producers, patrons, journalists – for you to impress.

Master Radcliffe, perhaps you could make suggestions for the program."

"Certainly." The Master beamed at each of his students in turn, seemingly unaware of the tension crackling around the table. "Heather and Elena, you'll each perform sonatas. Elena and Ivan should tackle the Liszt piece they've been working on. Dorien and Faye, I'd like you to perform the composition Faye has written. Titus, Aroha, Faye, and Elena will delight with some Beethoven, and then we will finish with the world premiere of my newest concerto." His shoulders squared with pride. "I have the sheet music ready. You shall start learning it today."

Heather dominated the conversation about the party, gushing over the Master's choices. Madame Usher offered Aroha a grant from her husband's endowment fund to pay for her parents' flights from New Zealand. I noticed no mention was made of doing the same for Elena and Ivan.

I escaped as fast as I could to the safety of the deserted Red Room. It wasn't safe for long. Elena let herself into my private practice, choosing the seat by the window again. There was no trace of the broken girl hiding in the shadows this time. She smiled as I played through my parts of Radcliffe's concerto until I was certain I had them perfect.

I set down my violin. "Why are you here? Did Madame Usher or Heather send you?"

Elena opened her mouth, as if to speak, then snapped her it shut. Instead, she shook her head.

I advanced, hands on hips, looming over her. "Then why?"

Elena's eyes widened with fright as she stared up at me. No, not at me. *Behind me.* I whirled around.

The door hung open. Elena must've forgotten to lock it after she came in. Ivan stood in the frame, his expression stony.

"Elena." He gestured to her and barked something in Romanian. She shook her head. He repeated the command.

"You are not the boss of me," she announced in a haughty

voice, rising to her feet. She floated across the room to face him, and I was reminded of what he told me in the garden, about their mother being visited by the fairies.

Elena stuck her tongue out at her brother and slammed the door in his face.

"Please, play the concerto again," she said, folding her hands into her lap and settling back with a contented look on her pixieish face.

~

Elena wasn't the only one acting odd. Ever since Master Radcliffe told us we'd be playing together at the recital, Dorien made excuses not to practice with me. Finally, I cornered him. "I know you don't give a fuck what your parents think of you, but I need this to go well. If you're not willing to play with me, I will perform on my own."

I didn't have the power to make those decisions, and we both knew it, but Dorien's shoulders sagged. He flashed me a smile tinged with sadness at the edges, the kind of smile that could shatter a girl's heart from a million paces. "I'll behave, Sprite. I promise."

As we played through the piece, I could tell his head was a million miles away. His fingering lacked its usual aplomb, and the result was wooden, devoid of the emotion I desperately needed to convey in the piece.

I scratched the bow across the strings, creating an almighty screech that echoed through the room. Dorien jumped, his fingers tumbling over the keys.

"Fuck." He pounded the lid of the piano.

"That got your attention." I glared at him. "I told you not to fuck this up for me. Yet, here you are, fucking it up."

"I know." Dorien rested his head in his hands. "It's my parents. I've played for sold-out crowds in some of the greatest concert halls in Europe and Asia without breaking a sweat, but the thought of playing in front of them with *you*…"

"Just tell me what's got you twisted up so you can cry about it and get over it. They probably won't even recognize me from all those years ago."

Dorien shook his head. "They'll remember you. They remember everything. And they will want to know why I'm playing with you and not Heather. Fuck." He slammed his fist on the lid again. The tension in his shoulders could launch an arrow into space.

"Maybe they won't come?" I tried. "If they're as into this cult thing as you say, then maybe they're not allowed out to enjoy a recital?"

"They'll come. Madame Usher will make sure of that." Dorien's eyes glinted. "I can't hide you from them, and Heather won't let me *pretend* to be her girlfriend. She demands the real deal. They've painted us into a corner, and they know it."

"I wish you'd tell me instead of talking in riddles. I can help, you know. I'm quite clever."

"You are." Dorien lifted my fingers to his lips and laid a searing kiss on my knuckles. "But right now, the truth is dangerous to you. Unless I can find a way to convince them… *yes.*" A spark of brightness shone through the storms in his eyes. "I think I have a way this could work out, for all of us."

52

FAYE

The whole house buzzed with excitement about the recital. Aroha danced around singing traditional Maori songs when she heard her parents would fly over. Heather seemed to have declared a truce with me and the Muses – or at least, she was too busy focused on improving her playing to put any effort into her torture attempts.

Elena slipped into my practice room again.

"You play beautifully," she whispered after I finished my as-yet-unnamed composition.

I snorted. "Sure. When people aren't hiding my instrument or ruining my performances."

Elena nodded but didn't offer up any kind of apology or explanation. People like her never had to do that.

"Do you want something?" I snapped the words, trying to show her that I wouldn't be intimidated by her beauty like others.

Elena winced. "I can accompany you. Would that be okay?"

The words 'Go to hell' danced on the end of my tongue. For a moment, I relished the satisfaction of denying Perfect Elena something, of seeing her face when she realized the whole world didn't automatically bend over backward to her whims.

But she was the one who warned the Muses about Heather's attack. I was so desperate for someone, *anyone,* to talk to. Not even a friend – just someone friend-adjacent. This was the first time since I'd bummed smokes from Aroha that someone at Manderley had reached out. Dorien and the Muses didn't count because I couldn't tell what was going on in their fucked-up heads.

I shrugged. "Yeah, sure."

Elena walked over to the piano and opened the lid, raising her hands to the keys with soft wrists, like a witch conjuring a spell. Without asking me what I wanted to play, she launched into Beethoven's *Violin Sonata No. 9* – a piece I loved for its raw beauty and that richness of musical color Beethoven gave to all his music.

She slowed the tempo from what I was used to, giving the opening an even more melancholy air. When she reached the lightning-fast *Presto,* her fingers danced along the keys with impossible lightness, like a butterfly flitting between flowers. I tried to match her deft, light style, but it was tough just keeping pace with her.

Halfway through, as the sweat pooled on my brow and my fingers nearly slipped from the strings during a particularly diffi-cult bar, I realized this was a test. A kind of Manderley initiation. But something else occurred to me that made a smile play on my face.

I'm playing with Elena Nicolescu. The Elena Nicolescu, daughter of the Romanian fairies, who will one day become the greatest Classical musician of our age. Life goal, realized.

As we played, I snuck glances at her, admiring the way her graceful neck drew up as she threw her whole body into the performance, the placement of her fingers on the keys, every movement perfection. Elena *lived* the music in a way that awed and slightly terrified me.

We reached the final movement – a crushing A major chord on the piano, and then we soared together, ending on a jubilant flourish of contrast and light. I threw down my bow in triumph. Elena's hands slid from the keys. I beamed at her. A faint smile tugged at the corner of her lips, its momentum broken by the tears streaming down her face.

"Elena, are you okay?" I slid onto the end of the bench. There was something about her – that innocence, those pixie eyes, that made me instantly want to care for her.

She shook her head, dabbing at the corners of her eyes with her fingers. "I'm sorry. I don't know what came over me. I—"

"If you want to talk about something, I'm listening." I glanced toward the door, wondering about the significance of the lock. She always locked the door when she came to watch me. Was it to keep someone out? Her brother, perhaps?

I remembered their harsh conversation on the steps. *Is something going on between them?*

Elena sniffed. She must have sensed my inquiry, because she said, "Ivan likes you very much. I can see why."

"Is that why you've been coming to see me?"

She nodded. "He has never shown interest in another girl. Not ever. I wanted to make sure you were good enough for him. But now I'm wondering if he is good enough for you."

A knock sounded at the door. "Elena?" It was Master Radcliffe. "Are you in there? I wish you to go over the Brahms again."

Graceful as a cat, Elena rose. She wiped her face on the hem of her sundress, and when she lowered the cloth, her expression was blank, serene. I recognized it for what it was – a mask.

We all wore masks at Manderley. It seemed the only time we stripped ourselves bare was when we played. Elena didn't need to tell me what was wrong, because she'd just played her sorrow for me to hear.

"I must go," Elena whispered. She swept from the room as gracefully as she did everything else, but there was a fragility to her movement that betrayed her terror.

What is she so afraid of?

53

FAYE

After that, Elena started coming to more of my practices. We played together – Beethoven, Brahms, and a Romanian composer she loved named George Enescu. At mealtimes, she saved the seat next to her at the table, even going so far as to ask Heather to move over for me. Heather's face could have boiled an egg, but she moved. I found that interesting.

Elena rarely spoke to me, but each gesture spoke of a desire to break the silence Dorien had imposed. I wondered if he'd made some official lifting of his ban on interacting with me, or if everyone had sensed the shift in dynamics between us.

I knew better than to hope this was the start of a friendship, but I hoped anyway. Loneliness has a way of seeping into your bones.

Two days before the parental recital, Elena swept into our practice room (how quickly I'd started thinking of it as ours, even going so far as to write both our names down on the reservations board). Her cheeks flushed with happiness and she practically glided to the piano. I didn't think I'd ever seen her so happy.

"You must come with us next Saturday," she announced.

The weekend after the party, Dorien, Elena, and Ivan were

booked to play a recital in New York City. They didn't want to drive back to Manderley in the dark, so they'd obtained special permission to stay over in a hotel. It sounded like an excuse to party to me, and I'd secretly been seething with jealousy about it, but I never imagined I'd be able to go.

I shook my head. "I have to clean the rehearsal rooms top to bottom. It's easier while you're all away as there will be fewer people using them. Besides, even if I wanted to, Madame Usher would never let me go."

"She will listen to me." Elena took my hand. I could practically feel her excitement sizzling through her veins. "I have already called ahead, requested you be added to the billing. We shall perform our Beethoven together. And I've booked us a suite. Please, say you'll come. I am tired of doing everything with Ivan. I want to have some girl time."

Aside from the fact that a night away from Manderley with my three Muses meant all kinds of delicious possibilities, no way could I say no to Elena. It would be like kicking a puppy.

Besides… I rubbed my bloodshot eyes. Another sleepless night listening to snatches of that music filtering from the room next door made me dream of a decent night's sleep in a non-haunted bed. If this was a horror film, Freddy Kreuger would have sucked me into the dream world by now.

Maybe I am *in a dream world – that would explain why three muses want to share me.*

The rest of the week sailed by in a blur. I was so excited for the recital that even cleaning the bathrooms and serving food to spoiled rich kids didn't seem so bad. Dr. Nelson called to say the preliminary tests on Mom had been extremely promising, and they were stepping up the treatment. I'd know in a few days if she'd be able to come off life support.

So what if Heather looked at me like I was a bug? So what if that obnoxious midnight concerto kept me awake? During my weekly hospital visit, I gushed about Elena to Mom (I decided to leave out all the naughty stuff about the guys. I wasn't sure she'd want to hear that). I even played her the second movement of our Beethoven. Dr. Nelson and some of the nurses came in to listen, and they clapped and cheered. I was too happy to tell them that people weren't supposed to applaud for classical music.

I crawled into bed the night before the party, my stomach churning with excitement. I knew from the square of bright light from the full moon and the buzzing in my veins that I'd struggle to sleep.

Sure enough, I wriggled down into the sheets and willed my mind to shut off. I counted Beethoven jumping over sheep. I pictured calm waves brushing against a white-sand beach. I touched myself and thought of the guys. But still, my mind reached toward the storage room, listening for signs of life.

After midnight, the footsteps paced across the floorboards. *Creak, creak, creaaaaak.* I had to hand it to Heather, even when she was pretending to be a specter, she moved with a certain musicality.

Then silence for a time. A long time, long enough for me to start to question myself again. *It's not footsteps – it's just the old house settling.*

I'd just started to drift off to sleep when the creaking started again. The footsteps moved across the storage room, then stopped. I strained to hear a sound, like the scraping of a piece of furniture. Then I didn't hear anything else for a long time except my heart hammering in my ears.

Then, the first mournful note sounded.

I peered at my phone. 3:02AM. Yet someone was playing again. That same haunting tune, over and over. Vaguely familiar, but impossible to place.

I threw the covers off, circling the room and pressing my ear to the walls, trying to figure out where it came from. I opened the door and stood on the landing, straining to listen. No, it wasn't someone practicing downstairs. It was definitely louder inside my room.

It doesn't make any sense. I circled my room again, straining to hear where the sound was loudest. Not in the bathroom. Definitely beside the bureau, and around the clothing rack...

My stomach tightened with fright. I held my ear to the wall. A tremble started in my legs and moved through my whole body.

The music was coming through the wall, from the other side.

From within the locked storage room.

FAYE

The music continued.

I banged on the wall. It didn't stop.

At 4AM, I tossed aside the sheets one final time and slid out of bed. If I wasn't going to sleep, I might as well get up and finish my chores.

As I padded downstairs, using my phone as a flashlight, I strained to hear the violin – but it was as if it stopped dead outside my room. The only time I'd heard it anywhere else in the house was when I stepped inside Madame Usher's private chambers. I didn't know what that meant except that she was probably to blame for it.

Down in the kitchen, I prepared spicy sausage, beans, and scrambled eggs for breakfast burritos. A treat to start our day. As I bent over the dishwasher, emptying last night's dinner dishes, the kitchen door banged open and Titus appeared.

"Nice view." He wiggled his eyebrows in a way that made me burst out laughing.

I straightened up, shoving the tray of burritos in the oven until I needed them. "Why are you up so early?"

"I wanted to get in a little morning practice." He nodded toward the woodshed. "And I heard you on the stairs and I thought you might like some company."

My heart pattered, but this time it wasn't fear. I remembered what Dorien said about Titus wanting to ask me out.

"The others told me what happened when I was gone." His eyes darkened. "I wanted to… I guess I wanted to say that you've obviously got your hands full with the two of them, but if you wanted to add a third guy to your harem, I'm game."

"My… harem?"

"Mmmm." Titus leaned toward me. His fingers trailed along my arm, raising a line of fire that scorched through my veins. He loomed closer, his breath kissing my neck…

…as he grabbed an apple from the bowl behind me, bringing the fruit to his lips and taking a bite. Fuck, how did he make eating an apple look so hot? A shiver ran through my body that had nothing to do with the draft blowing through the window.

I backed away from Titus until my ass pressed against the dishwasher. "It may shock you to know I am not used to this kind of attention from guys. I'm not sure what to *do* with a harem."

"You can do whatever you like with me." Titus was on me in a moment, his bulk hemming me in, blocking any possible exit. I didn't mind. Not in the least. Now it was my turn to trail my fingers over the skin of his arm.

His expressive eyes begged for more. He wasn't going to make a move – he wanted me to be overt with my consent and control. This was his apology, his way of making things right for being in my room. He wanted to hand me back my power.

I took it, fisting my hands into his shirt and dragging him the final inch, until our lips met in a searing kiss.

He tasted fresh and tart from the apple. Beneath it, his distinct scent – the myrrh and musk, the roses dappled with early morning dew – swept me into the sheer force of his being. If Ivan was a dark elf, then Titus was some kind of ancient forest god – dark and chaotic and fiercely protective.

A floorboard creaked, and my eyes darted across the kitchen, nervous about who might walk in and see us. My eyes rested on the herbs on the windowsill above the table, their tendrils spilling over their pots and snaking down the wall. From between the leaves, a pair of vicious green eyes stared out at me from a pale face.

I pulled away, struggling for breath. *Fuck.*

I blinked, and the face was gone.

Titus frowned. "Is everything okay?"

I nodded, willing my heartrate to return to normal. I thought about telling Titus about the face, but it seemed pointless. It was just a trick of the light. Manderley had a way of crawling under my skin, making me believe impossible things. "I don't want us to stop, but if I don't get this baking done—"

Titus nodded, but he didn't release me from his arms.

"Have you ever heard violin music late at night?" I tried to reach around behind him to free myself. "I hear it in my room, but nowhere else in the house. It seems to come from the storage room, except that it's not loud enough to be someone playing in there, and when I go out onto the landing, I can't hear it through the door. Oh, once I heard it in Madame's chambers, too."

Titus' eyes darkened. "I've never heard this music. I have an explanation, but you're not going to like it. Consider who used to occupy your room."

"Who used to—" I folded my arms and glared up at him. "I'm too tired and stressed for riddles. Explain."

"Didn't Dorien tell you? Clare played the violin."

"Clare? You mean, the dead maid?"

Titus nodded. "She was talented. She worked for Madame for peanuts in exchange for free lessons. The only time she could practice was late at night, when we'd all gone to sleep. I know you don't believe in ghosts, but…"

...but why would I hear mysterious music in the dead of the night, music that could only be heard in my room?

It's impossible. It can't be.

Ghosts aren't real.

Are they?

55

DORIEN

I hummed a few bars of 'Confessions of an Opium Eater' under my breath as I buttoned one of my baroque dress shirts, debating whether to go the full Monty with my tailored frock coat. I never felt this cheery about seeing my parents, but for the first time in decades, my heart was light. I had a plan. I could fix it. I could make life better for all of us.

Faye was mine.

Yours and Titus' and Ivan's, I reminded myself. But I didn't mind sharing her for now. If anyone could handle the three of us, it was Faye de Winter. Besides, she would choose me in the end. Faye and I – we were written in the stars.

She'd walked back into my life by complete chance, and I wasn't going to let her go again.

There was a knock at the door. "Come in." I finished tying the knot in my cravat. "I've got—Heather?"

I'd expected to see Faye's gorgeous curves sashaying through the door. Instead, Heather stormed inside, her prissy nose high in the air. She shut the door behind her, threading the bolt into the lock.

"Dorien, we need to talk."

"I've said all I have to say to you." I turned back to the mirror and flicked my hand like I was flicking away an annoying bug, which Heather definitely was. A cockroach. Or a dung beetle.

Heather didn't like that one bit. The false smile dropped from her lips, replaced by a scowl that did nothing for her looks.

"I know your secret," she hissed. "I know all about what's going on at Valencourt Manor. Or should I call it, The Temple of Earthly Truths."

My blood froze in my veins. That was the first time I'd heard that name uttered outside the walls of my home.

There was no use pretending I didn't know what she was talking about. I fixed Heather's reflection with what I hoped was a terrifying look, even as my heart pounded against my chest. "How?"

Heather came up behind me, placing her hands on my shoulders. "It doesn't matter how. What matters is that I have the information. I'm still deciding what to do with it."

"What do you want, Heather?"

"Isn't it obvious? You don't need to be at Manderley, Dorien. You're too talented to be wasting away behind these walls. Master Radcliffe can't teach you anything new. You should be back in the spotlight where you belong. And you should have the right woman by your side."

Heather leaned forward to lick my earlobe. I couldn't stop the shudder that rocketed through my body at her touch. "It's what your parents wanted."

"I don't care. I won't do it."

"You'll do it," she whispered. "Or I'll be reporting your parents to the authorities. And where will that land your brother?"

Shit. Fuck. Shit.

She knows. How can she possibly *know?*

"Leave him alone," I hissed. "He has nothing to do with this."

"Tsk, tsk. All this is your fault. You shouldn't have lost your temper, Dorien. Aggravated assault. Someone with a serious felony conviction can't be appointed as a long-term guardian. Luckily, as a long-term friend to the family with an impeccable record, I'm happy to step up."

"Stay away from him," I growled.

"There's that temper again. Go on, Dorien. Hit me. Add another assault to your record. All you'll be doing is giving me more ammunition. I'll take your brother away from you, and what will you have? That trash whore *Faye* to warm your bed? I hope you've had your shots."

I sat on the windowsill, my head spinning. "You've made your point, Heather. Give me your terms."

"Faye is not playing with you on Saturday. My parents give a lot of money to this school, and they expect certain standards. They won't accept anyone else by your side, especially not a painted heifer. She will step down, and you and I will play together instead."

"You can't play Faye's composition."

"*Please.* Modesty doesn't suit you. There's no way that fat cow could write something like that. It has Dorien Valencourt stamped all over it." She stopped in front of my mirror, turning her body to admire herself. "I should say, Dorien Valencourt and Heather Danvers."

"Faye won't let you get away with this."

"She won't have a choice." Heather's smile could have chilled a penguin. "I intend to make it so that Faye de Winter never sets foot in Manderley again. And you're going to help me. Or *else you'll never see your brother again.*"

56

FAYE

When I went down to the kitchen to finish prep for the party, I noticed several sandwiches and meat-balls missing from one of the platters.

Gah. I've got to remember to tell those boys not to steal food. If they're hungry I can give them something to devour—

Argh. I grinned stupidly at myself. *One night with Dorien and Ivan and even my internal monologue has become filthy.*

I shuffled the meatballs around, but now I had a big gap on the side of one of the platters. I racked my brain for something simple to fill it with. *I saw some crackers at the back of the pantry. If they're not stale, they'd be perfect.*

Humming Beethoven to myself, I went to the pantry and shifted the boxes aside, tossing anything that smelled funky. As I shoved aside a giant box of salt, I noticed something smeared on the wall near the back of the shelf, half-hidden in darkness. I took out my phone and shone the light on the wall.

What I'd thought was a smudge of ketchup or something was words scrawled in whiteboard marker in the same writing that had been on the noticeboard. *Clare's handwriting.*

The words chilled me to the bone.

THE WALLS ARE TALKING.

FAYE

The walls are talking.

What the fuck did that even *mean*?

Clare wrote it there for a reason. She knew that the next maid would find it. No one else would have any reason to go into the back of the pantry.

It was a message for me.

I looked again at the words, and my stomach twisted. I'd been afraid enough times in my life that I could recognize fear. When Clare wrote these words, she felt afraid.

And then she fell down the stairs.

I believed Dorien's story, that he'd already been halfway down the staircase. I didn't believe he killed her. So who was Clare afraid of? Why did she say this?

Could someone else have pushed her?

I scrambled to my feet and snuck out the door under the stairs into the entrance hall. My boots padded on the thick carpet as I ascended to the first floor. From the top of the stairs, I looked both ways down the hall, and my heart sank. There was no vase or piece of ugly antique furniture large enough to hide behind, no conveniently-placed curtain. Madame Usher's apartments were right at the end of the hall. Dorien would have seen someone else standing in the hallway as he went past. There wasn't enough *time* for someone else to reach the top of the stairs and push Clare.

I couldn't see how someone could have pushed Clare, and yet... I felt certain her death wasn't an accident. *So what the hell happened?*

FAYE

I worked all day, scrubbing down the ballroom before the party and thinking about Clare's message. Madame Usher demanded everything be perfect, but obviously, she refused to hire extra help or ask the other students to lift a finger. Titus snuck into the kitchen while I was prepping food and trapped me in the pantry for half an hour, his enormous hands reducing my body to jelly as he kissed me until my lip bled. Ivan winked at me across the classroom and I felt like I was naked. Dorien passed me in the hall with a stack of clean towels for the guest bathrooms, and seeing no one else around, pinched my ass.

By the time I'd finished everything on my list, I could barely drag my feet up the stairs to change into my concert dress. I'd left the attic landing light on for myself, but the bastard ghost had turned it off. As I stepped toward my room, a rush of icy air engulfed me, driving the breath from my lungs.

Weird. It's never cold up here.

Unease prickled at the back of my neck. I hated being up here, knowing there was someone in the house trying to scare me. It was almost better when I thought the Muses were responsible for my haunting. Now…

Just ignore it. It's a draft from somewhere in the house.

I fumbled in my pocket for the key. As my hand closed around it, someone stepped out of the shadows in front of me, sending a fresh wave of ice curling around my body.

"Wha—" But I couldn't form words. My breath died in my throat.

The brown hair tied up in a bun. That button nose. Eyes that once sparkled with life but now burned with hatred.

Clare.

She stared at me, her head twisting to the side at an impossible angle, one eyebrow raising in a ghastly expression.

Through her skin, the wood grain of my door was visible.

Run. I commanded myself. *You have to run.*

But I remained frozen with terror.

Silence stretched between us. Clare opened her lips, but no sound came out – her mouth opened into a maw of terrifying darkness that swallowed all light and hope.

I staggered back, my chest exploding with panic. Shadows spewed from Clare's mouth and circled her body – reaching, grasping, *crawling* toward me. One grabbed my arm. Before I could tear myself from its grasp, something hot and hard closed around my mouth, pressing a sweet-scented cloth between my lips.

Then everything went black.

TO BE CONTINUED

Find out who – or what – is after Faye in book 2 of Broken Muses of Manderley Academy, Haunted.

~

I should have kept my mouth shut.
I should have let them win.
Now the kings of the school are out for my blood,
... and they're not the only ones.

Need more dark, gothic, and delicious reverse harem bully romance in your life?

HP Lovecraft meets *Cruel Intentions* in the paranormal reverse harem bully romance readers are calling, "The greatest mindfuck of 2019". Warning: Not for the faint of heart – this story of three broken bad boys and the girl who stood her ground contains dark themes, crazed cultists, books bound in human skin, high-school drama, swoon-worthy sex, and potential triggers. Grab book 1, *Shunned,* in KU now.

When Faye popped into my head, fully formed and stomping her foot for her story, I pushed her aside.

Not because she isn't badass – she is. Not because she didn't deserve a chance to live and fight and love – she does. Definitely not because 'fucktrumpets' as a swear word should never see the light of day – that shit should be shouted from great heights.

But because I was afraid.

Faye needed to be a classical musician. She needed to live and breathe and love the music, and I… I am a classical *philistine*.

I was raised on a diet of heavy fucking metal. I'm more at home in the mosh pit than in the concert hall. I've always seen classical music as something for the rich and snooty, where everyone pretends they're having fun because it's *culture*. I didn't think I was the right person to do Faye justice.

But Faye's a stubborn bitch. She wouldn't go away.

She led me to a book called *Rock Me Amadeus*, by Seb Hunter – the story of an ageing rocker (Seb wrote this hilarious history of heavy metal called *Hell Bent for Leather* I highly recommend) trying to uncover what there was to like about classical music.

Sadly, the book is out of print now – I tracked down a second-hand copy.

In it, Seb explores the history of classical music in chronological order, including many bizarre road trips across Europe, strange encounters, and a Wagner drinking game. Through this book I discover that (d'uh) musicians like Bach, Beethoven and Liszt were the rockstars of their day – wallowing in the excesses of drugs, drink, and women. Paganini sold his soul to the devil for his musical talent. And the music… phew. Where have you been all my life?

All music fans can recount their 'Come to Jesus' moment – the exact point when they went from not knowing a musical thing existed to loving the thing with their whole heart. I remember exactly the day I first heard Metallica's 'Enter Sandman' and realised music could be deeper and richer and more powerful than I ever imagined. And I remember when I first cranked Beethoven on my speakers at Seb's suggestion and fell in love with classical music.

Meanwhile, Faye's flashing me a satisfied smirk.

Told you so.

The interesting thing about being a writer is that when you work on a story, you give a piece of yourself to the world, to your readers. But it's not a one-way thing – the story gives something back. You can never predict what that 'something' will be. Sometimes it's a sense of peace, or closure on trauma that's haunted you. Sometimes it's righteous anger, or a sense of purpose, or a desire for action. Sometimes it's confidence, or chaos, or acceptance.

Sound the fucktrumpets – Faye gave me music that lifts my soul.

I've created a playlist for the Broken Muses of Manderley Academy series. You'll find it on Spotify here. I've tried to include every song I mention in the text, as well as some I love that I feel Faye and the Broken Muse boys would adore. I've included some more modern music, too – a bit of goth, a smidge of metal (for many metal musicians, like Titus, are classically-trained and heavily inspired by classical roots). Maybe it will spark your own 'Come to Dories' moment, or you'll find some cool new tunes to jam along.

Writing *Ghosted* has been a joy and a pleasure, but as always, it takes a village to bring a book to life. I'd like to thank my cantankerous drummer husband, for reading this manuscript and giving me so many ideas to make it better. And for being my lighthouse. And for putting up with me blasting Bach at full volume.

To Kit, Bri, Elaina, Katya, Emma, Jamie, Kim, Mila, and Jenna, for all the writerly encouragement and advice. To Meg and Eveis for the epically helpful editing job, and to Amanda/Aria/Lori for the stunning covers. To Sam and Iris, for the daily Facebook shenanigans that help keep me sane while I spend my days stuck at home covered in cats.

To you, the reader, for going on this journey with me, even though it's led to some dark places. Warning: if you thought book 1 was tough, book 2 is a whopper. Get it here.

If you're enjoying *Broken Muses of Manderley Academy* and want to read more from me, check out my new dark reverse harem bully romance series, *Kings of Miskatonic Prep.* HP Lovecraft meets *Cruel Intentions* in this dark paranormal reverse harem bully romance that's definitely not for the faint of heart. Hazel is the most badass FMC I've ever written, and I think you'll love meeting her.

I've also got two other reverse harem series. The Nevermore Bookshop Mysteries is what you'd get if you crossed Agatha Christie with Black Books and added a harem of famous literary men. It's my most popular series to date, and it's a lot more light-hearted and fun (despite all the murder). Start book 1, *A Dead and Stormy Night.* If you turn the page, there's a short excerpt from book 1.

The Briarwood Witches series is about a science nerd heroine who inherits an honest-to-goodness English castle, complete with five hot British/Irish tenants, a fas problem, and some magic she can't control. It's a little bit dark and angsty and sexy, and complete at 5 books. You can grab the box set here.

If you want to hang out and talk about all things Broken Muse, my readers are sharing their theories and discussing the book over in my Facebook group, Books That Bite. Come join the fun.

I'm so happy you enjoyed this story! I'd love it if you wanted to leave a review on Amazon or Goodreads. It will help other readers to find their next read.

Thank you, thank you! I love you heaps! Until next time.
Steff

EXCERPT: KINGS OF MISKATONIC
PREP, BOOK 1
READ THE FIRST CHAPTER OF SHUNNED

Read Shunned now

Who the hell builds a school on top of an inaccessible cliff?

Whoever built Derleth Academy, my new school. I answered my own question as the car's wheel skidded over the rough gravel on the way up the steep peninsula. A scream escaped my lips as the car lurched toward the edge of the cliff, one wheel spinning completely free.

Muttering under his breath, the driver for the school slammed the car into reverse and backed us onto the road before slamming on the gas again. We continued our wary climb along the narrow gravel path.

Surely the Academy can't be completely *cut-off.* The school had to bring up food and supplies. Parents must visit on the weekends. My driver was certainly giving it his all, tearing around the corners like he was on a Formula 1 racetrack and not a goat path hugging the side of a mountain. I gritted my teeth and gripped the back of the seat as rocks rolled from beneath the wheels and clattered over the sheer drop into the raging waters below. One wrong move, and we'd tumble down a two-hundred-foot cliff and be dashed against the cliffs so hard and fast that boats would mistake our remains for rock paintings.

Not the way I ever imagined I'd go.

We passed into thick vegetation, the cliff and ocean on one side giving way to looming trees that blocked out the grey sky. I let out the breath I'd been holding. Branches scraped the sides of the car, and my phone beeped with protest as we moved out of cell range. *No contact with the outside world,* the school brochure read. *At Derleth Academy, we foster a competitive academic program requiring the full attention of our students. Distracting technology or personal items will not be tolerated.*

In other words, I couldn't call for help. It was the opening sequence to every horror film, ever.

Not that I had anyone to call. Not anymore.

"Almost there," the driver said, swinging the car around a hairpin corner and launching my stomach into my throat. It was the most words he'd spoken to me the entire trip. "You can see the school through the trees."

I squinted into the forest, trying to make out some kind of building that might pass as a school. But I couldn't see a thing. We rounded another corner and—

Well, that's terrifying.

We rolled between two towering stone pillars obscured by creeping vines, past an ornate sign that read DERLETH ACADEMY. A wide, pristine concrete drive flanked by an avenue of towering trees and wide, manicured lawns led up to an imposing stone building, stretching in all directions with narrow arched windows, spiky towers, and a row of leering gargoyles along the roof.

What is this place? It looked more like Dracula's castle than a prestigious preparatory school.

I couldn't believe the wealthiest people in the country sent their children up that winding road to get educated. *Who's the headmistress, Morticia Addams?* But according to the brochure, that was exactly what they did. In droves. Derleth Academy had a waiting list a mile long, and you couldn't even pay to get in. You had to be *invited*.

Somehow, I, Hazel Waite – an overachieving orphan from the wrong side of Philly – ended up on their radar.

I flashed back to the day two weeks ago, when a banging on the door of my dingy apartment dragged me from a deep slumber. A woman with coiffed hair and a designer suit that cost more than a car staggered backward in surprise when I glared at her through the chain wearing only my pajamas and what must have been a terrifying scowl. Well, *she* wasn't the one being dragged from a pleasant Jason Momoa sex dream during the four-hour reprieve between night shift at the diner and cleaning rooms at a retirement home.

"Are you Hazel Waite?" she asked, her brown eyes wide and curious.

"No. Piss off." I glowered, slamming the door in her face. She was probably from CPS, trying to force me into foster care. Fuck that. I only had seven more months to survive before I turned eighteen. No way was I going to spend it in the hell that had killed Dante.

The woman didn't go away. She sat out on the road in her sports car and waited me out. I had to leave for work or I'd lose my job, and it wasn't easy to find work when you were underage and using an obviously fake ID. As soon as I left the house, she ambushed me.

"I'm not here to hand you over to the authorities," she said hurriedly, shoving a thick envelope into your hands. "I'm a scholarship administrator from Derleth Academy in Arkham, Massachusetts. Your current school put you forward for one of our four senior scholarship positions – a fully funded year at a first-class prep school, where our students go on to attend the top colleges in the world. I know the first quarter has already started, but it's taken me this long to track you down. You've only missed a week so far."

I stared at the envelope in my hands, at the red, black and gold school crest – a crooked five-pointed star inside a shield with some kind of Latin phrase beneath it. *This has got to be a joke.*

"I know what you're thinking," the woman said. "It's not a joke or a trick. I promise you that it's not. If you come to Derleth, we will assume guardianship duties until you turn eighteen. You'll be housed, clothed, and have all your schoolbooks and other needs met, as well as receiving a first-class education. You're a promising student, Hazel, and I know you've been dealt a cruel lot in life. This could be where you turn everything around. Don't answer me now. Read over the paperwork, and I'll return tomorrow for your decision."

And now, just ten days after I signed my soul over to this school in exchange for paid tuition, room, and board, I stared up at the imposing facade and wondered if I'd made a terrible mistake.

Sure, my life was miserable. I was drowning in grief, and even working two jobs I could barely pull in enough money to survive. College was out of the question, because I couldn't finish high school without going into foster care. But at least all that was familiar territory. That was the world I'd grown up in – the world of pain and struggle and loss. Derleth Academy was the exact opposite. Every element of this building screamed wealth and privilege and *you don't belong here.*

The driver pulled to a stop on the wide circular drive beside a towering stone fountain. A black woman in a drab grey smock darted out of the shadows of the porch and approached the car. I held my hand out to her. "Hello, I'm Hazel Waite—"

The woman ducked her head, avoiding me. She popped open the trunk, hauled out my heavy suitcase and bookbag, and hurried off to the house with them before I could offer to help.

Weird much? I swiped a dreadlock off my face. My friend

Dante's foster sister had done them for me last year, back when things were perfect and the most I had to worry about was whether my mom would ground me for getting dreadlocks.

An awful feeling twisted in my gut. I wished Mom was here, hating my loss, right now. But she was gone, gone, gone, and so was Dante, and it was just me and this terrifying school and no other options.

Three figures descended the grand stone steps toward me: A woman with translucent skin and a flowing black dress, flanked on either side by two students wearing the Derleth uniform. Fallen leaves skittered away from the woman's hem, and she moved with such poise that she appeared to float over the steps. With her severe features and a gauzy black ribbon pinned in her hair, she looked more like she was attending a funeral. Behind her, the two students – a guy and a girl – glared at me, distrust emanating from their every pore.

The woman stopped on the second-to-last step, peering down her nose at me as if I were a bug that wasn't even worth squashing. "You'll have to do something about that hair. We enforce a strict dress code in my school, Ms. Waite. I'll not have you flouting it on your very first day."

This must be the principal, Hermia West. My Morticia Addams guess wasn't far off. This woman looked like she drank the blood of students to sustain her beauty. The way her grey eyes stabbed right through me sent a cold shiver through my body.

There was nothing in the student handbook about dreadlocks. Although, of course, I'd only skim-read the thing on the bus from Philly. The handbook was boring. And *long*. "I'm sorry, Ms. West. I didn't know—"

"Ignorance is no excuse. That's 3 demerit points for you. And you're to refer to me as Headmistress."

Beside her, the boy sniggered. I turned my gaze to look at him, and my heart nearly stopped. *Wow, he's beautiful.* I had no idea boys that hot existed outside of magazines and Hollywood movies. He stood practically the same height as Ms. West, his broad shoulders accentuated by the tailored cut of his red-trimmed blazer. Prefect and merit badges decorated both lapels. Dark brown curls caught the grey light filtering through the clouds, throwing back beautiful shades of russet and silver. His clean-shaven face and high, majestic cheekbones appeared angelic, but his ice-blue eyes were cold and cruel.

The girl moved closer to him, touching his arm and shooting me a possessive glare, like a cat in heat. She had the appearance of a cat, too – slanted green eyes accentuated with heavy makeup, pointed chin, and the lithe body and long legs of a panther. Beautiful but deadly.

"This is Trey Bloomberg and Courtney Haynes," Headmistress West said. "I've appointed them as your student guides. They will show you the dorm, library, and dining hall, go over your schedule and classrooms, and ensure you understand *all* our rules. You will dine with the student body in two hours' time, and tomorrow you begin classes. I've had a copy of your schedule and the school handbook placed in your room. Memorize them, for failure to comply will result in further demerits. Here's your dorm room key."

In my pocket, my phone gave another defiant chirp. *Great.* I'd practically worn down the battery looking for a signal on the death road.

Headmistress West descended the last step to drop an ancient-looking metal key into my hand. Her pointy black boots lined up with my scuffed Docs. She loomed over me, her disapproval seeping into my bones. "You have a phone in your pocket." It wasn't a question.

"Yes."

Behind her, the boy smirked. I felt naked, exposed. My legs itched to make a run for the woods. Headmistress West held out her hand, unfurling long fingers topped with red-painted nails, the tips pointed like talons. "Hand it over. We don't allow outside technology on campus."

Instinctively, my hand flew to my pocket. "I won't use it to call or text. It doesn't work here, anyway, so what's the—"

"Ms. Waite, failure to obey a teacher's command is an automatic loss of 10 points. You seem most anxious to find out what punishments await the students at the bottom of the class list."

A lump rose in my throat. My phone contained photographs – snaps of my mom smiling demurely or brushing her hair in the mirror before she went out to work at the strip club. Of Dante and I hanging out around the neighborhood, smoking on the rusted playground beside his house, tagging the concrete wall behind the boxing gym on the corner. Every other one of my possessions had been destroyed in the fire. Those photographs were practically all I had left of them.

Trey and Courtney covered their mouths with their hands, barely disguising their laughter. Courtney leaned over and whispered something to Trey. They both cracked up. Despite myself, my cheeks flushed. *Better get used to this.*

Headmistress West, of course, ignored them. She wasn't backing down on this phone thing. My fingers closed around it, the comfortable weight of it in my hand reminding me that it was one of the last connections to my old life.

What does it matter? They're gone. Looking at their photos won't bring them back. But this school could be the only chance I have at a real future.

My hand trembling, I dropped my phone into her talons. As soon as it left my hand, I itched to get it back. Headmistress West slipped the phone into a fold of her dress, where it disappeared from sight.

"Follow me." The headmistress swirled on her heel and floated up the stairs. Numb, I fell in step behind her. Trey came up beside me. His arm brushed mine, and a jolt of warmth rocketed through my body. I dared a look up at his face. As we moved into the shadow of the porch, the colors in his hair changed, becoming a deep brown and blood red. A curl flopped over his eye, and I noticed flecks of silver on the edges of those arresting blue irises. My fingers itched to reach up and swipe that curl off his face, to touch his smooth skin, feel his cheek move beneath my fingers, to cut myself on his cheekbones. A familiar longing pooled in my stomach, an ache that I'd never been able to sate before, and now never would.

I'd never seen a boy that *perfect*.

Trey's fingers brushed me again. My breath froze in my mouth as his hand lingered on my elbow. To anyone looking at us from a distance, it would appear as though he was helping me, steadying me up the steep steps. The touch on my skin was white-hot, lighting up parts of my body that hadn't felt anything since Dante… since before the fire. *How can this boy with such cruel eyes have this effect on me?*

When he caught me looking, Trey's perfect lips curled back into a sneer. His fingers tightened on my arm, squeezing my skin. Tighter, tighter, until he was cutting off circulation. I yelped in protest.

"You don't belong here," he murmured, his perfect lips forming hateful words. "You should leave now."

He said it so casually, like he was chatting about the weather, and that self-satisfied smirk never left his face. My stomach twisted, the air driving from my lungs as though he'd punched me.

"No thanks," I said brightly, pretending that I misunderstood him. "I'm good."

"We don't want you, and we're used to getting what we want. We're going to eat you alive, new meat." Trey flashed me a smile that was all teeth and violence. The venom in his eyes frightened me. *This is not a guy to mess with.*

Too bad he seemed to already have it out for me, and I hadn't even got inside the school yet. My plan to keep my head down and stay invisible fizzled before my eyes. Already I could see how the school year was going to play out. *We don't want you here.* Trey spoke for the entire student body. He was a King in this school. It was written in his smile, dripping from the menace in his words.

I'd pissed him off. Just by existing. Just by setting foot on the hallowed grounds of his kingdom. *Well, fuck you, Trey Bloomberg.* I could handle a year of insults and loneliness if I got my diploma at the end of it. My life was already hell on earth – if Trey Bloomberg thought he could break me, he'd have to try a lot harder.

I wrenched my arm away from us. "Don't touch me." Behind us, Courtney giggled.

"Yeah, Trey. You should know not to handle garbage. She's a gutter-trash whore who's probably fucked so many guys that your dick wouldn't even touch the sides."

The comment stung. I thought of my sweet mother, all candy smiles and sticky skin as she stripped off her sweat-soaked lace g-string and six-inch heels after her shift and pulled on the cloud-pink pajamas I found for her in a thrift store. A hard lump rose in my throat. I shoved the image aside. *Not now.*

Wait until you get to your room, until you're alone, then you can break down.

"I guess we're not going to be braiding each other's hair," I muttered to Courtney.

"I wouldn't touch that rat's nest on your head if someone hid a *Faberge* egg inside," Courtney sneered. "I bet it's got real eggs in it, though. Insect eggs, laid by the gross things crawling around in there."

Instinctively, my hand flew up to my face, to touch the dread-lock that always fell over my eye, to tuck it behind my ear – a gesture that Dante would so often do when he noticed my loss in my eyes, which was all the time because I liked them unruly. Ever since the fire, I'd been touching my own hair more and more, seeking the comfort of the familiar weight of a hand moving the dreadlocks. But it wasn't the same. It would never be the same.

Courtney wrinkled her face in disgust, while Trey continued to smirk at me. The force of his loathing sank my stomach to my knees. He didn't even know me, but it didn't matter.

At the top of the stairs, the headmistress turned and frowned at me. "Don't dawdle," she snapped. "The school doesn't bite."

"She's wrong," Trey whispered. "Are you ready to find out just how bad we bite?"

The lump of hard, bitterness burned at the back of my throat. They were right. I didn't belong here. I was the poor gutter-trash girl from the wrong side of the tracks, and they were *royalty*. They were the monarchs. *They're going to make my life miserable, and there's nothing I can do.*

Read Shunned now

Tough luck, bully boys – I won't hide away.
I'm not afraid.
But maybe… *I should be.*

HP Lovecraft meets *Cruel Intentions* in book 1 of this dark paranormal reverse harem bully romance. Warning: Not for the faint of heart – this story of three broken bad boys and the girl who stood her ground contains dark themes, crazed cultists, books bound in human skin, high-school drama, swoon-worthy sex, and potential triggers.

START READING NOW
books2read.com/shunned

What do you get when you cross a cursed bookshop, three hot fictional men, and a punk rock heroine nursing a broken heart?

After being fired from her fashion internship in New York City, Mina Wilde decides it's time to reevaluate her life. She returns to the quaint English village where she grew up to take a job at the local bookshop, hoping that being surrounded by great literature will help her heal from a devastating blow.

But Mina soon discovers her life is stranger than fiction – a mysterious curse on the bookshop brings fictional characters to life in lust-worthy bodies. Mina finds herself babysitting Poe's raven, making hot dogs for Heathcliff, and getting IT help from James Moriarty, all while trying not to fall for the three broken men who should only exist within her imagination.

When Mina's ex-best friend shows up dead with a knife in her back, she's the chief suspect. She'll have to solve the murder if she wants to clear her name. Will her fictional boyfriends be able to keep her out of prison?

The Nevermore Bookshop Mysteries are what you get when all your book boyfriends come to life. Join a brooding antihero, a master criminal, a cheeky raven, and a heroine with a big heart (and an even bigger book collection) in this brand new steamy reverse harem paranormal mystery series by *USA Today* best-selling author Steffanie Holmes.

READ NOW

ABOUT THE AUTHOR

Steffanie Holmes is the *USA Today* bestselling author of the para-normal, gothic, dark, and fantastical. Her books feature clever, witty heroines, wild shifters, cunning witches and alpha males who *always* get what they want.

Legally-blind since birth, Steffanie received the 2017 Attitude Award for Artistic Achievement. She was also a finalist for a 2018 Women of Influence award.

Steff is the creator of *Rage Against the Manuscript* – a resource of free content, book, and courses to help writers tell their story, find their readers, and build a badass writing career.

Steffanie lives in New Zealand with her husband, a horde of cantankerous cats, and their medieval sword collection.

STEFFANIE HOLMES NEWSLETTER

Grab a free copy *Cabinet of Curiosities* – a Steffanie Holmes compendium of short stories and bonus scenes – when you sign up for updates with the Steffanie Holmes newsletter.

Come hang with Steffanie
www.steffanieholmes.com
hello@steffanieholmes.com

www.ingramcontent.com/pod-product-compliance
Lightning Source LLC
Chambersburg PA
CBHW031934110726

47902CB00001B/168